The Pigeon Catcher

EA Bundy

Summary: Kevin Conners climbs up a Gothic house at night to remove a pigeon nuisance. Peering in an attic window, he sees the dead body of a girl about his age, plus a man dressed all in black, and brandishing a wicked knife. Attacked, Kevin falls two stories, and that should be The End, but it is just the beginning.

"A book for the dreamer in everyone. Atmospheric, with very believable characters; Kevin, Haley and Misty will stay with me for a long, long time." –Sarah Neufeld, author of the YA illustrated novel *Visibility*.
"Parts are creepy…but can't wait for the next…" –NH
"I looove Haley…" –NMC

Text Copyright © 2012 Eugene Allan Bundy
Cover illustration © 2012 Eugene Allan Bundy
Cover design © 2012 Singing Winds Press

~Singing Winds Press~

P.O. Box 131, Dallas, Oregon 97338
(Singing Winds Press is closed to submissions)

Library of Congress Control Number 2012901760

Paperback Edition ISBN: 978-1-61955-000-1
Electronic Edition ISBN: 978-1-61955-001-8

THE PIGEON CATCHER

DEDICATION

This work of fiction is dedicated to all dreamers, everywhere, and especially to those who think they don't dream, but do.

IMPORTANT NOTICE

The characters and incidents in this novel are products of the author's imagination and are used fictitiously. They are not to be construed as real. Any resemblance to actual events or persons living or dead is purely coincidental. Nothing in this novel is meant to be taken as advice, neither psychological, psychiatric, or medical advice. If anyone reading this work of fiction suffers from night terrors or some other malady, they need to seek competent professional help. The Senoi people described in this work of fiction did exist. However, the original ethnographic descriptions by an anthropologist, as regards their dream techniques, was later questioned. The books on dreaming mentioned in this novel are made up, but for interested readers there are many good works on dreaming, including books on lucid dreaming.

~Singing Winds Press~

Dallas, Oregon
Printed in the USA

CONTENTS

Author's note:

Working in public schools, I have made a great many young friends, some of whom will likely try to read anything I have written simply because they know me. This novel is perhaps my edgiest at this time. I think of it as a psychic thriller. Another author named Nathalie who read this said she only did so at night *if* her husband was there with her, in case she became too frightened. I didn't think it was that scary myself, but please, if you don't love scary stories, wait and read one of my others because this book is not for everyone. In fact, for some people it won't be scary enough.

For more information about *The Pigeon Catcher*, or my other novels, please visit my website:

www.eabundyauthor.com

ACKNOWLEDGMENTS

The following people, and some I may have forgotten,
contributed to my completion of this work in many ways:
Noël was the first reader and gave invaluable feedback.
Richey, author of *The Unseen* series, gave really helpful
suggestions regarding my novel's beginning.
Sarah, author of the captivating story *Visibility*, graciously and
meticulously critiqued the entire novel.
Current or former writing group members who also helpfully
critiqued *The Pigeon Catcher* were Marian, Andrea, Charlie,
Carmen, and Ian.
Nathalie is a writer and friend who added her suggestions.
Elinor and Lani are my former classmates who also read and
gave feedback and encouragement.
Diana is a retired high school employee in The Dalles who
helped with accuracy of school details.
Marie at PSU's first annual Writer's Conference gave feedback
and encouraged me to find a *small* publisher.
Jonathan helped with invaluable technology assistance.
I also owe a debt of gratitude to the author of the book
On Writing.
Plus, an appreciative thanks to Haley, a fictional ten-year-old girl
who appeared unexpectedly in chapter eight of *The Pigeon Catcher*
—and to the Muse who brought her.

MANY THANKS TO YOU ALL

1: FIVE YEARS AGO

In a Portland, Oregon dream laboratory, Ed Bridger felt a shiver run down his back and stopped mid-sentence, turning to view a young pair of piercing eyes. There was something mysterious about the small, dark girl.

"Want to help," she said.

At first, he mistakenly believed she was asking *him* for help. He tried to mentor Haley until he understood more fully, then their roles reversed. In fact, he learned so much from her, articles appeared in professional journals sharing the new concepts. His coworkers were flattered as top researchers around the world contacted them. One renowned "expert" even came to Oregon and suggested Haley should have the opportunity to profit from their advanced facility in Virginia. "Just imagine," he said, "what might occur if she could work with us?"

Regardless, her parents said, "No."

There are half a dozen cutting-edge sleep laboratories in the United States but the Portland facility was a more typical enterprise, staffed by specialists from allied fields who came together part-time, aiding persons with sleep disturbances. At least, that was their sole purpose until that fortuitous afternoon when a five-year-old, multiracial girl with black hair and obsidian eyes came through their door.

At the present time, Haley has been Kevin Conner's neighbor in The Dalles for a whole year, although he knows nothing of her dream activities or the difference between dreaming and reality. In seventeen years, he's given no thought to that question —until now.

2: DREAM OR REALITY?

Kevin's original fuzziness cleared despite the darkness. Reaching around his back, he checked to be certain the gunnysack holding his flashlight was safely through his belt. He took a final look across the night-blackened yard and then gazed at his friends, one heavy-set and the other slight of build.

Cal, the bulky one, asked, "What you waiting on?"

"If they were home," Kevin replied, "I'd just go out a dormer window like I planned. That's why I was thinking—"

"Dormer?" Cal asked.

Jake whispered, "You know what that is."

"Do not."

Kevin said, "Little roof poking out of the main one...now stay here and be quiet." He turned to his task, moving stealthily across the dark lawn toward the large house. Sometimes he wondered about Cal. Why had he even brought him along?

Kevin had familiarized himself with the rose trellis stretching high up to the second-story rain gutter. Initially, the trellis was to be his back-up method for gaining access to the roof because it was more dangerous than going out the dormer. Yet, the risk enticed him as he moved toward the trellis base. Locating a cross-board, Kevin began scaling the structure.

The rose became much thicker near the top of the first story. He guessed the gardener didn't relish pruning so high off the ground. Wishing he'd worn a long-sleeved shirt and pair of leather gloves, Kevin rubbed at the stings where thorns had cut his hands and arm. "Oh well," he whispered, "I'm halfway up."

As Kevin neared the projecting roof of the second story, he paused, catching his breath. Sucking in the surprising fragrance of early blossoms wafting on a warm air current, he smiled at the knowledge his sometimes girlfriend, Carol, loved roses. She'd be sighing right now at the smell of this natural perfume.

Keep to the task, he thought, refocusing his attention. Getting past the roof's edge would be difficult. It extended farther out than he'd realized. Jerking strongly on the metal gutter, it was sound, but climbing past would be a challenge. To make things worse, the image of Carol's face began to haunt Kevin. Her flashing green eyes set in freckled skin seemed to admonish him, "Are you crazy?" Her voice sounded again in his mind. "Get down from there right now."

It wasn't enough the strawberry-blonde nagged at him in person. No girl, no matter how pretty, was telling him what to do. He shook his head. What were the two of them thinking? This would never work out—them getting back together.

No more delays. Filled with determination, Kevin pulled himself waist-high to the gutter so his legs dangled unsupported above the yard below. Glad he couldn't look down, he swung his body upward—arcing onto the slanted roof. Turning on his back, he nervously placed his heels in the gutter and rested on the steep slope. Fit as he was from soccer, telltale sweat trickled down his neck. The sign of exertion, or fear?

Carol's voice berated him again, "If you fall and kill yourself, Kevin, I'll never forgive you." He smiled, knowing that was exactly what she would say. He'd better remind Cal and Jake to keep their mouths shut, especially Cal. If word got back to Carol, Kevin would never hear the end of it, although he was doing this for her—sort of. On the other hand, he'd seen signs she was going to dump him, again. Why'd he let her talk him into going out with her once more, anyway? Maybe he should just let Cal tell her about this outing and be done with it.

Pigeons moved nervously beside the dormer above him as Kevin lay there on his back, panting from his adrenaline rush. The male bird began cooing to its mate and Kevin knew they were beginning to settle down. While adjusting the flashlight in his gunnysack so it wouldn't jab, he detected weak illumination shining out of the attic's dormer window onto the roof beside him—invisible from down below where his friends waited.

Kevin heard his buddies whispering in the yard, but ignored them, grateful they hadn't started yelling up to him. Turning over on his stomach, he verified that the pale light flooded through the trio of dormer windows. The middle section was stationary but the other two were for ventilation during eastern Oregon's hot summers. He stretched his arm upward, touching the dormer's edge.

The large recessed area to the right was pitch-black, so there'd be no difficulty catching the troublesome birds. He sold the common pigeons he caught to bird hunters for training their gun dogs. They paid a dollar and up for each one. Invariably destroyed, the pigeons did not return to pester their former "landlords." In that way, Kevin didn't have to cull them—a task he avoided.

Placing his hands flat on the roof, he edged his way up to the dormer. Nearing it, he heard one of the birds make its alarm call, a pigeon grunting sound. Kevin knew they wouldn't take flight yet due to fear of injury in the dark. He wondered how he would get down off the roof with these pigeons in his gunnysack. If he didn't need the money for taking Carol to the movies tomorrow night, he might have waited to do this job.

Curiosity compelled him to peer through the diamond-shaped panes in the attic window. A portable electric lantern sat midway across the floor and he quickly adjusted to its brightness. He thought it odd there was a light on in the attic of this otherwise unlit house.

Kevin glimpsed his faint reflection in the glass. His mussed-up hair appeared much darker than its actual light brown. His eyes, staring from his oval face, didn't reveal their blueness. Although he was seventeen, he looked younger—downright immature.

Small hairs stood on the back of his neck, as the reflected glimmer from another pair of eyes seemed to appear. It couldn't be his friends. Cal was afraid of heights and even Jake would have made noise climbing up. For a moment, it seemed as though a dark, female head was visible beside him. He closed and then reopened his eyes. No—just his own faint reflection. How silly, letting his mind get carried away like that.

Pressing his face against the glass, Kevin rubbed the painful thorn nicks on his arms. If the owners were home, he would have climbed out the window, avoiding the scratches. Focusing on the interior, he saw the messy attic was mainly a storage area. A large brass bed was the only piece of furniture. Its mattress was heaped high with excess bedding and clothing, including an old-fashioned mink stole. A set of golf clubs leaned against the back of the bed, plus boxes and other storage containers sat randomly about.

Kevin was turning away when a movement caught his eye. What he'd perceived as a shadow beyond the lantern was now a shifting shape. He blinked, thinking his eyes were playing another trick on him. No. The dark shadow became a moving specter, hunched-over and carrying something—a small metal box?

Not only was that presence dressed in black, it wore a dark ski mask. The hair on the back of Kevin's neck prickled again, and he gulped as the mysterious head lifted, revealing cold black eyes. Kevin was too shocked to move. His logic and all his senses reacted. That person shouldn't be there. The figure crept close to the lantern, his body-shape and motions revealing he was a male.

Still crouched, the man opened the container and removed something. A brilliant necklace dangled from the shadowy hand and myriad facets highlighted the room with reflected sparkles of light. The man's attention interrupted and he straightened, turning toward the descending stairwell. Moving furtively to the top of the steps, he cocked his head to one side, listening. Replacing the jewelry, he hastily returned the metal box to the hole in the floor, sealing the cavity with a short floorboard.

Kevin sat there, riveted. He'd heard nothing that should have startled the dark figure. His friends were silent far below. What was really happening inside the attic?

The man moved suddenly forward, glancing around as though he realized someone was watching. For no apparent reason, the mysterious form leaped closer. Had Kevin been spotted?

In his haste, the man tripped over debris, crashing headlong into the bed and knocking things to the floor. As a result of that flurried activity, something was revealed causing Kevin to gasp—

A pale arm extended from beneath the dislodged bedding. It connected to the upper-half of a young woman's unclad body. She appeared to be about Kevin's age. Bright blue eyes stared fixedly, punctuated by her unnaturally white skin—nearly as light as her ash blonde hair. Only minor blotches and the thin, reddish-brown line of dried blood on her neck marred her skin's pale surface. Her pink lip-gloss looked out of place, vibrant and alive on someone who was…. Despite everything, Kevin couldn't help thinking how pretty she'd be if she wasn't dead.

He cringed, lurching back from the window's lifeless form. Turning to get away, he thought he glimpsed the dark figure covering the young woman's naked body with blankets. Why would the guy bother? Hadn't he seen Kevin after all?

Pausing beside the entry to the roof alcove where the pigeons hid, and driven by a compulsion to know what was happening, Kevin forced himself to lean around the corner for another glance in the window. Perhaps the light glaring off the glass had kept the ominous figure from seeing him.

What Kevin witnessed, however, was the black silhouette striding directly toward him, brandishing a wicked knife. Impulsively darting under the dormer roof's overhang, Kevin scrunched as far back as he could and heard the frightened pigeons scurry deeper into the narrowing nook. As the window was forced open, Kevin's ears were assaulted by the scraping sound of its latch and the protesting creak of un-oiled hinges. The dark shape lunged around the corner. Kevin felt one of the pigeons brush by, then fly into the darkness, startling the aggressor. The remaining bird would likely attempt the same maneuver. Hearing that second pigeon moving past, Kevin grasped it, causing a frightened grunt.

The knife was thrust into the alcove just as Kevin hurtled his feathered captive directly at the assailant's head. It was a forceful hit by the flapping bird.

The man swore, sliding down the steep roof.

Kevin moved out from his confinement around the edge of the dormer, continuing toward its peak. There, he paused. Somehow, the man had kept from falling or Kevin's friends would be screaming their heads off. The loud commotion had gained their attention, however. Cal's hoarse whisper floated up.

"Kevin, you okay?"

There was no answer since Kevin didn't know where the dude in black was and hoped the man didn't know where he was, either. What to do? His mind raced to make sense of the scene he'd witnessed. The ski-masked man was undoubtedly a burglar. Perhaps the young woman had interrupted his larceny and been killed. In that case, there would be no hesitation to murder a witness. Too bad Kevin hadn't seen the guy's face because even if he got away he couldn't identify the murderer—

Bang. The window crashed shut, perhaps flung by the darkish man, or The Dalles' fierce winds. There were only two escape routes off the roof. Kevin had to descend by the trellis or somehow get into the attic and race down through the house.

Cal hollered. "You okay, Kevin?"

Kevin remained silent and followed his strong premonition to move back down the roof. Descending the dormer's sloped valley, he heard an eerie whisper from the peak, and halted.

Mocking and threatening, it hissed, "Kevin, are you all right?"

The words were too soft for his friends to hear. Already removing the gunnysack from his belt, Kevin reached inside and retrieved his flashlight. It had a powerful beam and was rugged enough to serve as a weapon. He could barely make out the dark shape atop the dormer peak and hoped the man was staring at him. To be certain, Kevin scuffed his foot to draw attention. Closing his eyes, he turned the light on the burglar.

"Ah." The startled utterance confirmed Kevin's past experience. A brilliant light could temporarily blind far more than pigeons. Switching it off, he opened his eyes and moved rapidly to the front of the dormer, pushing the window open. Leaping inside, he flung it closed and fastened the latch. Running carefully to the brass bed, he pulled back the re-piled covers, but the body was gone. Only mounds of clothing remained.

A creaking floorboard caused Kevin to turn. The dreadful figure was there between him and the stairway. From the corner of his eye, Kevin saw an opposite dormer window was now open. He'd been lured into a trap. Why hadn't he called to his friends to get the cops when he had his chance? The sheriff's office was just down the street.

The sinister voice whispered again, "Are you all right, Kevin?"

Backing around the bed, Kevin clutched his flashlight as a weapon. Bumping into the golf bag, he pocketed his light and grabbed a metal club. The assailant hesitated as Kevin shuffled forward, raising the iron threateningly, while carefully avoiding debris on the floor. He backed the man toward the stairway. A black sneaker slipped over the edge, dropping his adversary to one knee.

Maybe Kevin could still alert his friends. He raced left toward the open window, partly-tripping over a box. Attempting to leap to the roof outside, he lost his balance as the golf iron snagged the window frame. Kevin slid feet-first on his back down the steep roof to the gutter. Legs careening over the edge, he dropped his makeshift weapon and managed a desperate turn, somehow grabbing the metal gutter's fluted edge with both hands.

The club and then his flashlight crashed loudly below. His left hand slipped loose and he dangled by his right. The gutter's lower edge cutting into his wrist.

The man chuckled, "Let me help you, there."

Fingers pried loose, Kevin fell, screaming uncontrollably—a horrible sound—plummeting…. Down…down…down….

3: LIGHTED TUNNEL'S END

Kevin's fall and the darkness were broken by the light. Eyes tightly closed, mind fuzzy and disoriented, illumination surrounded him and somehow permeated his eyelids. His arm ached and pains stabbed his wrist.

His mother's voice called faintly….

Was he dead—or in the hospital? He tried to focus on her words.

"Kevin, you had a nightmare. It's all right…you can wake up now. You're okay."

His eyes remained tightly closed as he rubbed his sweaty face with his left hand, feeling the soft stubble of still-maturing whiskers. His heart pounded in his chest and his breath came in gasps.

"You were only dreaming." His mother's voice spoke softly from close by.

Yeah right, he thought, and groaned, "Oh. I can barely move my right hand." He feared to look at his wrist; afraid to find imprints made by the gutter that was supposedly part of a dream. He couldn't make himself glance down. What if the marks were there? How would he deal with that knowledge? Maybe he could see it…later.

"You probably slept wrong," his mother suggested. "Your arm's just tingling from a pinched nerve."

When his eyelids fluttered open, he was definitely in his bedroom, but the morning sunlight—way too intense—jabbed at him.

"I'm glad you've finally awakened," his mother said. "I'll make you some breakfast. Hurry along so you won't be late for school."

School, he thought, and asked, "What happened to Saturday and Sunday?"

She gave a small laugh, "I know the weekends fly by but you have to go to school today. Come on, let's get moving."

Lying on his bed in a daze, he dimly observed his mother's salt and pepper hair as she exited the room. What he'd experienced couldn't have been a dream. It was too real. On the other hand, he wasn't dead. The awful fall should have killed him or at least put him in the hospital. He wouldn't be lying at home in his bed if the fall was real. The whole thing was too freaky.

Having no appetite for breakfast, Kevin grumbled something unintelligible to his mother on his way out the door. She called him back. Her voice was soft, plaintive. "Why don't you go in and talk to the counselor at the high school?"

"No. I'm not talking to a shrink again."

Ever since his incident at school last year, Kevin's mom thought about sending him to a counselor over every little thing. After all, his nightmare was just a dream—wasn't it?

Halfway to the high school, realization struck, he'd forgotten to shave. What a start for my day, he thought. Awakened out of the nightmare from hell, he'd skipped breakfast and neglected to remove his soft whiskers for probably the fourth day in a row. His right wrist still throbbed, plus his whole arm was sore. Two times before arriving at his destination, he stopped and nearly went back home.

School didn't go much better. Arriving late, he received a tardy slip. By third period, he had two referrals, one for teacher disrespect, and the other for an altercation with a friend. Those were his first of the year, which was nearly over. He racked up a second tardy when he spent time in the bathroom trying to talk himself into skipping school. On his way out the boy's room door, a student aide caught up with him and said he needed to report to the office. Probably about my referrals, Kevin thought.

In the school office, Mrs. Tedry the secretary called to him before he could sit down in one of the detention chairs. "Mr. Bridger wants to see you."

Preoccupied and anticipating the worst, Kevin automatically moved in the direction of the principal's office, not fully registering what she'd said.

"No," she interrupted. "Go to the counseling center. Mr. Bridger wants you."

As if everything else wasn't screwed up, now he needed to go to the shrink's office. Kevin made his way upstairs with his head drooping down and feet dragging the floor. He'd met Bridger only once, briefly, though he'd seen him around.

Sitting there in Bridger's office, Kevin thought he seemed an okay man. The guy was tall, of medium build, with thinning, sandy hair—probably in his mid-forties.

"You aren't in any trouble with me, Kevin. In fact, I've heard you typically don't have problems at school—this year. But because of what happened last spring, you're more than a blip on our radar screen today."

Kevin recalled the pepper spray he'd accidentally released in the lower hall when he headed for the gym his sophomore year. It was really all Cal's fault. Once the spray caught in an air current from an outside door propped open for maintenance, most of the school had to evacuate because several students had allergic reactions.

Some A-hole set off the fire alarm, making things even worse, because the police and fire trucks soon arrived. Whispers of, "Do you think it was terrorists?" filtered through the ranks of disgruntled students milling about outside the building.

Mr. Bridger said, "The staff's worried. They described you as being surly and taciturn, words never applied to you before. Mrs. Wetzel told me you've been disrespectful to adults and hurtful to your friends. Melody spent third period in the girl's restroom she was so hurt by what you said. A friend brought her to my office, and they asked me to speak with you."

Kevin, whose body was already at slouch maximum, let his head droop onto his chest. He and Melody had been good friends for a long time—three years at least. The realization he'd deeply hurt her solidified his decision to go home when he got the chance. She was just trying to help, he guessed, but why'd she have to say he should go see the counselor?

"Has something major happened to you recently?" Mr. Bridger's genuine concern almost caused Kevin to say yes.

"No…" he replied. "I had a restless night. Didn't get much sleep and somehow hurt my arm. I'm just having a bad day." He couldn't tell the truth—the guy'd think he was whacko.

Last year, the principal had insisted Kevin get a mental health evaluation after the pepper spray incident. That was messed up because Cal was the one who brought the little spray canister into the school, threatening to set it off. Jake got it away from Cal and handed it to Kevin, who was attempting to stuff it in his pocket when Cal tried to wrestle it from him. The potent spray went everywhere.

The next thing anyone knew, a teary-eyed teacher was half-choking, half-yelling in Kevin's face. The damning evidence was still clutched in his hand, and he wouldn't rat out his friend. Cal never came forward to reveal the truth. Not even when the police arrested Kevin. Thank goodness they hadn't hauled him off in cuffs. He and Cal didn't speak for a long time after that.

"We all have an occasional bad day," said Mr. Bridger, "so I'll assume that's what it is. But if tomorrow starts out the same, I want you to promise you'll come in and talk with me. Do I have your word you'll do that?"

Kevin thought that one day like this was awful, but two would be living hell. He decided he really would come in if that occurred, and replied, "Yes."

"Just so you know—if you decide to come in later—I don't force people to talk about things if they aren't willing. Now, to be on the safe side, I'm giving you a pass to the counseling center for any time during the rest of today and tomorrow. Just think of it as your Get out of Jail Free card. Show it to any teacher and come on down. Okay?"

Kevin nodded yes.

"You need to know, coming down here doesn't necessarily

eliminate consequences but it helps you stay out of more trouble. Understand?"

"Yes." Kevin left the counseling center feeling a little bit better. At least he wasn't being ordered for another evaluation at mental health. Since his visit there last year, his mom seemed to think everything he did indicated he needed counseling. She hadn't even believed it was Cal's pepper spray.

Downstairs, Kevin meandered through the long hall toward the west side of the building. At the far end of the dim corridor, an unaccountably bright light attracted his attention. It was so intense that the long hall resembled a tunnel.

When he arrived at the juncture formed from adding the newer wing, Kevin decided to go out the side exit for home. Hurriedly, he forced the door open to make his escape, accidentally banging into someone who was attempting to enter.

"I'm sorry," he said. "Are you all right?" He gazed more directly at the other person, his initial concern transforming into stricken shock.

"Don't worry," she said. "I'm not hurt."

He stood there unable to reply, looking down into animated blue eyes. There was a healthy pink hue to her cheeks, accentuated by her rose colored lip-gloss. Her mouth crinkled into a warm smile that lighted up her rounded face, which was haloed with medium-length blonde hair.

Unbelievably, hers was the very image he'd seen sprawled on the brass bed in his nightmare. Now, however, she was fully clothed and appeared vibrant and very much alive.

She asked, "Do I know you?"

"No, I don't think so."

"You look familiar," she said, "and it seemed like maybe you recognize me from somewhere."

"You look a lot like someone I used to know," he lied, feeling lame. His mind worked wildly, trying to understand things that made no sense.

"We just moved here," she said, "and I don't know my way around. My stepfather signed me into school but I need to find the office and see about my classes. Can you tell me where it is?"

He pointed and replied, "At the other end of the hall." He couldn't imagine why she'd come in this door. She was *really* lost.

"Thanks, I don't know anyone here and I'm a little nervous. I've never had to move before…it's my senior year." Her tone had turned somber, but then brightened as she added, "My name's Misty, by the way."

"Nice to meet you. My name's Kevin. Too bad you had to move before you could graduate from your old school, but as you'll see, students here are friendly." He thought this was the worst possible day to meet such a pretty, new student. His hand migrated to his face, detecting the few days' worth of whiskers— well, kind-of-whiskers. Had he combed his hair? He must really be a sight. Also, she was a senior and he was a junior.

Misty stood there, seemingly reluctant to walk down the hallway to the office.

"Oh," he said, "I'll show you where it is."

"Would you? I know it seems silly but I'm really nervous about starting a new school. I keep telling myself I should quit being a baby."

They walked slowly down the hall.

"Where did you move from?"

"Coeur d'Alene, Idaho. I've lived there my whole life…till now."

"How come you moved to The Dalles?"

"My stepfather sold a business in Coeur d'Alene and bought one here. He said we could delay our move. Due to something else, I thought it would be better to come here now, but I miss all my friends."

"Yeah…" Kevin nodded.

Coming down the hall behind them was a young man built like a super-jock. "Hey, Conners. New student?"

"Yes…just moved here," Kevin said.

The other guy added, "Why don't I show her around?"

"Kevin's already helping—thanks."

That didn't faze the newcomer. "I'm Brad, the unofficial greeter. I orient all the new students. He won't mind." Brad gave

Kevin a threatening look as he attempted to move between him and Misty.

She said curtly, "No," and intertwined her arm with Kevin's. Moving down the hallway again, they left Brad standing in uncomfortable silence. Kevin knew the athlete was accustomed to getting his own way—especially where girls were concerned.

"Hey," Misty said as they put more distance between themselves and the would-be interloper. "We just moved into our home down by the courthouse. Want to come over later? You're the only person I know here."

Kevin's brow knitted as he realized the girl from his nightmare had apparently moved into the very house from his dream. He struggled to refocus. "Yes, I can do that." He thought she might change her mind anyway, by the end of the day, once she met other students and felt more secure.

"I know," she said, "why don't you come over right after school, if you don't have other plans?"

"I don't, but you may be busy this afternoon once you meet more kids."

Misty stopped and turned, looking into his eyes. "So…you think you might show up at my house and find it already full of other guys?"

"No," he replied, thinking she must have read his mind. "It's just that—"

She broke in, "I guess the guys in The Dalles will turn out to be as dense as the ones in Coeur d'Alene, so let me put it this way…do you want to hang out with me this afternoon?"

"Yes."

She asked, "Where do you live?"

"On Sixth Place, just a few blocks from your house."

"Cool." Reaching into her bag, she found a little notepad and a pen. "I'm going to put my phone and address down for you. We don't have our new mobiles yet but the house line is in. I want you to write down your home number and address for me. Okay?"

From nightmare to dream come true, he thought. One of the prettiest girls he'd ever met was giving him her number without being asked. Maybe his worst-starting-day would turn out ending the best—and yet, a shiver ran down his back.

When they'd exchanged information, Misty looked at him and said, "I feel a little better about this new school now that I've met you."

She studied his face curiously, as though she saw something familiar there. "I'm not certain why, but it seems like we already know each other. After school, I think I'll...." She seemed suddenly unsure of herself. "Maybe I'll come visit. Is that alright?"

"Sure." He felt giddy that she wanted to spend time with him and yet uncertain how to deal with the reality of this young woman, and his nightmare. Another chill erupted.

They walked to the office in silence. Inside, Mrs. Tedry glanced up and began helping Misty. Kevin absently scanned a copy of The Dalles Chronicle lying nearby. He was startled to see the headline. Search for Cat Burglar Continues.

Mrs. Tedry gave Misty her class schedule. "Your school records should be here next week. We requested they rush them because it's so close to the end of the year." She turned to Kevin as the phone began to ring. "Where do you need to be young man?"

He held up the counseling pass.

Misty turned. "Thanks. See you this afternoon."

Kevin found himself moving toward, of all places, the counseling center.

4: THE SHRINK

Kevin waited for Mr. Bridger to finish meeting with another student. He tried to figure out what was happening, and wondered what he would say to the counselor. Could he trust the man? At least the guy hadn't freaked out when they talked earlier. Certainly not like the principal had the previous year about the pepper spray occurrence.

Eventually, Kevin decided that discovering what was going on by himself was fruitless. He couldn't talk to Carol about this. They would undoubtedly break up, and when they did, she'd betray him with the nightmare information. Probably by her retaliating in some way he could barely imagine.

What about talking to Jake? He was a great cross-country runner and fun to play video games with, but not a person you could just sit down and talk to. Cal? He'd belly-laughed last year about Kevin having to get checked out by a mental health therapist because of the pepper spray incident. No one but an idiot would confide in Cal.

Out of boredom, Kevin began studying the posters and diplomas on the wall. A certificate stated Bridger was a Licensed Clinical Social Worker. Kevin had assumed only a school counselor would be working there. Peering closely at a large photograph, he guessed by the familiar-looking landmarks that the picture had probably been taken in London. There were teenagers clustered together in the foreground. In the background, a bridge's towers soared above a river. On closer inspection, he could see Mr. Bridger at the edge of the group. Intrigued, Kevin decided he would ask about the photo.

Looking farther around the room, he puzzled over the

meaning of a hand-calligraphied banner that hung on a wall. It read: Believing is Seeing.

Weren't those words turned around?

When Mr. Bridger met with Kevin, he explained that whatever they talked about was confidential—with a few exceptions. The ones that stuck in Kevin's mind were child abuse and safety issues like suicide and homicide. At length, Mr. Bridger asked, "What do you want to discuss?"

"I don't know what's happening. I hope I'm not going crazy." Kevin sat there in surprise at the way he'd blurted that out.

Mr. Bridger relaxed against his chair's back. His eyes studied the floor for a moment before he spoke. "That's a pretty scary word, crazy. Using it seriously as you just did says something big is happening. What makes you wonder about your sanity?"

Those words were spoken so calmly that Kevin was reassured. "It started with a nightmare. One so real, I...." Kevin subconsciously rubbed his wrist. "My right arm still aches."

While fingering the sore area, Kevin saw his crossed leg bouncing spasmodically, and realized Mr. Bridger had noticed as well, though he hadn't said anything about it.

"That sounds like a powerful dream," said the man, "and we'll discuss it in a minute, but first I want to reassure you about something. I've worked in clinical settings in the past, and if I thought your sanity was a real issue, I'd have you sign a release form and conduct a mental status exam. You'd get questions like, 'Do you hear voices from the TV even when it isn't turned on?' Or, 'Do you know what time of day it is?'"

Kevin laughed nervously. He'd already been asked those questions last year when the school administration insisted he not return to classes before an assessment at mental health—all because of the stupid pepper spray mess. No need to mention that now, though.

"I realize," Mr. Bridger said, "those questions sound preposterous, and 'The time of day' one threw me too until I encountered people who got it wrong—told me it was nine at night and dark outside the window when it was actually mid-day and the sun was shining."

Mr. Bridger asked, "Would you say you have more or worse nightmares than other people you know?"

"I don't think so—except for this last one. It was intense."

Mr. Bridger said in a soothing voice, "It's scary when people think they might be, as you said, 'going crazy,' but you aren't showing any obvious signs of mental illness. Besides, most people who actually have such a diagnosis think they are normal —at least initially they think that."

Kevin was relieved.

"Now, let's figure out more about what *is* going on. Why don't you start at the beginning, or wherever you feel comfortable, and tell me what you experienced?"

Kevin recounted the details of the nightmare, followed by his strange awakening, and feeling pain in his arm. He reminded Mr. Bridger of the catastrophic morning which had followed. Kevin told him that just when he began to think he could get past the nightmare, he literally bumped into a new student coming into the school. She turned out to be the "dead girl" from his awful dream. He'd never seen her before in waking life but she apparently lived in the same house he'd dreamt about, where she'd moved during the past weekend. According to the newspaper, there really was a burglar in town. Kevin finished recounting his story and saw his foot still bouncing uncontrollably. Once again, Mr. Bridger had noticed it too.

"What you've related seems puzzling," the soothing voice continued. "But let me show you something." Rising from his chair, Mr. Bridger selected two books from a shelf, and displayed the top one's cover, *Dream Loose, Dream Lucid.*

"This book," said Mr. Bridger, "is focused mainly on one aspect of dreaming, the lucid dream. Technically, what you experienced wasn't true lucidity, because you were not aware you were dreaming. However, your nightmare had a clarity associated with such dreams. There's another part in this book about False Awakenings. I mention this because people who experience them believe they are fully conscious. When they finally wake up, they wonder if they're still in a dream. I don't know how to classify your nightmare, but it fits with known dream phenomena."

Kevin breathed hard from retelling his experiences, but felt relieved talking about them and knowing he wasn't going crazy. But why was his foot still jerking about?

Mr. Bridger asked, "What are your biggest concerns?"

"Well, I don't want to go through something like this again, and I'm freaked out by actually meeting the girl in my dream."

Tapping meaningfully on the book in his hand, Mr. Bridger said, "There's growing conviction in the field of dream research indicating ESP—particularly telepathy and glimpsing the future—are linked with dreaming. Many people have shared identical dreams, especially nightmares. Still, we needn't take most of them too literally. For instance, you didn't see the body of a murder victim today, you met a live person."

"Thank God," whispered Kevin.

Mr. Bridger reached down for the other book, titled *Creating Your Own Dream World.* "It may surprise you that experiencing nightmares is fairly common with high school students. Many people think it's mostly little kids who get them. I've used this book to help people of all ages control dreams and nightmares." Mr. Bridger leafed through the volume and then looked at Kevin.

"I consult part-time at a sleep lab in Portland, working mostly with children. You'd be astonished to hear how much control over their dreams some youngsters have developed, and one in particular I can think of." He handed Kevin the book.

"I'm loaning this to you. Focus on chapter five about the Senoi dreamers. It has helped many students I've worked with and I'm certain it'll be useful to you."

Kevin sat up and nodded.

Mr. Bridger added, "You'll be working primarily on building awareness of the dream you're in and confronting anything frightening. If you overcome a nightmare enemy, you may demand a gift from him. And even if he overcomes you, he must then be your ally in future dreams." Mr. Bridger paused.

"If the guy in the ski mask returns in your sleep, let him have it with whatever is at hand. Remember, it's a dream. Make him yield and demand he give you a gift."

That sounded so preposterous, Kevin smiled.

"You'll see what I mean when you read that chapter in the book."

Kevin left the counseling center feeling somewhat better, once again.

5: MY HOUSE AND YOURS?

Kevin had been home for more than an hour after school. He'd showered, shaved, changed his clothes, and waited—

Eventually, he decided Misty wasn't coming over. He lamented not learning more about her and their strange connection through the nightmare. There was relief also, because he worried where the dream's influence was leading him.

To relax, Kevin went out behind his family's multi-car garage where he'd built his racing homer loft, with its wire-mesh aviary. His moderate-sized home was surrounded by an immense yard composed of three lots. A rocky bluff topped with trees ran along the south, continuing into the neighbor's yard.

If he'd thought Misty was still coming to visit he would not have gone to the bird pen. Many people disliked or feared pigeons, a fact he'd become sensitive to over the years. He entered his homer loft, inspecting the grit container and the waterer. They were full. He didn't check the feeder because he wouldn't feed again until later when his birds returned from their evening flight. He looked over the nest boxes to see how his baby pigeons—the squabs—were developing. He could almost see them growing.

Kevin was talking to a young bird he held when his old black lab, Molly, sounded off with her combination whine-bark. Her friendly greeting was an alert to the family that someone was approaching the house. She was hard of hearing, however, and sometimes just slept-away, letting people walk right past.

A feminine voice called out. "Is anybody home?"

"Uh, yeah. Just a minute…." Startled, he nearly dropped the squab and unceremoniously returned the ruffled youngster to its nest before exiting the homer loft.

"Hi," he said, hoping he didn't look surprised or embarrassed, but also wondering how she'd found him.

Fawning over his dog, Misty looked even prettier than she had earlier in the day. She now wore a light pink top that matched her lip-gloss and her blonde hair was in pigtails. She continued to pet Molly, who loved the attention. "You probably thought I wasn't coming over, right?"

Kevin hesitated, not wanting to lie, but not wanting to tell the truth, either.

"Unfair question?" She looked at him. "Hey, you didn't get slicked-up just for me, did you?"

He felt more than a little off-balance, and guessed his face was turning red.

She smiled mischievously. "The reason it took me so long to get over here was that I couldn't find Sixth Place. For a while, I thought it didn't exist, but that's not the whole truth. I wanted you to notice me, so I primped. I tried not to go overboard. How'd I do?"

Kevin stood there trying to figure out what he should say.

"I keep asking unfair questions, don't I?" Not waiting for his answer, she walked over to view the flying pen. "What's in here?"

"Those are just my racing homers," he replied, purposely leaving off the word pigeons.

"You race them?"

"Yes, there's a local flying club for homers."

"Where do they compete?"

"Well, its long distance, not like what you see at a horse track. Homers under a year old—what we call young bird racers—they fly up to one hundred and fifty miles their first year. Old birds go out to five hundred. We take them mostly to the south and southeast. Over in the Midwestern states, they fly up to 1,000-mile races, but our terrain's too rugged."

"Can I see one up close?"

"Yeah, I'll catch a youngster and bring it out."

"Can't I come with you? They won't attack will they?"

"No," he laughed. "They'll fly around and try to get away but they won't hurt you. They're used to me but they'll be skittish of a stranger."

Entering the loft, he cautioned her, "Move slow...and stand still at first, until they get used to you." He smiled, knowing he had several pure white homers. Most racing fanciers frowned on owning light-colored birds, and perhaps with good reason. The flashy pigeons seemed to attract hawks. Kevin knew that people who saw a white pigeon often believed they were looking at a dove. Everybody liked doves even if they hated pigeons, and despite the fact they are the same species.

As a white homer flew by, he snatched it from the air.

She asked, "How'd you do that?"

"It just takes practice."

He tucked the bird's wings under the fingers of his right hand and held it out to Misty, encouraging her to grasp it two-handed. She did pretty well, and he guided her movements until she was holding and admiring the pure white racing homer.

"How pretty. Its feathers are so soft…. What's his name?"

Kevin laughed. "Whitey Ford."

"Really?"

"No," he said. "I just made that up. Whitey Ford was an old-time pitcher for the Yankees. I have over fifty birds and I only give names to a few. Some get lost or killed in races, so I only name my breeders, which I don't race. You can pick a name for that one, though."

"I can?"

"Sure, if you want to."

"Is it a boy or a girl?

"That's a young bird. Too early to tell. Probably a hen, but why don't you pick a name that's for either male or female?"

"Wait a minute. I see why you don't name these white ones… they're identical."

"No. I can tell them apart, except a few youngsters before I get to know them."

"That's hard to believe."

He said, "Yes, but it's true."

"I guess, but it seems impossible." She held up the pigeon and looked into its dark eyes. "What shall I name you?" After thinking for a moment, she said decisively, "Mist, because it can be a boy or girl's name and it's short for mine, too. You are White Mist." She laughed when she spoke, startling the pigeon. It gave a mighty burst with its wings, freeing them from her grip. Surprised, she let go with a yelp and it flapped to a nearby roost.

"Shall I catch it again?" he asked.

"No, I'd rather hold one that's not so strong—a baby?"

He moved to the nest box containing the three and one-half week squab. "This little guy will be leaving the nest in about a week. If you let him loose on your hand, be sure which way his rear-end is aimed or you'll get a little present you won't like."

He pulled the reddish-brown squab from its nest, wondering about the wisdom of his idea. Visions of Misty screaming and running from the homer loft with bird poop in her palm played through his mind. He decided to position the squab carefully, monitoring it for a happy conclusion. Kevin nestled the small bird in her extended hands. His fingers rested with hers as he watched her staring intently at the squab. The contact felt so nice he almost continued, but pulled away after lingering longer than seemed warranted. Glancing over at Kevin's arms, Misty said, "Do you have a cat?"

"No." He wondered what had prompted her question.

"Where'd you get all those scratches on your hands and arms? I noticed them when you handed me this baby."

He looked down in bewilderment. "I don't know—can't remember." Why hadn't he noticed the scratches before? How long had they been there? His mind flashed back to his nightmare. That was too unsettling and he pushed aside his memory of climbing the rose trellis and receiving thorn pricks. Instead, he stared at the squab and moved his arms behind him.

Changing the subject, he said, "This youngster's color is sort of brownish but we call it red. The gray pattern that sets it off makes what we call checkering, so he's a red-check." Kevin tried to ignore the sweat trickling down his back.

"You're pretty good at catching these. Can you catch wild pigeons?"

"Well, I've had fair luck—so far."

"I hate to mention this and I didn't know you raise pigeons, so that's not the reason I came over. I've only slept in my attic bedroom a couple of nights but there are wild pigeons on the roof that drive me crazy. Sometimes, they start cooing way before the sun comes up."

"They can be a nuisance." His mind raced as he guided her to the squab's nest box. The coincidences flooded him: the girl from his bad dream, the same house, attic, and a burglar. And now the problem with pigeons, plus her request for his help....

He brought his thoughts back to the task at hand and directed her to hold the squab about a foot from its nest. The little feather-ball leaped back into its home and peeped with happiness, turning round and round.

Misty laughed.

Kevin might have laughed with her under other circumstances. Instead, he lowered a flight-training box from the top row of nests and showed her how to open and close the single-bird entrance. It was an attempt to distract her and buy more time to consider the new facts.

One after another, he caught half-a-dozen pure white birds and Misty opened the small door for him to deposit each of them through the wooden crate's side entrance. That task completed, he carried the training box outdoors. Misty closed the loft door and followed to the expansive backyard area. When he set the container down, Molly sniffed at it briefly before losing interest. Kevin arranged a couple of lawn chairs nearby.

Misty asked, "What are we going to do?"

"When you're ready, flip the little catch and open that lid. Those homers will race for the sky, so step back when you do that. It makes an awesome sight, the pure whites against the blue."

"I'm ready."

"Go ahead."

She pulled the top up and back. The six white racers flapped out of the crate, rising straight into the air. Molly, lying nearby, lifted her head and then returned to her afternoon nap. The pigeons circled higher and higher, gaining altitude until they leveled off and flew giant rings above Kevin's home. He reclined on one of the lawn chairs. "If you lay back and look up, you won't strain your neck. It's easier to watch them this way."

She did as he suggested and breathed a peaceful sigh.

His mind wasn't really on the birds. He wondered what Mr. Bridger would say about all these developments. What had he meant by the words "glimpsing the future?" Did these coincidences indicate something could happen to him and Misty?

He subconsciously reached down to rub his right wrist and found it spasmed with pain. Once his attention focused there, he realized how much it hurt but tried to conceal his discomfort from Misty.

"They really are beautiful, aren't they?" she remarked.

"Yes, unless they're being a nuisance on your roof." The minute his words came out, he realized his blunder. What a moron I am, he thought.

"I almost forgot," she said. "Do you know of anything I can do to get rid of the wild pigeons…?"

Her voice sounded strained as she changed direction in her thinking, "Er...I thought about not telling anybody, because I was trying to run away from it, but I'm going to tell you and probably only you. My mother died a few months ago. It was messed-up— a totally bogus thing."

"I'm so sorry…," he said.

She added, "I haven't felt safe ever since. That's why I decided to leave Coeur d'Alene before I graduated. I had too many awful memories to deal with up there."

"Uh huh." He swallowed with difficulty, having no idea what to say. The pulsing in his wrist intensified again.

"I've felt unsafe for so long—until just today when I met you."

The two of them lay there on the lawn chairs in silence, each lost in separate thoughts. Staring into the sky at the white homers flying above them, Misty sighed.

Kevin struggled to pull himself away from negative thoughts and scary connections between the beautiful girl and his nightmare.

"Can you come over now and take a look?" she asked, "the ones on my home are really obnoxious."

"That's why I built my loft out by the garage away from the house. We can't hear them from indoors." Keep talking, he thought to himself, wondering how she could focus on the wild pigeons right after talking about her dead mother. The thought of a dead person reminded him again of his nightmare and Misty's body lying uncovered on the bed. He jerked his mind away from that horrible image.

She stood up. "Ready?"

"Yeah, I guess," he said, still lying down. "I can come and see what the roof looks like. But I can't catch them in the day, only at night."

She reached out her hand. When he accepted, she pulled him to his feet with surprising strength—way more than he'd anticipated.

As they left the yard, he gave Molly the command to "Stay," and tightly closed the gate. She'd been known to sneak out and follow at a discreet distance.

With a few upward glances at the white pigeons circling overhead, they made their way toward her house. He was totally distracted by an apprehension that became stronger as they approached the dwelling.

His attention was interrupted by the sound of her voice as Misty said, "I don't want to become a bother, so I'm telling you ahead of time. Let me know if I start hanging out with you too much."

"Okay, now I'm warned." His mind returned to thoughts of her large house as his eyes were drawn upwards to the roof. What was he thinking about...in coming here?

She said, "I'll want to hang out with you, probably all the time. I feel safe around you. Haven't felt like this for months. It's such a relief."

Despite growing fears, he smiled, thinking of them spending

a great deal of time together.

"What are you smirking at?"

"I was thinking that I could get used to having my own groupie."

"I'm not a groupie!"

"Just teasing."

She asked, "Are we going to make anyone jealous?"

"There's a couple girls who might sharpen their claws." He felt guilty as Carol's image flashed through his thoughts.

Misty reached out, grasping his fingers. "What if they see us holding hands?"

"We may both be living dangerously."

She squeezed and let go, "I don't want to cause any problems."

Recalling his nightmare, Kevin said, "I don't think we can avoid problems altogether."

"Maybe we'll get lucky."

He replied earnestly with a sly smile, "I hope so."

6: THE ATTIC

With the Wasco County Courthouse looming large to the north behind him, Kevin stepped into the road to get a better look at the attic windows and asked, "Some of those open up, don't they?"

"At least two do…on the front, and the near side."

"Is the noise coming from under one of the dormer eaves?"

"I guess."

"Pigeons aren't good home builders and tend to nest in that type of protected spot."

"You sure know a lot about them."

"Compared to most people, I suppose, but not in comparison to other fanciers." Kevin pondered a while and then said, "Although, my advanced biology teacher had me give talks on them to his classes when we were dissecting pigeons. I guess I do know quite a bit about them."

"Do you want to come up and test out opening a window?"

"Uh-huh." His artist's eye couldn't help imagining the sketches he could make of the picturesque building. "I've always wondered what those dormered attics look like on the inside. It's a really cool house. I like all the leaded panes above the main windows."

Despite that, he couldn't understand why he was agreeing to go inside her house. Why was he letting her take him to the attic, of all places? Then, realizing how attracted he was to Misty gave him a clue. He subconsciously massaged his right wrist, feeling discomfort there.

"What's wrong?" She'd apparently noticed a troubled look on his face.

He changed the subject. "That rose trellis is only about ten feet high. I thought it'd go clear to the roof." He made a mental note that the trellis differed from the one in his dream, though the location on the house was the same.

She stared thoughtfully down at the pavement. "It's a neat old house, better than we had on Sherman Avenue in Coeur d'Alene. There's too much traffic there in the summers. I used to love hanging out at the lake and then…" her voice trailed off.

Kevin took hold of her hand. They climbed the front steps from the street and went up the second set to the porch. Misty pulled the screen back, turning the brass knob. The door swung open, revealing an entry alcove.

"Don't you lock your house?"

"Only at night. Who'd be stupid enough to break into someone's home this near to the courthouse?"

For the moment, he didn't comment.

The formal living room sat off to the left but the bright and cheery sitting room to the right boasted a beautiful, wood-paneled staircase, curving to the second floor. Still holding hands, they traipsed up the steps. The beveled windowpanes in the upper windows acted like tiny prisms, reflecting mini-rainbows all about them.

When they arrived at the next level she said, "I don't know why, because this house is totally beautiful, but some parts, especially the basement, give me the creeps. And I don't like coming home alone. Isn't that the dumbest thing?"

"Not really," he said.

Misty looked grateful and gave him a quick hug. She self-consciously straightened and dropped her hands to her sides. Slightly tilting her head she whispered, "You always manage to say the right thing."

Shrugging with embarrassment, he smiled at her. He liked Misty a lot—but where was this heading?

"Okay, let's go see the attic." She led him to the right, bypassing the upstairs great room and proceeded down the hall toward the second floor's small kitchen. She halted at a door recessed in the wall a few feet before the kitchen. Kevin felt a tremor, realizing they would soon see the attic. She opened the door and led the way up. From the bottom, the cramped stairway curved steeply to the right and a distinctive attic smell greeted them. Nearing the top of the stairs, it was more open, and light flooded downward.

He shuddered at the view as they stepped into the expansive chamber. The brass bed was there, nearly in the same location as in his dream. Clothing and extra bedding lay neatly on top, mostly-folded—instead of piled high in a jumbled mess as he'd seen before. There was no sign of the golf bag but the battery-powered lantern rested on an end table beside the bed. Misty stood in front of Kevin, not noticing his reaction.

They remained quiet, lost in their separate thoughts. Kevin was overwhelmed by similarities to his nightmare, and slumped quietly to the floor, a sickening feeling in his gut.

The sound of a cooing pigeon interrupted the silence. Misty laughed, turning to wink at Kevin. Her ready smile said it was the pigeons that brought them to the attic—wasn't it? She stopped in mid-laugh, looking concerned. Kevin wasn't where she'd expected. She stared at his form crumpled on the floor.

He looked back into her stricken eyes and tried to stand.

"Kevin. What's wrong?" She knelt beside him, taking hold of his arm.

"There's stuff I didn't know how to tell. Or if I should. Now, seeing all this…"

"What is it?"

"Last night I had a terrible nightmare."

Kevin recounted his story in detail up to the point where he thought he'd seen a shadow move as he peered through the attic window from the roof.

"A moving shadow?"

"Yes, and that lantern sat over in the middle of the floor."

"I brought it up here for light before I replaced the burned-out ceiling bulbs."

He continued, "The shadow was a man in black, wearing a ski mask and doing something with the floor. Over there…" Kevin pointed. "Then the guy brought a trinket box to the lantern…looking at jewelry in the light."

"You mean—like a hole in the floor?"

Kevin rose slowly, examining the wooden surface as he proceeded. "Yeah, it was over this way." He stopped, a startled look on his face as he peered down at an unnaturally short floorboard. Most of them were six feet or longer, and a few were four feet, but none were only a foot long. Except that one.

Kevin straightened, fishing a quarter from his pocket.

"Is that the spot?" Misty asked.

He knelt. "Let's see."

As Kevin used his quarter to pry up an end of the board and pull it free of the floor, Misty gasped.

Despite everything he'd already told her, Misty said, "How'd you know about this?"

He placed the board to one side and peered into the dark cavity. The shadowy space was the width between floor studs and likely ran the length of the room. He gingerly reached his hand in.

"Watch out for spiders." she cautioned. It was a wise thought in a region known for black widows. He hesitated, resuming his search with a grim smile, and feeling somewhat secure in the knowledge that spiders were not part of his dream. He withdrew his hand, disappointed.

"Nothing. My arm's too big. It's so cramped in there I can't reach out in either direction." He wondered if the cat burglar was that much skinnier.

"Let me try." She slipped her arm into the opening. There was a scraping sound and she used both hands to withdraw an old-fashioned metal box from the hollow. "Look at this."

"Like the one from my nightmare."

She pried it open and it was nearly full of jewels. She asked, "Who do you suppose left this here?"

"The masked guy?"

She walked to her bed, spreading out the jewelry on the

cover. He moved beside her and they took turns sorting through the contents of the container.

She whispered in amazement. "How much do you suppose this is worth?"

"I don't know, but these are real pearls. Those ones there are black pearls. I know because my mom has a pair of earrings from my grandmother. And look, here's diamonds. This stuff's got to be genuine, and there's several thousand dollars worth at least."

"Eeeeeyyyyeeeee. We're rich." She held up a sparkling necklace like Kevin had seen in his nightmare. His mouth opened as he inspected it, apparently the very one the burglar had held up in the bad dream.

She reached down, hands scooping, and turned to him with a display of gemstone and jewelry items. "Let's run away."

"You're the one girl I might want to run away with." He said impulsively. Even as he spoke, he couldn't believe his own words.

She stopped, dropping the jewels on the bed. "Do you mean that?"

"Yeah. In a way."

Her enthusiasm dampened when he vacillated on his reply. "Oh well," she said. "I don't know if running away is my best idea. What do you think of all these?"

He lay back on her bed, eyes gazing at the ceiling, wanting to evade her question, "There's more to know and a lot I haven't told. Things in my nightmare make me…. I need to tell you the rest, but I don't want to."

"I won't interrupt. Go ahead."

The persistence of coincidences—dream-to-reality—caused Kevin more apprehension by the minute. "Shouldn't we put the jewelry back?"

"I suppose, but let's each keep something. Maybe we can find out if they're real. The rest could disappear but we can prove what we've found."

"Good idea. Let's hurry and put this stuff away. I didn't want to say it, but this house is creeping me out now."

She picked a black pearl pendant on a gold chain, and, pulling her hair to one side, put it on. "This chain doesn't match the pearl's fitting," she noted, as she dropped the small pendant down the v-neck opening of her top. "Does it show through my clothes?"

"Not really," he remarked, trying to keep his eyes focused mainly on the area where the pendant should be hanging. "If you wear it with something fluffy, it'll never show."

He chose a diamond ring with a large, faceted stone surrounded by small ones. "We can't let anyone see these. There's a good chance they're stolen. We might get blamed for the burglaries."

Kevin had a flashback of the man with the wicked knife. Chills raced down his back. "What if the burglar returns?"

Misty, still engrossed by their find, didn't seem to hear him and selected an ordinary-looking ring with a small, red stone. Taking off the gold chain, she lowered it down through the band until the ring rested on the pendant. Replacing the chain around her neck, she said, "This one's safer to get checked out by a jeweler, if we decide to."

They returned the rest to the jewelry box, depositing it into the hidey-hole. That accomplished, a compelling curiosity caused Kevin to test out the window near where the pigeon sounds originated. Sure enough, the latch scraped and hinges squealed, but it swung open. The bird's long, mournful coo fell silent. Leaving the window ajar to furnish a breeze, he returned toward Misty.

Stopping uncertainly, he wondered what he was doing. That's the window from my nightmare, he thought. It even sounds the same.

Lamentable cooing began again, sounding louder through the open window. He realized, even while feeling an ominous premonition, that when Misty smiled, he forgot his fears and became sidetracked.

As seeming proof of his thought, the next thing Kevin knew, he was lying beside her on the bed and staring up at the curved ceiling while he recounted seeing the man in black and noticing him race forward. Kevin told how the man had stumbled over debris on the floor and careened into the bed, knocking away much of what had been piled there, to reveal….

Kevin forced himself to say, "There was a body on the bed."

Suddenly aware that they lay on the very spot he'd seen her corpse, Kevin sat up with apprehension. What would Mr. Bridger say to all this?

"Who was it?" Misty asked. "Did you recognize them?"

Kevin hesitated too long.

"Me? No wonder you freaked when we first met."

"I'm sorry; I didn't want to tell you."

"It's so scary. But you had to. What are we going to do?" She looked around the room as though she feared the man in black was lurking somewhere, ready to pounce.

Kevin said, "I was so worried, I went to the school counselor. That's where I learned dreams can be a source of seeing the future." He paused. "I think we should get out of here."

She sat up, agitated. "Finish telling what the counselor said; then we'll go."

"He told me that two people sometimes have shared nightmares and occasionally dreams are so life-like you can't tell them from reality. He gave me a book to read describing how some tribe of people controlled their dreams. He said lots of folks have been helped by learning to alter bad dreams."

"That's cool."

"The book is on my bed at home. We can get it and read more, but let's—"

A loud noise sounded somewhere lower in the house.

Kevin jumped at the sound. Gripped by renewed fear, he wondered why he hadn't left earlier. It was as though an invisible force held him.

Why…had…he…stayed…?

7: THE STEP-DAD ENTERS

Kevin and Misty jumped up as a husky male voice called from the floor below. "Are you home?"

Misty whispered, "That's my step-dad; he better not find you here." She smoothed the two indentations in the bedspread. "Hide underneath. I'll get rid of him."

A creaking sound issued from the steps below as Kevin slid hurriedly into the ample space under the bed. Discovering the golf bag, he gulped hard and carefully slid it over—using it to help him hide from the possibility of prying eyes as they crested the top step.

"I'm up here." She seated herself on the bed. Kevin thought she was probably pretending to sort her clothes into tops and bottoms that went together.

"I didn't think you'd be home. I never see you," the man appeared at the top of the steps. Kevin didn't get a clear look but could tell the guy was big, like an ex-football lineman.

"Well, I'm here now, what do you want?" Her tone was harsh and to Kevin's mind, surprisingly disrespectful.

The man said with a measure of suggestion, "Oh, you know what I want."

"Not that. Not since my Mom died. I've told you before."

"What difference did her death make?"

"Since Mom died, I can hurt you worse than you can hurt me. We haven't *done it* since."

In the uncomfortable silence, Kevin lay under the bed in shock.

She spoke impatiently to the man, "What…?"

"I'm taking some people out for dinner tonight. Would you like to join us? You could meet the ones I've hired and others I'll be doing business with."

"No. I have plans, plus I'll probably turn in early. In case you forget, I'll be locking the door from *this side*. I can't tell you how mad I'll be if you ever try to sneak up here in the middle of the night again."

"I understand." He sounded apologetic as he approached the bed and stood beside her. "You don't usually wear necklaces; where'd you get that?"

"It's just a chain. Reminds me of my mother if you must know. I wear it sometimes…when I miss her."

There was a struggle—feet scooted about, and they bumped into the bed.

"Take your—" her half-screamed next words were garbled in the struggle, "…hands off me."

Kevin bumped his head on a cross board under the bed while scooting out from underneath. He paused at the edge opposite them when he heard the man scream.

"Ouch! You little *bitch*. I ought to…. You *bit* me."

"Don't even think about it." There was derision in her voice and more control than Kevin could believe. She said, "I bet I can scream loud enough from here to bring the Sheriff from down the street. The window's open. Shall we test it out?"

The man's thudding footsteps receded to the stairway.

Kevin glanced from his new position mostly out from under the bed. He saw the bulk of the man descending the steps and then Kevin laid back in shock.

Misty followed behind her stepfather and the latchkey turned noisily in the door at the foot of the stairway.

By the time she got back, Kevin had again slid mostly under the bed, lying in a curled-up position.

Her soft voice whispered, "It's all right to come out now."

Kevin didn't know if he wanted to, but he made his way from under the brass bed anyway.

"I never meant for you to hear that," she apologized. "I really didn't. Now I've got so much explaining."

The slamming of the front door interrupted her. They heard the sound distinctly through the open window.

She continued her explanation, "When I was fifteen, I had a crush on a football star, John...at the local college. I hung out at the beach near his school, and maybe I filled out a swimsuit a little too well.

"John noticed me and I lied, saying I was a senior in high school. Anyway, he came onto me and I was in way over my head. One thing led to another that I later regretted, but you can't really undo things like that."

She was silent for a long moment.

"Thank God I didn't get pregnant," she whispered. "My step-dad figured out what was going on and had us followed. He threatened to go to the police, ending John's career in sports and putting him in jail. His life would be ruined."

"What happened?"

"I didn't know what to do. I was afraid my mom would find out and John would be jailed. I told my step-dad I'd do anything to keep my mom from finding out. Now you know what he wanted from me so he'd keep quiet. The next couple of years, every time my mom was away...." She broke down crying.

Regaining her composure, she said, "This room is as far away as I could get from him in this house." Her head sagged forward. "The master bedroom's on the first floor. That's the only place he'd ever sleep, except in my bed, but I won't let him."

She continued with a frantic note to her voice, "My mom died in a bogus sailing accident on Coeur d'Alene Lake. You're telling me about a nightmare and seeing me dead. If I die, everything goes to him. Until I'm twenty-one, he's executor of my parents' estate."

When Misty spoke again, her voice was so low Kevin barely heard her words. "The stupid thing about moving here is I know everybody in Coeur d'Alene, but I don't know a soul here except you. I wouldn't even have the guts to tell you about this if you hadn't overheard."

"Since before mom died, my life's been hell. I've wanted to tell somebody. Will you still be my friend?"

"Nothing's going to change that."

She whispered, "Do you think I'm an awful person?"

Despite his conflicting emotions, Kevin managed to say, "I think you're brave to stand up to your pervert of a stepfather. He's an awfully big guy. I started to get out from under the bed, to help you."

"I'm glad you didn't, because he doesn't know I have a friend. I think that's best."

"We should get out of here." Kevin said. "We can study that book on dreams and you can spend the night at my place."

"Okay. My step-dad will think I'm still up here. He's unlikely to check for some time. Let's go."

She gathered spare clothes, her hairbrush and other items into a backpack. "I'll go down and make sure he left. Then we'll slip out the back door just to be safe."

Kevin waited nervously in the attic while she checked-out the house to be doubly certain her step-dad had left. Misty called for Kevin to come down, and removed the key sticking out of the stairway side of the door, locking it from the hallway. Putting the latchkey in her jeans' pocket, she stopped in the kitchen to throw snacks into the pack. Her knapsack bulged from the addition of an apple, a part-bag of chips, some cookies and a small packet of peeled carrots.

"We can sneak down the alley toward your place."

"No," he said, "let's go the other way, cutting over the hill past the library. It'd be pretty hard for anybody to follow without us spotting them."

"Okay."

They descended the staircase to the ground floor and out the rear exit. Across the blacktop paving, past the garage-turned-rental, they traveled on around the hill to the library.

In no time, they arrived in Kevin's backyard. The lawn chairs were still sitting on either side of the racing homer's transport box. Molly, looking plump as ever, wagged her tail as she wiggled her way toward them.

"What's your mother going to think about this?" Misty asked.

"I wasn't planning on telling her. If she knew the whole story she'd let you stay, but probably in her room instead of mine."

"Has a girl spent the night before?"

"No, I've had girls over, but that was mostly when I was in junior high and we were working on reports together."

"I'm glad you're not afraid to tell me the truth…without making stuff up."

He reflected that if he wasn't feeling so flustered by the nightmare and recent events he might not have been so honest. He entered the house alone, found it empty and returned for her.

While inside, he'd thought about their situation and decided to ask a question. "Might your step-dad be planning to have you killed and make it seem like a cat burglar did it? Maybe that's what my nightmare suggested."

"In your dream," she said, "how'd you know I was dead and not just sleeping?"

"Your skin was awful pale, not the light pink you really have and…" he paused and said quietly, hoping she wouldn't hear, "Your throat had been slit."

"Oh." There was a sharp intake of breath and her right hand tightly gripped his fingers while her left moved protectively to encircle her throat.

They stayed quiet, standing beside his house until neither knew how to break the silence.

Wordlessly, he led her through the kitchen door on a refrigerator raid before going to his bedroom.

8: KEVIN'S ROOM

"I like your house," Misty said, "it's so homey."

"It is kind of comfortable." Kevin was pleased she felt at home even though she was used to a more opulent lifestyle.

As they entered his room, his homemade study-wall came into view. A desktop PC was in the center of the handmade desk that ran most of the length of the south wall. He'd cut the top lengthwise out of an eight-foot long sheet of plywood. Four file cabinets supported it. An iPod rested in plain sight on the desk's top. The shelves above it held his boombox style music player and a small TV. From his bed, he could watch television across the room.

There were rows of music and movie discs, plus stacks of video games. The top shelf was littered with 4-H ribbons from various event divisions, along with the trophies he'd won with his racing homers. A special cubicle held his favorite signed soccer game ball. Soccer was Kevin's primary sport, though he also loved playing basketball with his friends. Relegated to a spot under his desk, his basketball sat beside his seldom-used cycle helmet. The actual motorcycle stood dormant in one of the unattached garages, waiting for him to replace its muffler. His laptop peeked halfway out of his backpack, which rested on the floor.

Misty noticed an arrowhead dangling on a string attached to the cluttered bulletin board and asked about it.

"My friend Billy made that and gave it to me. I believe he's descended from Chief Tommy Thompson, who lived to be over one hundred."

Misty noticed papers tacked to the upper right corner of his bulletin board. On closer inspection, they turned out to be a stack of rifle targets. They contained tight hole-patterns in the bull's-eyes made by his .22-rifle. Glancing around the other three walls of his room, she saw posters displayed, along with his artwork. There were drawings of two different dogs—plus Molly. Several sketches of pigeons…and then, as her eye roved, a series of comic book type illustrations caught Misty's attention. They formed a collage in a space about four feet square. Most were simple pencil or ink drawings but a few were in color. Kevin noticed where she looked and said, "Those are a female superhero my neighbor wanted me to make. She invented the character and I made the drawings based on her ideas."

Two of Kevin's largest pencil efforts on another wall resembled rubbings of Native American petroglyphs. He displayed them because they looked rustic. Those drawings were made from reference photographs of etched rocks, taken during one of his far-flung mountain bike outings.

What particularly seemed to catch Misty's eye as she meandered about inspecting his room, weren't the drawings, although she stopped to admire them. Nor did she focus on his Bluegrass band posters or the timeworn picture of Pele`, the famous Brazilian soccer player. What captured her attention was the poster of Mother Theresa.

"I bet you're like…are you going to be a religious hermit or something?"

"No."

"What's with the Mother Theresa picture?"

"She's…well. Her and President Obama, Nelson Mandela and a few others are sort of my heroes."

"Like, who else?"

"Oh, Steven Hawking, Princess Diana, J.K. Rowling, Michael Moore…"

He got off his bed and selected several music CDs, which he placed in the changer. The sound of Alicia Keys floated across the room.

"You got any DMB's stuff?" she enquired, still inspecting the contents of his room.

"Somewhere," he said uncertainly. "I went to their concert in the Columbia Gorge once."

"So did I. What if we were there at the same time?"

"It's doubtful." Turning toward the CD player he said, "I just put on some music so if my mom comes home she won't hear us talking."

"Good thinking. What's on is okay."

While she inspected his room, Kevin realized he felt disappointed she had overlooked the racing homer trophies.

Then he wondered about all the strange events since his nightmare. Why had he experienced such a horrible dream? Was Misty in danger of being killed by her step-dad? Would such a creepy guy as that pursue her to Kevin's house if he knew where she was?

Turning away from things on Kevin's desk, Misty asked, "Are you one of those, like…really smart guys?"

"I don't think so," he said slowly, wondering what had prompted her question. "My grades are all right."

"Let me guess. You probably have a B average but you don't spend all that much time studying."

"Well…" He hesitated a bit too long. "I've got lots of other interests…."

"I knew it," she laughed. "You're probably a frickin' genius."

"No way."

"Yeah, right. Let's see…. So you don't have a report you did for some class, where the teacher wrote, 'This paper was not done by a sophomore in high school.' They probably thought you got it off the Internet or some stupid thing, right?"

Kevin laughed despite himself. "Okay, I'm a little bit guilty. How'd you know?"

"Because I got the same kind of comments on my papers," she said, before keeling over on his bed with laughter.

"Next thing I know," she giggled, "you'll be running off to join some weird, think-tank thingy. No, wait." She sat up and glanced around the room again. Her eyes returned to the Mother

Theresa poster and she mumbled, "Obama, Mandela…. I got it. You're probably going to join the Peace Corps. I bet you already got the forms half filled out."

"Yeah—right. In your dreams." He was disconcerted by how close to correct she was. He had seriously researched the Peace Corps. But his reference to dreams stopped their conversation.

"Oh crap," he said, "we got side-tracked. I set that book over here…somewhere…." He rummaged around through a pile by his pillow.

"So this is where you had the nightmare, right?"

"Uh-huh, I woke up and I believed it was real. After finding that metal box, it had to be true in some way. Uh, here it is." He held up the paperback book titled *Creating Your Own Dream World.*

"How'd your nightmare end, anyway?"

"I guess I sort of died," Kevin said. "I left some things out. I should tell you the rest."

"Yeah, but how'd you sort-of die?"

"Let's start where I left off and you'll see. It was when the guy bumped the bed and a bunch of stuff fell to the floor, uncovering her…."

"I'm going to say her—and not you—because otherwise it'll creep me out." He continued after a pause, "Her arm was sticking off the bed and her…. I mean, the upper half of her body was exposed as well."

"What was I wearing?" Misty asked. "Do you remember? Was it like what I've got on now?"

"Nothing."

"Not like this?" She looked down at her pink top.

"I mean the upper half of her…I don't know how to." He looked away. "Her top part didn't have any clothes on and I couldn't see the bottom half."

"Well, thank God for small favors."

"I started to get away," he continued, "but something made me look back and the guy was piling bedding and other stuff on top of her. Then he started coming after me."

Kevin told Misty the details from the remainder of his nightmare, finally concluding, "I got knocked sideways going through the window and slid down the roof. I dangled by one hand until the guy in the mask undid my fingers and I fell. It was so damn scary. Too real. My right arm is still sore from it." He absently traced the thorn scratches.

"How will this book help?"

"I don't know for sure. Mr. Bridger at the high school told me to read chapter five about...." He flipped to the table of contents, "The Senoi Dreamers. Bridger talked like I should learn about dream control. How to confront enemies and get a gift from them."

"You're supposed to receive a gift?"

"Yes...but let's read the book and find out."

She asked, "Are you mostly a visual learner?"

"I guess so, why?"

"Because," she continued, "I'm more auditory and we've only got one book so you should read aloud and I'll listen. That way, we both get what works best for us."

Side-by-side, they propped themselves up with pillows on Kevin's double bed to study the counselor's book together.

"Maybe there'll be pictures." She positioned herself closer beside him, snuggling her head into his shoulder.

"Maybe." He didn't care what her reason for getting close was; he enjoyed her nearness and the smell of her hair.

As he flipped through the pages, she commented, "You know what?"

"Huh-uh."

"This is my first sleepover in The Dalles."

"I think we're going to have a lot of firsts."

"I like that idea."

He read aloud about the Senoi, whose society revolved around the use of dreams in waking life. It began with children recounting their sleep experiences in the morning. If they had a nightmare, perhaps of a fierce animal attacking, they were encouraged not to run, but to turn and fight with whatever weapon was available—or even barehanded.

Whether they won that struggle was not the objective. The goal was to turn and face what was scary. Confronting one's fear was of paramount importance. Should they be defeated or even killed that was still their victory. They could call on any former enemies to help them in future dreams. Facing fear was the goal. In essence, the Senoi had devised the ultimate win-win dream strategy. If they defeated the enemy, they won a gift. If the enemy defeated them, they acquired a dream ally.

Misty said, "This Senoi stuff is interesting but maybe we don't need it."

"Why?"

"Your nightmare was so real, we learned from it, like where the jewels are."

"Yes."

"Does this Senoi idea mean the bad guy is your ally now? Does he have to help you in future dreams?" She thought for a moment, "How will he help? If the book is right, I think he has to because you made him back off with the golf club, even though he seemed to kill you in the end."

"I see. I wasn't looking at it that way. Not sure if that makes him my ally or not. What else can we learn from my dream?"

She sat up. "We know there's a cat burglar and the jewels are hidden under my attic floor. It seems like someone wants to kill me. Probably my step-dad, maybe with the burglar's help. Mom died unexpectedly and that creepy stepfather of mine was the only one there. He can't be directly involved in my disappearance —too suspicious. He needs an accomplice."

"The guy in the ski mask?" Kevin asked.

"Yeah, probably. I wonder? If we get rid of one, do we still have to worry about the other?"

"I think so," Kevin said. "Everything else seemed right about the dream so that means the masked guy plans to kill me as well as you."

"I guess so. But why?"

"I might be a threat by telling someone what he's up to," he guessed.

"If we got rid of the masked guy," Misty said, "my step-dad would just find somebody else to replace him. If we somehow get rid of my stepfather, I think we'd still have to deal with the dark dude."

"We need to remove them both from our lives, otherwise, they'll come back to haunt us." He rested the book on his chest.

She agreed, "Uh-huh."

"For some reason, the masked-guy wanted to hide her body. But why was it naked? Neither of those things makes sense. If they have the cat burglar thing going on to make it seem like a burglary-related murder, why wouldn't they want the body to be found?"

"One of those things makes sense," she commented.

"Which one?"

"Except in the coldest part of winter when I totally bundle up, I sleep nude."

He was momentarily taken aback, but regrouped quickly. Trying to look casual, he quipped, "Oh, then I have something to look forward to...tonight."

"I usually sleep in the nude but I'm revising my sleeping habit now that I've heard about your nightmare."

"Me and my big mouth." He said, "That still leaves the question of why hide the body?"

"That'd be good to know," she said. "I've been trying to figure how we can find out more. There's probably information at my house. Let's plan where to search if we go back."

"Yeah," he agreed, "we should have a plan."

There was a sudden rapping sound—loud and demanding—that startled them. Kevin nearly knocked Misty off the bed as he jumped up.

9: THE VISITOR

The persistent rapping began again. Kevin held up his hand toward his bedroom window in a halt signal, as he said, "I've told you before, Haley, knock once and then give me a second." He crossed to where a young girl's dark head showed through the glass. She stood tiptoe on the ground in order to stare in. He brusquely raised the window, noting it was partway open. How long had she been listening? "I'll talk to you in a minute."

As he closed the window, her sing-songy voice slipped its way through. "Does your mother know you got a girl in your room?"

He sat back on the bed beside Misty. "That's my neighbor. Her folks got killed in a car accident so she lives next door with her aunt and uncle. They don't have kids of their own, haven't a clue what to do with her and so they send her over here. She's a pain in the butt, yet she grows on you. I'm letting her in since she overheard. If we don't, she'll tell the whole world."

Misty asked, "Is it a good idea, involving a little kid?"

"No, but it's the best I got for now, and she can be trusted."

"We don't want her to get hurt."

He nodded, shrugged resignedly, and went to the window, opening it all the way.

"Here's the deal. If you keep your trap shut, I'll let you in to help with what we're planning." He paused for dramatic effect. "If you snitch, I'll never speak to you again about anything important."

"Gee," she said, holding her dark arms in the air to be hefted through the window, "tough choice."

He seized her hands and pulled her inside.

"I'm Haley. You like Kevin, don't you?" Before Misty could answer, Haley added, "Nah, it's beyond that, it's like, way beyond that." She turned her head, surveying the room. "Looks bigger from inside, doesn't it Kevin? I thought girls aren't allowed in your room. Or did that just mean me?"

"Misty, this is my neighbor—and sometimes friend—Haley. She practically lives outside my bedroom window and I don't know how I neglected to mention her."

"Yeah, how did that happen?" Haley turned to Kevin and said in a derisive voice, "Are you trying to get into her pants?"

His face reddened, "Haley, you're ten years old—"

She cut him off. "Ten-and-a-half."

"I'm not talking with you about the birds and the bees. Now, do you want to find out what's going on here, or not?"

She mumbled defensively, "I kind of already know."

"Well, listen up because we might need your help, but we've got to keep quiet. My mom will get home any time now."

"I'm all ears," said Haley, plopping herself down on the bed beside Misty.

Kevin could barely refrain from making a joke about her elfin-shaped ears once she'd mentioned them. Their shape was hard to account for. Her racial heritage was mixed. Her mother had been white, while her father was Native American, Hispanic and African-American. Haley's features were an interesting fusion of all three, except for her small, pointed ears, which were a mystery.

Her curly black hair was cut about medium-length, just barely long enough to pull back into the ponytail she wore. In order to make the ponytail work, she had to yank her hair very taut. That tightened the skin of her narrow face, skewing her ears and pulling the ends of her eyes and eyebrows slightly out of alignment. The total effect made her look like a dark pixie.

Kevin ignored his impulse to joke with Haley and began his explanation. He described his nightmare and subsequent encounter with Misty at the high school. He told Haley what a shock it had been bumping into a person in real life whom he'd only dreamt about and thought was dead. Then came the real life discovery of the attic and the many things in it, including the jewelry box. Lots of the objects from his dream were real.

Misty pulled the gold chain from around her neck, displaying the black pearls and reddish ring.

Haley examined them as Kevin retrieved the diamond ring from his pocket, which his small neighbor soon appropriated. She placed it on her finger, then her thumb but it was too large even for that. "Maybe I'll grow into it," she said wistfully, returning the ring to Kevin.

Misty revealed the suspicious circumstance of her mother's death, adding the final concern that if Misty died, her step-dad would inherit her estate.

"What about your father?" Haley asked.

"He died in a plane crash when I was eight."

Haley put her arms around Misty. "Both our parents died, huh?"

Misty nodded agreement.

"But we got Kevin," said Haley, "and we got each other."

Misty folded her arms about the little girl and squeezed.

After the hug, Kevin continued recounting events, adding the information about the book on Senoi dreaming.

When he finished, Haley sat up and said, "I'm your girl."

"What do you mean?" Misty asked.

"When it comes to dreams, I got us covered."

 Kevin said, "How?"

"They had me in a sleep lab in Portland for like a whole year and never did catch up to me."

Kevin continued feeling puzzled.

"It's like I know more about dreams than guys who are supposed to be experts. It all started when I was five. I had terrible nightmares. 'Night terrors' they called them. Had them so bad, I feared going to sleep. Used to lie awake on my back because if I turned over I'd fall asleep. My folks took me to all kinds of specialists. But they couldn't do anything to help.

"By myself, I learned to control nightmares. Then night terrors. They're different. Night terrors aren't in REM sleep like regular dreams and nightmares. I learned about that in the sleep lab. Controlling nightmares was just the start. I did all kinds of weird things, even poltergeist stuff. You name it and I've done it.

"They think when I hit puberty the poltergeist stuff will stop but they don't know for sure."

"What's poltergeist mean?" Misty asked.

"Like—weird noises, and stuff moving without being touched. Sometimes, objects just appear or disappear. Things like that."

"Wait, wait, wait," Misty interrupted, "you're doing all this in your dreams?"

"No, poltergeist stuff's in real life."

Misty seemed to think it was all in dreams. She spoke out with assurance, "Nothing just appears out of thin air. Everyone knows that."

Kevin was more familiar with the concept of poltergeist happenings. He looked at Haley with new curiosity.

"Yeah, when it comes to dreams—I got us covered. They started worrying I'd go crazy and it'd be their fault." Haley laughed. "So, I quit going to the sleep lab. But I helped lots of kids with their bad dreams, night terrors and such." She sat up with her arms crossed proudly over her narrow chest and said with enthusiasm, "I'm definitely your girl."

Kevin didn't know what to think about Haley's assertions.

"How do you know so much about dreams?" Misty asked.

Haley's deep exhalation indicated she had no patience for people who didn't keep up with her rapidly flowing thoughts. She smiled and then said in the voice of a strict grammar school teacher, "Pay attention this time and that means both of you." She looked intently at Kevin. "Just because you think I'm only ten, well, when it comes to some stuff—like dreams—no one knows as much as me. In this, it's like I'm eighteen and you're both ten. Nah, better make it five years old. If you want my help, treat me with re-spect. Not like some dumb kid."

Kevin looked at her. "I'm sorry. I didn't mean to treat you like a dumb kid. Sometimes we tease each other or I make fun of you but it doesn't mean anything. My life would be pretty drab if you weren't in it and if I…."

"Knock it off. Apology accepted." She turned to Misty, "You don't need to apologize—yet, but listen up, okay?"

"Sure."

Haley hauled off and slugged Kevin in the chest. "That's for letting this other girl in your room first and making me stand outside, like forever. But I sort of forgive you. I like her and she likes me. I'm not going to get kicked out in the yard again, right?"

"Right." Kevin and Misty said as one.

"When I was five, I had terrible nightmares. But if I thought about a good dream while I was lying there—you know, one I'd had before—it would become real. I was kind of like daydreaming it."

Misty got a questioning look on her face but didn't interrupt.

"I'd go to sleep in the daydream and that way I'd have a good dream that night. So I didn't have to worry about having nightmares anymore."

Kevin asked, "You fell asleep daydreaming about a good dream you'd already had?"

"Yeah. Then I learned to change the good ones, not just be in them again."

"What do you mean, change them?" Misty asked.

"If I wanted one about riding horses but in the first dream I was by myself, I could make it different. You know, add friends or something. Maybe put you guys in it. Or I could change the place of the dream—"

Kevin interrupted her. "This is really cool, Haley."

"Yeah," added Misty.

"It's only the start, from when I was five. I'm sort of filling you in."

He said, "Thanks."

"Or else," Haley said with a grin, "you'd stay clueless. And, yeah, I realize I have pixie ears, but get over it."

How'd she know about that? he wondered.

Haley continued, "I messed around and sort of created my own...kind of like a computer-thingy. You know. A data-thingy for dreams. Only, it was in my head, not in a computer."

"Database?" Asked Misty.

"Yeah—that. When I went to bed at night, I'd start looking through my old dreams until I got to one I wanted to have again or to do different. Then, I'd start playing the one I picked for that night. It was kind of like my own movie—whatchamacallit?"

"Archives?" Misty asked.

"Yeah, that's it."

Haley no longer seemed like just another ten-year-old kid to Kevin.

"Then, I got into flying dreams and flew in any of my old dreams that I wanted to. Learned to fly right through one and then into another. Sometimes, I'd fly through them all, making changes as I went. Nightmares weren't a problem. I just flew away from anything I didn't like. Made things happen to bad guys. Poured mud on them, stuff like that."

Kevin asked, "Have you heard of the Senoi dreamers?"

"Yep. Told me about those dudes in the sleep lab. But I didn't have nightmare problems by then. They wanted to learn from me how to help kids. At least, Mr. Bridger did. I liked him. Some others thought of me as their little secret weapon. Mr. B said, for safety, I should stop going to their lab. He worried about what those government guys were planning for me. But, I could take care of myself. Especially in dreams."

Kevin asked, "You know Mr. Bridger?"

"Yeah, he and I are buds. We hang out. He learned a lot from me and I learned from him, too. Like, not to get a big head just because I'm smart." She glared at Kevin and he wondered why.

"Back to before," she continued. "It was easy to get in other kids' dreams and show them what to do, not just tell them about it."

Misty asked, "You were entering other people's dreams?"

"Yes, I figured it out once, after flying through my own dreams and not finding anything I wanted to do. Figured, why not go in other people's dreams and see what was going on there. It was pretty easy. If they had any trouble, I'd stop and help. I took stuff from their dreams to put in mine. Made up my own new dreams, too."

Misty said, "You went inside other people's dreams?"

"You already asked that." Haley reminded. "When I learned about video games, that changed my dreaming a lot. My dreams got to be sort of like the games. It was cool. Putting powers and weapons and all kinds of new stuff into them. Tons of monsters —more levels. I took stuff from lots of different places."

Misty and Kevin exchanged bewildered glances.

"Finding demons in somebody's dream, I taught kids how to tame them. Then I'd make another one to put in my dream."

Misty asked, "You wanted monsters in your dreams?"

"Yes, you know, guys with big fangs and blood dripping down the chin. That kind of stuff."

"Whoa," Kevin shook his head. "This is going a little fast. By six you were creating video games in your dreams and making them better. Then you started creating dreams and added things from other people's?"

"Yeah."

"Well, before you go any farther and totally freak us out, what can you tell me about my nightmare? It has us worried."

"You won't get it, without what I'm telling you."

"It's late," said Kevin, "and you'll have to go home soon, so explain what you can about my nightmare—now please."

"Naw, I want to stay here tonight."

Kevin decided to let that go. The main thing was to get more information. Molly began to bark.

Kevin went to his window and looked out. "Just some kids going by. I've got to go to the restroom and mom should be here any second, so keep it quiet.

10: COSMIC WHAT?

After returning from the bathroom, Kevin asked again. "What can you tell me about my nightmare?"

"It wasn't exactly a nightmare," Haley said slowly.

"What was it?"

"Bringing together the dream world and a…." She struggled for words. "Different sort of thing. More like a place. It was not a real dream—that other thing. Which is pretty rare. It gets into stuff like precognition. That's seeing the future."

"I know what precognition is." Kevin said.

Misty said. "I don't."

"He doesn't either, just thinks he does." Haley continued, "When stuff happens and it seems likely to turn out in a certain way—even that's not for sure. There are other possibilities. Ways that things can turn out. Nothing is for certain. Each likely outcome makes another kind of place, sort of like this one, but a little different.

Misty reached out and took hold of Kevin's hand for reassurance.

"What Kevin did," Haley continued, "is he went out through his nightmare and bumped it up against one of those other place-thingies. He doesn't know it, but he did it on purpose, just like meeting you was on purpose. You both decided to get together but you don't know about that, yet.

"Without your nightmare, and if you hadn't met Misty, she would have been killed tonight. It would've been a done deal."

The other two sat in a state of alarm and Kevin squeezed Misty's hand.

"It was a nice piece of work," said Haley. "Your nightmare. I couldn't do any better. I was surprised when I saw it."

"Saw what?" he asked.

"Watched you make your nightmare and guide it to the alternate zone. That other place you picked out. Boy, that masked guy is pissed at you, messing things up for him like that."

"Are you saying you saw me? You witnessed my nightmare?"

"I see pretty much all your dreams. I keep an eye on you. You're my...." She struggled for a word, then gave up and continued, "But that nightmare, you did it all on your own. It was cool. I didn't know you could. Way to go, Kevin."

"You watch all my dreams?"

"I know about them, but I only pay attention when they're interesting. This one was real interesting."

Kevin wasn't sure what he could believe and felt the need to test her. "Then tell me about another of my dreams that you found 'interesting.'"

"Better not." She had a sly look on her face.

"Humor me."

"Okay, let's see...one of your dreams with Carol. How about when you were dreaming about you two parked in your mom's car and you both hopped into the back seat?"

"I give up." he said, "You *can* tell me things you shouldn't know. How about my nightmare? Can you tell something that I might have missed in there, which is important? Like, when and how did the body disappear?"

"And why did it disappear?" added Misty.

"I could tell, but I'm not going to."

"Why?" Misty begged. "Please."

"If you had let me take more time—the longer way of telling —you'd already know. There are reasons why you left stuff out on purpose. That's why you don't know. It's not right, me messing with that. I'll tell you this much, though, I won't let anything bad happen to you.

"Put yourself in my place," Haley continued. "I'm a geeky ten-year-old. I've got no one else to really talk to. Kevin puts up with me but I've never been able to discuss dreams and stuff, even with him. I tried. Even got him to make me a comic book but he just didn't listen."

Kevin cut in. "That Dark-Dream-Girl comic you had me draw?"

"Yep." Haley glanced at the sketches on the wall and Misty followed her gaze.

"I thought that was just make-believe," Kevin said.

Haley continued. "I know about stuff bigger than you learned in physics. I looked through your book. Didn't understand some words, but I couldn't ask you because you don't take me serious-like."

His hand rose to the top of her smoothly stretched hair and rested briefly.

"I'm not mad at you," she said. "Nobody understands. I talked to scientists. Told them things they didn't know. Stuff they never dreamed…." She laughed at her own joke.

"Then I was supposed to go home and—what—play with Barbies? Well, sometimes I did."

Kevin had a puzzled look on his face. "I thought it was odd, finding my physics book open in places I didn't leave it turned to. One time in the living room I thought mom had been looking at it. You must have visited her when I wasn't home."

The look on Haley's face showed disappointment. "Your mom at least let me in the house."

"The thing is," he said, "it's hard to figure this out because in a lot of ways you are a ten…" He caught himself, "…and one-half-year-old. I've seen you play with dolls and you're into comic books, video games, and skateboarding…."

"You're not?"

His face betrayed he'd been caught. "I don't play with Barbies —usually."

"I bet you sneak over to my place and play with them when no one's looking."

"Okay, you caught me." He confessed so genuinely, Misty laughed. Kevin sputtered, "What can I say? I was a big dope."

"Yep." Haley returned to her previous topic. "Before your nightmare came along, a dream combined with a—you know what I said. I thought that only I could make one. You didn't create it my way but I never saw anyone else do it before. Last night, when I watched, I thought, Kevin you totally rock. So, I'll help you, but not too much or you won't learn what you need to know. And you won't get to be what I'm hoping for."

"What's that?" whispered Misty.

"Two more cosmic players."

They sat still—stunned.

"I told you, I'll watch and won't let anything bad happen. We need to let this be sort of natural so you can learn what you need to know."

Misty added, "And for you to get what you want."

"Yes."

Misty put her arms around Haley, pulling her in tightly. Laying her head on top of the small girl's, she said, "I pray you'll get what you want. I know what it's like to feel there's nobody you can turn to. We both know what that's like."

Haley's smile disappeared and she began to cry. "Mr. Bridger said that's the reason I got my talents. To make sure I won't have that kind of loss again. Like, from when my parents died."

Kevin observed, "They just died a couple of years ago, way after you started to develop your abilities."

"Mr. Bridger thought I was doing that because I saw the probable futures that told me a disaster was coming. I tried to stop it but I just couldn't grow my gifts—he called them—fast enough."

Misty said, "Oh, you poor thing."

"Now you know why I won't let anything happen to you. I don't need to stay here tonight but I'm going to, no matter what you think. But it's not to keep you from doing stuff. I know that's in both your minds."

"How do you know that?" Kevin asked.

"Like I said, if we'd taken the slow way, you'd already

understand. Lots of times I can tell what people are thinking—and if you had let me do this my way, you'd know why that is."

He said, "Can you read everybody's minds?"

"No, too much static. Mostly, I hear the ones I care about or those close by. I try to keep out the bad junk, especially yucky feelings. All of those hurt me.

"Some things I can't tell, and don't know about because I'm not supposed to see them until they happen."

She looked suddenly concerned, "Like right now, Aunt Fran just called your house. Your Mom's going to come banging on your door to see if I'm here. Misty better get in the closet—fast."

Misty disappeared behind Kevin's closet door.

Kevin looked dumbfounded. "My mom's home? I didn't hear her drive up."

A sharp knock sounded—

"Kevin, is Haley with you?"

Swinging the door wide, he revealed Haley sitting on his bed with a comic book in her lap. "Yes mom, she came over to spend the night with our family."

"Hi, Mrs. Conners," Haley said. "Thanks for letting me stay over with Kevin. He doesn't usually let me hang out so much but it being the anniversary of mom and dad's deaths, and all…he's being real nice, and I don't have to stand outside the window anymore."

Mrs. Conners said, "I don't know that we can have her spend the night in your bedroom—just the two of you. I understand it's a difficult time…."

"Mom, this is Haley, and it is just once a year. It's not like she's an eighteen-year-old girl or something."

"Well, I know, but…"

"Would you like it better if I invited an eighteen-year-old girl I know to come over and spend the night with us as a chaperone?"

"No, Kevin. We can't talk about this now. Haley will have to sleep out on the couch and that's my final word."

He heard something new and different—foreign thoughts in his head coming from Haley. He felt the intent of her ideas and formed them into words.

'Don't let her kick me out. I need to be here tonight. Make it happen.'

"Mom, Haley hasn't asked one other thing of me all year—except the comic superhero. I already said she could stay. I didn't know it'd be a big deal. She needs to be here. If that means poking your head in every few minutes, or us leaving the door open because you don't trust me, then that's what we'll do."

"Kevin, I…." She backed partway out into the hall. "The phone's ringing. It's probably Fran again. I'll go see what she wants."

Mrs. Conners padded away with the phone blaring insistently in the distance. Haley turned toward Kevin, her hand raised and extended for a high-five. He completed it noiselessly, with flair. In the distance, they heard Mrs. Conners talking to Haley's aunt.

"Yes, Fran, she's here. It looks like she'll be spending the night." There was a pause in the communication.

"What did you say?

"Haley's with you…? She just came back?

"Okay, I'll…uh, talk to you later, Fran." She shuffled slowly down the hall. Poking her head in Kevin's doorway, she looked uncertainly around his room. Haley was nowhere to be seen. Shaking her head, she announced, "Supper's in a half-hour."

"Right."

Mrs. Conners slowly pulled the bedroom door shut behind her, still shaking her head.

Haley's black hair poked out from beneath Kevin's bed.

Misty slipped quietly out of the closet but left the door open, in case. "What just happened?" she asked Kevin.

"I'm not sure." He glanced questioningly at Haley as she slid from under the bed, brushing dust bunnies off her clothing.

"That was you talking in my mind, wasn't it?"

"Yes."

Misty asked, "What was that like, mentally hearing her?" Misty's tone made it sound as though she wasn't sure she believed him.

"More like the impression of her than her voice," he answered. "I knew what she wanted me to know. Not really in

61

words. I put it into words to make it more understandable. You know, like what I'm used to." He turned and asked, "Haley?"

"You would have convinced your mom because she wasn't sure what to do. But Aunt Fran wasn't going to let me stay. She has to think I'm over there."

"She does think that," Kevin said. "How come?"

"You're not ready—yet. I'm going home to get Misty and me something to eat." She opened the window to slip out. "I'll be back...soon."

"Why didn't you convince my mom to let you stay over? It seems you could have done that easier than me."

"Then...you'd of learned nothing."

He tilted his head to look at her sideways. "Are you sure you're only ten-and-one-half?"

"It's sort-of no, and sort-of yes." She slipped through the window and was gone.

In the meantime, Kevin ate a hurried dinner and returned to his room just in time to see Haley climb back in the window. Two bags hit the floor before she finished wriggling inside.

"We're going to learn a lot from you, aren't we?" Misty said, as she accepted the sack Haley offered and wrapped an arm around the small girl.

"Yeah," Haley sounded pleased. "Will you hold me for awhile?"

"Sure," Misty pulled Haley onto Kevin's bed, leaving the food resting on the nightstand.

"Hey," said Kevin, "what about me?"

The other two grabbed him, pulling him down with them.

After a while, he said, "I think we better play a video game or something like I usually do."

"Oh," said Haley, "can I play your new one, the—"

"Yes."

Misty added the food Haley had brought to the stash from her own backpack and began to eat. Haley played video games for a while, which was frustrating because she didn't allow herself to demonstrate the level of competence that she had developed.

After Misty had eaten, she and Kevin lay whispering on the bed. She asked softly, "How did she get her aunt to think she was over there?"

"I don't know," he whispered back. "She can't be in two places at once. Can she?"

"This is scary…."

They looked across at Kevin's young neighbor.

Haley's head glowed in the light from his monitor. She had removed her hair tie, freeing the ponytail and releasing her wavy locks. She paused the game and turned toward Kevin's bed. Her black hair was highlighted around the edges with traces of red and green from the monitor's illumination. "No," she said, "I'm only here with you guys."

They stared at her shadowed face. Mostly, they saw the aura of her hair's outer fringe. In their minds, they heard an intense sound.

'Aunt Fran heard me calling to her from my bedroom. See?'

Haley turned back around and resumed her game. Kevin and Misty lay there silently, holding one another. Had Haley's voice been only in their minds or had it echoed loudly about the room? They hadn't seen her mouth move but it was in the shadows.

Eventually, Haley gave up on the game and went over beside the other two.

"It's time to get ready for your dream tonight," she told them. "And remember. Nothing bad can happen to you. You'll learn…and have fun. Even if it's a nightmare, you're creating it for a reason. Don't race through trying to beat-up the bad guy."

"It's lame to hurt the dude in the ski mask?" Misty asked.

"Yep, he's your worst enemy, but also your best friend."

Kevin asked, "How do you figure?"

"Not sure I want to tell you." Haley became thoughtful. "Okay, suppose a guy in a mask brought the two of you together? And as a pair, you have a chance to do something special, maybe even awesome—the most important thing in your whole lives. It wouldn't be happening except for the masked man bringing you both together. And anyways, you're sort of using him. Also, if you hadn't met, Misty would be dead."

She let them think about that for a while. "How do you feel about the burglar-guy now?"

"Scared," said Misty, "but grateful."

Kevin added, "Me, too."

"There you go," said Haley, "you got a new way to see it. We can get into the real meaning later. It'd stretch your minds too much for now."

She continued, "Tonight, we got to trust each other and see what we can learn from our dreams. Follow your hunches even when they don't make sense."

They reluctantly agreed to be guided by their intuition.

Kevin dug his sleeping bag out of his closet and played the chivalrous role, insisting he would sleep on the floor. He spread the bag on top of his oval rug. Misty was about to turn out the light when she said. "Just a minute, I don't want to sleep in my clothes; I brought pajamas in my backpack." She gave Kevin an impish, knowing smile.

"It's safe to leave your room," Haley told them. "Your mom's reading and your dad's not home."

One after another, they tiptoed into the hall to the bathroom, preparing for bed. Afterward, Haley in her cartoon pajamas curled beside Misty on Kevin's bed. "Hey guys," she said, why don't we take some of Kevin's homers to the park tomorrow? We haven't done that for a long time, have we Kevin?"

"No," he replied as he slid down into his sleeping bag. "But that's totally random."

Haley begged, "Please."

"I suppose."

The small girl whispered as she snuggled deeper into bed, "This is my first sleep-over at Kevin's." After a silence she added, "It's my first since I've been in The Dalles." She yawned. "Remember. Trust your hunches…and sweet dreams."

11: THE BASEMENT

There was an insistent noise at Kevin's window. Tap. Tap. Tap.

"All right," he said, rolling out of his sleeping bag. He was most of the way to the window when he realized something didn't seem right. Turning back toward his bed, he wondered where Misty and Haley were.

The tapping returned.

"I'm coming...." He turned again and saw Misty's face peering in from outside, her hair aglow in the morning sunshine. He opened the window. "Where's Haley?"

"She went home. Come on, we've got to go, like we planned last night, remember?"

He wasn't sure he did. He stood, confused and disoriented, trying to decide what to do...and heard her say, "You might want to brush your hair."

He automatically ran his fingers through his hair and turned to see Misty smiling up at him, her chin resting on his windowsill. He impulsively leaned down and kissed her.

"That's more like it," she said with a big smile.

Kevin met Misty at the side of his homer loft, and then went in to throw grain into the feeder, not remembering when he had fed them last.

The young couple eventually retraced their previous route past the library and around the hill toward the back of Misty's house. They entered the alley and crossed the blacktopped area to the rear entrance. Passing quietly through the doorway, Misty turned left to circle up the stairs. Kevin grabbed her hand, looking at the steps that descended to the right, "What's down there?"

"That's the basement. I get scared in it, remember?"

"Let's take a look. Don't worry; I'm with you."

They spiraled to the right, down into the cellar. The distinct sound of a washing machine came from the laundry area. The basement lights were all off. In the dark, Kevin's sense of smell heightened and the musty dampness reeked of wet clothing, overwhelming his nostrils. He finally found a switch and flicked it on. The antiquated lighting system sparked to life, shining dimly. He assessed the noisy clothes washer. "Does your step-dad do his own laundry?"

"No, he sends everything except mine to the cleaners. He tried to get me to do his laundry. I refused."

"Anybody else living here besides the two of you?"

"No. Unless he moved somebody in yesterday."

"How often do you come down here?"

"As little as possible. I'll only do about one load of clothes a week. This is my second time here. Well, my third trip, actually. I just don't like this place."

"What's in there?" Kevin stared at a rectangular room projecting out into the basement.

"I don't know," Misty said. "I just rush down, put a laundry load in and race back up. You know, like when you're afraid the bogey man will get you."

"Why do you suppose there's a lock on the door?"

"No idea."

He moved closer to the entrance. "Can't be anyone in there; it's padlocked from outside. Let's take a quick look. We've got fifteen minutes before that wash load's finished."

"How're we going to—?"

"Any tools down here?"

She pointed to the semi-partitioned southerly end of the basement. "I guess so. There's an old tool bench over that way."

On the wall above the bench, Kevin located a screwdriver, a hammer and some vice grips.

"You're a carpenter, aren't you?" The way she said it was as much a statement as a question.

"Not really."

"Didn't you build your homer loft?"

He answered, "Yes," as he used the vice-grips to back the door's hinge pins out a bit.

"Probably made your desk and study area in your room, right?"

"Uh huh."

"Who else can break into a door like this?"

"Oh, probably lots of people," he replied, using the hammer and screwdriver to lightly tap the hinge pins out. "There." He smiled as he yanked the door open from the hinged side, leaving it connected only at the padlocked hasp.

"Couldn't have done it if the door opened inward."

He pulled the cord on the bare bulb dangling from an electrical wire in the center of the small room. "These walls are an add-on, not part of the original house."

She stood in the doorway as he went in and surveyed the interior. There was an unmade bed at the other side of the room.

After poking around, he decided someone had slept in it recently. There were bags, papers, and men's clothing strewn haphazardly about the floor. He said, "It doesn't look like someone intended to live here too long."

A backpack caught his eye. He moved a new pair of black sneakers that rested against it and began to undo zippers to get into the various compartments. There was a tiny flashlight in one, a dark navy blue sweater in the main compartment and he was startled to see a black ski mask. Speechless, he turned to show Misty.

Instead, he crouched in shock. She no longer stood in the doorway. In her place was a sinewy man dressed all in black and wearing a ski mask. Kevin felt suspended in time. He looked from the fabric in his hand to what the man was wearing.

Something like a wee small voice in Kevin's mind said: *'Ask him.'*

Ask him what? Kevin thought, feeling Haley's strong influence.

'Ask him a question, of course.'

He asked the first thing that came into his mind. "Are you going skiing?"

Kevin knew summer had nearly arrived and the ski season was over, but he voiced the silly question anyway, not knowing what else to say.

"Cute," the man replied.

Was he slightly amused? Kevin glanced around for something he could use as a weapon.

"Looking for this?" The fellow raised his right hand from his side, displaying the wicked-looking knife.

"Yeah," said Kevin flippantly. "Why don't you slide it over to me on the floor?"

The other fellow chuckled. "You're quite the wise guy."

"Are you trying to kill Misty?"

Haley's small thought-voice cheered, *'Way to go.'*

"It's part of the plan."

The little voice came again, *'What does he want?'*

"If," Kevin asked, "you could get what you want without killing Misty...?" He struggled to complete his sentence.

"Even better," the man said with interest.

Kevin queried, "What do you want?"

"I—"

The man's head came crashing down onto the concrete floor as his feet flew upward into the air behind him. Kevin looked at the inert form, thinking the guy must surely be dead. The knife had flung into the room, spinning on the floor. Kevin picked it up and dropped it down a large knothole in the wall. It hit the bottom with a metallic clunk. He went to inspect the fallen man, mumbling, "We almost had our answer...."

Misty leaned over the black figure. "Wants to kill me, does he?" Looking up at Kevin she said, "I'm sorry, I got carried away."

She ripped the ski mask off, revealing a very thin face, aged somewhere between thirty and forty years. She placed her fingers along his neck, checking for a pulse. "It's not the same, doing this on someone else. I've only checked my own heart rate in gym class. Looks like he's alive. I didn't think pulling that rug runner would work so well. I got scared when he said killing me was the plan. Then he raised the knife toward *you*...."

The basement lights went out. Kevin could hear the man moaning and Misty's heavy, frightened breathing.

A shocked "Oh," sounded as the washing machine shifted into spin cycle.

Why is the washer still on if the power is off? Kevin wondered. Worried about Misty, he tried to say her name but the word would not form on his lips. His mouth felt heavy as darkness engulfed him....

12: BACK TO MR. BRIDGER

The morning sun shone brightly through Kevin's bedroom window. He was the first to awaken, and felt a stinging in his arm where he'd pinched a nerve from sleeping on the floor. He began adjusting his position to restore circulation.

He wondered why he hadn't used his foam camping pad, but then he realized it was stored out in one of the garages with the bulk of his family's camping gear. He looked over as Haley turned and put her thin arm partway around Misty's head. He smiled despite the tingling in his own limb. They made a touching sight lying there peacefully on the bed. He glanced at the time on the alarm clock, which he'd forgotten to set, and said, "Better get up you two."

"Oh, Geez.' he called out in panic, "Haley, your aunt's going to miss you."

Haley turned partway over and tried to bury her head beside Misty's right shoulder.

"I mean it," he threatened, "or no more sleepovers."

She said sleepily, "Aw, you know you don't—"

"Up." he said, "we have to get up."

"Oh, oh," said Haley, coming wide-awake and looking at the door with anticipation. "We're too late."

Knock, Knock.

"Kevin," said his mother in a quiet voice. "Are you up? You're running behind schedule this morning. You should be all-ready for school by now."

Instantly wide awake, Misty silently leaped out of bed and crept into the closet, pulling the door shut behind her.

"I'm getting up," he said. "I'll be right out." Haley ducked out of sight just in case his mother stuck her head in through the doorway.

Kevin felt embarrassed realizing he was seventeen years old and Misty had just heard his mother check to be sure he was getting ready for school as if he was a third grader.

Moments later, at the outside kitchen entrance, Haley knocked, but then walked in without an invitation. Kevin was just coming through the interior door for breakfast.

"Hi, Helen." Haley yawned so big that Mrs. Conners laughed. "Aunt Fran said I could eat with Kevin."

"Oh, its Helen now, is it? Well, there's plenty of food so help yourself. Then you two better be off to school."

Haley smiled, nodded and grabbed a plate.

The rush to get to school took precedence over everything else. Especially since they had to take food to Misty, then get her out the window and across the yard without detection.

Once Kevin and Misty separated from Haley on their way to the high school, they decided to visit Mr. Bridger during third period to see if he could explain some things about Haley.

"I think we should tell him about your step-dad," Kevin said. "What he did to you. Maybe we can get that creep locked up until things get sorted out."

"That won't protect me and might make things worse."

"How do you figure?"

"Child Welfare might put me in foster care even if the police lock Shaine up."

"His name is Shane?"

"Yes, only it has an i in it. If he's in jail, he'll have an alibi for the other guy to kill me. We have no proof. If we turn in the jewels and they were stolen, the police might decide you're the cat burglar. In foster care, it'll be easier for the ski-masked guy to locate me. I think I'm safer the way things are, if I can stay with you. No one but Haley knows."

"Sure you can, but I don't think child welfare would put an eighteen-year-old in foster care."

Misty told Kevin that Mr. Bridger's office was a new experience for her. She had visited counseling centers on more than one occasion in North Idaho but this time she wanted to be present. Mr. Bridger had to finish a phone call before he could speak with them. He sat there with the receiver to his ear, nodding his head and occasionally saying, "Uh-huh" or "yes."

Misty puzzled over the seemingly backward order of a sign's words on the wall behind his desk. It read: Invention is the Mother of Necessity.

Soon he was off the phone. "So, this is the young woman of your dream," said Mr. Bridger. "I would have said nightmare but that didn't sound right."

They both laughed.

He continued, "And saying the woman of your dreams would be a bit presumptuous." Again they laughed, but Misty's voice was a little louder.

"I see you're in better spirits today, Kevin. What has changed since I saw you last?"

Kevin said, "Haley—our little friend."

"Haley Madsen?" asked Mr. Bridger. "A little girl about ten years old?"

"Yes, ten and one-half," said Misty. "That's her."

"In a way, I'm not surprised," the man said. "I had hints of this. How did you meet her?"

Kevin said, "She's my next door neighbor and she's been trying to hang out with me for a long time. Like my shadow, almost."

"That's right," said Mr. Bridger, seeming to remember something. "Although, I suppose she could have found you anywhere."

Misty asked, "What's up with that?"

"She's very gifted in a number of ways," Mr. Bridger said. "In some areas, I don't know of anyone who comes close to her." He gazed at Kevin and mumbled, "So you're the one?"

"The one…what?"

"The person who began to occupy so much of Haley's time. She up and quit her work with the sleep lab. Said she had a new...interesting project."

Misty said, "She told us you knew why she quit and it had something to do with government people taking an interest in her. But what do you mean by saying she could have found Kevin anywhere?"

"There is truth to that first part. I became concerned about the amount of interest Haley was generating. I worried how far people might go to further their own ends at the expense of a young girl. But that's something I hope to keep just between the three of us. I know confidentiality only works one way; I'm bound by it but you're really not."

Kevin said, "We won't say anything. Who'd believe us anyway?"

"Precisely," said Bridger. "Now for the second question. Whatever the reason Haley selected Kevin, it had to do with her dreaming, and I think she could have found him anywhere, whether they were neighbors or not. However, I don't want to elaborate right now. We've gotten sidetracked. What did you come in to talk about?"

Misty began slowly, "Well, we simply love Haley, but some of what she's telling us is hard to believe."

Mr. Bridger nodded agreement. "I don't know how enlightening I will be but I'll help if I can. Please understand that if someone off the street asked me these same questions, they'd receive evasive replies. Given your special circumstances, however, I'll be more open. What are your concerns?"

"Could Haley be a threat to us?" Misty asked.

Kevin was surprised.

"I see you're not leaving the hard questions for last," the therapist said. "In one way, the answer is 'Yes'. Anyone might hurt even someone they care about by a thoughtless word or act. I don't believe Haley would purposely harm either one of you. In fact, I suspect the opposite. She'll likely protect Kevin and her concern for him probably extends to you. She's not a threat in any ordinary sense of the word."

Kevin asked, "How much power does she really have?"

"Oh, man, you two aren't going to let me off easy, are you?" Mr. Bridger wiped a trickle of sweat from his brow. "I've struggled with that question myself and don't really know. She has more control of unseen forces than anyone I've met or heard about. What I've researched regarding Rasputin, the Russian fanatic who supposedly controlled the Czar and his family, indicates the famed 'monk' couldn't come close to what Haley can do."

Kevin sat up uneasily. "Whoa, that's heavy-duty. I've read about him."

"You've probably heard the phrase concerning absolute power…." Mr. Bridger suggested. "In the end, it corrupts—"

"Absolutely," Misty filled in.

Kevin had heard the saying as well.

"That," said Bridger, "is an ongoing struggle for Haley, as it would be for anyone. She could play God but she chooses not to. Though tempted to control people and situations, she doesn't. Because of her constant temptation, she struggles more with her own internal demons than with any from the dream world or waking life."

Misty asked, "Can you give an example?"

"Yes. I could make it simple, like the temptation to force her teacher to give a better grade than Haley deserves. Let's make it closer to home. Pretend she had a schoolgirl crush on Kevin that became a very strong desire in her. Let's just say that to feel secure she wanted him to care about her more than he does for anyone else. How many ten-year-old girls with the ability to make that happen would just let Kevin make up his own mind?"

Misty guessed, "Pretty much none."

"What if she thought another girl was getting in her way? How many young females would show restraint?"

Misty blurted, "Hardly any."

"Precisely. Yet, in Haley's case, she would struggle and overcome that desire. She would allow him to make his own decisions without her interference. That is her greatest strength."

"Wow," Misty sat back in her seat.

Kevin asked, with agitation in his voice, "You meant that as a hypothetical example, right?"

"Sort of," Mr. Bridger laughed, "but having worked with children in kindergarten through eighth grade for a number of years, I say we should never underestimate the power of a young girl's heart when she gets a crush on a guy, no matter what the difference in their ages. I had a third grader in love with me once and it was definitely unsettling. At the time, I was about forty."

There was a long silence in the room, filled with the separate mental journeying of each person. At last, Mr. Bridger spoke. "In some ways, I think Haley is the loneliest person in the world. She struggles with things we don't comprehend. That has to be difficult, especially for a ten-year-old.

"She seems finally to be reaching out to you two. She used to visit me frequently but now she rarely does, and then it's usually in my dreams. She comes and plays in them, teaching me about things I can do while dreaming.

Mr. Bridger took a deep breath and exhaled slowly. "I've researched dreams for nearly twice as long as she's been alive and I don't know a fraction of what she knows. Some of it, I've glimpsed and decided I don't want to venture there. Still, she has more fun in her dream world than anyone I know, but no one to share it with."

Misty reached over and squeezed Kevin's hand. "I think she has us to share with now," She said softly. "Thanks, Mr. Bridger, for being open. I know it's a sensitive topic and we respect that."

He replied. "I'm relieved to know she has someone to hang out with."

"It's confusing, though," Misty said. "I don't understand much of what she is talking about, like the other place-thingies."

"There are two complications here," Mr. Bridger said. "It's an obscure theory to begin with, which many physicists don't believe has credence. Plus, there's the fact that Haley has trouble articulating what she knows. Partly, it is because her speaking patterns reverted to an earlier age after her parents died. She's just now catching up verbally to her ten-year-old self. Bright as she is, she struggles to express her thoughts. If you persist in trying to understand, I believe you will. But let me warn you. Things are likely to get more intense than you can imagine. More even than I can picture. If you hang in there, you'll learn things no one but Haley knows."

The thought in their minds as they left the counseling center was, do we really want to be aware of those things?

13: GIRL TALK

Kevin stayed after school to catch up on missing work. Haley had the run of his house, and smuggled Misty into his bedroom where the two girls were lazing around. Misty had wedged a chair against the bedroom door and left the closet open for a quick retreat, although Haley said she would warn if anyone approached.

After a reasonable amount of small talk, Misty decided not to be coy. She came right out and asked Haley, "So, who's this Carol person?"

"Oh, her?" said Haley. "She's nobody. I mean, now she's nobody important."

"Are you sure they're over?"

"I make it my business to keep an eye on Kevin. I'm always checking out the competition, you might say."

Misty did her best to keep from laughing. She turned her head to one side making it harder for Haley to see her expression.

"I know how it seems, me watching Kevin and all. I just can't help it. Most girls he might like would want him all to themselves —not having me around." Embarrassed, Haley said, "You like me to be around him, but Carol doesn't. I'm better off with you here."

"Haley, you've got a crush on Kevin don't you? I know all about liking an older guy."

The smaller girl looked surprised that Misty had guessed she liked Kevin. Haley asked, "You liked an older guy?"

"Yeah and I was years older than you. I should've known better."

"What happened?"

"I don't think I should tell you."

Haley lay back on Kevin's bed and closed her eyes. Her face looked peaceful. When she spoke again, her voice was unusually soft—for her.

"He was in college. Real good looking. Hot. A jock who played football. He was…." She paused. "He saw you in your bikini and…."

Haley stopped. She looked at the young blonde woman whose eyelids were moistening. "I'm going no farther; that's your personal business. But if you want to tell me, that'll be cool."

"I'm glad Kevin isn't here," Misty said, putting her arm around Haley. "He doesn't know all about this. I totally threw myself at John at first and he tried to ignore me but I kept after him. What happened was mostly his fault but I have to live with knowing I was pretty immature."

"Like me."

"Not like you. Not like you at all. Besides, you're ten…."

Haley blurted, "Ten and one-half."

"Yes, but I was almost sixteen. Technically, I was fifteen, but my birthday was only about a month away. The thing is, John was almost twenty."

"Twenty? He was practically an old man."

"Yeah, he should have known better than to get involved with me."

"Did you guys *do it?*" Haley asked in the same voice she might have used when referring to a soap opera romance she'd watched on TV.

"Haley, that's an unfair question. I don't want to lie to you but I'm not sure—"

"You don't want me to make the same dumb mistake you made, do you? Besides, if you are covering it up, it means you did, and anyway, I can find out if I really want to."

"If I tell you about this, you have to promise me two things."

"What?"

"Promise you'll never make the same mistake I did," Misty looked earnestly at Haley.

"I Pinky swear." She raised her little finger.

"And never tell Kevin. He knows some of it, but not all. I may tell him eventually. I just don't know. It's so embarrassing."

"I won't tell, even though I try not to keep stuff from him. But this is, like...your stuff; not mine to tell."

"Yes, I did it with John."

"Oh." Fifth-grade Haley was shocked to hear for sure that Misty'd had sex—and with a much older guy—when she was fifteen. Haley thought of fifteen as being older than her, but not *that* much older. Her face twisted with consternation as though twenty seemed ancient. It was, after all, twice as old as Haley. The look in her eyes intensified.

"That's scary," Haley gasped. "Yuk." She must have come close to knowing about the romance on her own without being told, but then she'd obviously drawn back.

Misty was so involved in telling her story, she didn't notice the troubled look on Haley's face. The little girl's overall appearance was of someone whose dream-world experiences made her feel superior to others in many ways but whose limited real-life knowledge still hadn't prepared her for much that is in the world.

"My perverted step-dad found out about John and me and had us spied on—"

Haley interrupted. "You mean somebody else was watching you guys? Even besides your step-dad?"

"He hired a private detective. When the pervert knew we were doing it and had proof, he told me he'd have John put in prison unless I...did it with him, too."

"With your step-dad?"

Misty sighed. "Yes."

"How old is *he?*"

Misty thought for a moment. "He's like, forty-something."

"That's disgusting—sick'o."

"I didn't know what else to do. I knew I'd lied about my age and thrown myself at John and I didn't think he deserved to go to jail. I really loved him. At least, I thought I did. Plus, my mom would have found out. I couldn't let her learn about it."

"No. But…doing it with your step-dad? That's nasty."

Misty said, "Yeah, it was icky—the worst."

"So…then what happened?" Haley asked as she scooted even closer, clutching her arms tightly around Misty.

"That was the part Kevin knows."

"He knows about your step-dad?"

"Yeah, he was hiding when Shaine tried to make a move on me, but I bit the bas—

"But I bit him, and threatened to scream. He left. I didn't mean for Kevin to overhear but now I'm glad."

"Poor Misty." There were tears in Haley's eyes. "Poor Misty." She buried her head in the hollow of Misty's shoulder.

Feeling Haley's emotion catapulted Misty into the swelling tide of her own feelings. Misty and Haley rocked each other back and forth, crying together. It was quite possibly the best cry Misty had allowed herself since her mother died.

"I was afraid to tell Kevin because if he couldn't handle it and dumped me, I didn't know what I'd do. I don't know anyone else here. You and Kevin are all I've got."

"I must tell you," Haley interrupted, "Kevin's leaving school now. He's in a hurry to see us. Well, he wants to see—aw, his mind's full of you."

"Haley," Misty sniffed as she held the small girl out from her body and looked into her eyes, "I wish I could tell you I care for you as much as I do Kevin, but surely you know…."

Haley smiled and wiped away her tears, "Yeah."

"But, if Kevin adores me, it doesn't mean he doesn't care about you, too. Just in a different way. If I thought he liked you more, I don't know what I'd do. I need him so much right now."

They straightened up and then busied themselves preparing for his arrival. Misty used the small mirror hanging on the back of the door to help repair her smudged eyeliner and eye shadow. Mostly, she just wiped away where there were dark smears.

"In a couple of minutes," Haley warned, "his mom's going to poke her head in here to see what's going on. I'm heading over and check-in with Aunt Fran. For now, you need to hide in the closet, becasue I've got to leave. He may get back before his mom comes in. I'm not sure."

As an afterthought, Haley said, "If you guys ever need your privacy, just pull the blind and I'll know to stay away. It doesn't matter where you are or even if there's a window. Just see yourself covering this window, and I'll know what you mean."

They hugged and Haley departed. Misty hid in the closet and softly whispered a prayer that Mrs. Conners wouldn't come in and find her. Life was already too complicated. She didn't need the added problem of being caught hiding in Kevin's closet.

Entering his bedroom with great expectation, Kevin was disappointed at not finding Misty. He worried that something might have happened to her and wondered where she was.

There was a gentle rapping on his nearly closed bedroom door. Pulling it open, he found his mother standing there with a funny look on her face.

"Kevin, can you put up with Haley this evening? I hate to ask but Fran is panicky. It seems harder than ever before for Haley to deal with the anniversary of her parents' death. It would mean a lot to them if you'd let her spend time with you. I know you're probably getting behind on your schoolwork."

"It's no problem," Kevin said. "I stayed after and got mostly caught up. She isn't that much of a bother. Neither of us have brothers or sisters…and she's kind of like my little sister. When I think of how I'd be feeling if you and dad died when I was little…."

"Well, if there's anything I can do to help her, you know I will. Besides, if she starts to bug me, I'll tell her to go home and come back tomorrow. That's something you can't do with a regular sister."

"Oh, Kevin." Mrs. Conners threw her arms around him for a quick hug. She straightened self-consciously, knowing he hadn't been into hugs from her since junior high. "Thank you, I'm really proud, and Fran and Haley will be so happy."

She scooted off down the hallway and yelled back over her shoulder, "I'm going to call Fran and let her know it's all right. She'll be so pleased."

He tightened as he felt a pair of arms grab him from behind. Something about the softness of their intent told him it was Misty and not the man in black. Except for that knowledge, her intended greeting might have turned out much different, and not how she wanted.

"I missed you so much," she whispered.

He turned around and they hugged and kissed.

"We better close the door in case your mom comes back," she murmured.

He used his foot to push the door closed…but something interfered.

"Ow," said Haley.

Misty whispered. "How'd you get back so fast? Seems like you just left."

"What'd you two do," Kevin asked, "have a girl talk?"

"Maybe," Misty teased.

Haley finished entering the room and closed the door. "We aren't telling."

"Oh yes you are," He scooped her up and tossed her on the bed. She squealed with delight.

Arms raised menacingly over his head, Kevin descended toward her. Grabbing her sides, he tickled her unmercifully. "You're going to spill your guts and tell me everything."

What he hadn't anticipated was Misty.

Leaping onto Kevin's back, she wrapped her arms and legs tightly around, effectively immobilizing him. He teetered, off-balance, which allowed Haley to vigorously tickle his ribcage.

"Truce," he laughed, collapsing onto the bed with the girls clasped to him. "I give. No gut-spilling today."

"Yeah, and don't forget…" Haley chortled, "We can take you."

Misty cautioned, "We better keep it down, your mom might come back."

"I wish my mom would come back," Haley lamented.

"I meant Kevin's mother."

Haley became tearful. "I know what you meant, but sometimes it doesn't take much for me to miss my mom."

Her words reminded them that the death anniversary was not altogether a ruse.

"Closet time," Haley interrupted, hastily wiping her eyes.

Misty launched herself in that direction.

There was a light rap on the door. "It's dinnertime, you kids."

Haley leapt up with disheveled hair, and grabbed a pillow before she opened the door.

"Sorry, Aunt Helen," she said, half out of breath. "We were having a pillow fight. It was all my fault—but I got to tell you— Kevin's pillow-fighting really sucks. I'll be coming over a few more times to get him up to speed. Just wanted you to know."

"Yes, dear, thanks for telling me." Kevin's mother closed the door and went down the hall chuckling. "Oh, those two. Now I'm Aunt Helen. What will it be next?"

14: HALEY'S ERRAND

The next day allowed everyone time to think about recent revelations. The threesome had been lounging in Kevin's bedroom when Haley looked anxiously around. Search as she might, she couldn't spot his alarm clock. "What time is it? Never mind...I got to run an errand."

Before either one could answer, she added, "You two go for a walk. But not too far. I'll see you in a little bit."

She ran off, leaving the couple alone. Kevin's mother was conveniently away visiting a friend in the nearby town of Mosier and wouldn't be back until late.

Haley took the most direct route from Seventh Street to Tenth, where the high school was located. As she neared the large building, she whispered, "He's still there, but he's about to leave."

Once in the high school office, she looked toward Mrs. Tedry, whose name was posted prominently on a brass plate sitting atop her desk. Having run most of the way, Haley was still taking big gasps for air as she told Mrs. Tedry, "I got to talk with Mr. Bridger...it's important."

Suppressing a smile, Mrs. Tedry said, "I'll see." She buzzed his office and said, "Mr. Bridger, there's a young lady here to see you." Turning to Haley, she asked, "What's your name, dear?"

"Haley." Taking a gasp of air, she said, "Haley Madsen."

After a brief exchange on the phone, Mrs. Tedry informed her, "He says you may go and see him, it's that way and up the..."

But Haley had already left. Before she could really get started, Mr. Bridger appeared as if by magic. "Hello, Haley. Long time no see."

She ran forward and threw her arms around him. "So glad you're here. I got to talk about something real important. A friend of mine—and of Kevin's...."

Kevin and Misty elected to do as Haley had suggested. They slipped out of the back entrance and crossed the yard hand-in-hand. Passing under a large, spreading oak, they climbed the gentle slope toward the rim-stone bluff that faced Seventh Street. The hilltop was a secluded setting where no passersby could observe them and it was also well shaded by trees. Having learned from past experience, Kevin brought a blanket for them to sit on.

They made small talk for a while—partly, they wondered what Haley was up to. Her absence was puzzling since she usually spent every available moment with them. They were lying back and enjoying each other's company when Misty felt compelled to talk with him about the sordid parts of her past. "You know that little 'girl talk' Haley and I had while you were up at the high school?" she began.

"Yes," he replied, "I was just kidding...about trying to find out what you'd said."

She laughed nervously, "I know, but it's something pretty big. I feel awkward talking about it, yet I'd feel bad if I didn't."

"You told Haley something you're afraid to share with me?"

"Not really. I told her about John and my step-dad, though."

"She's only ten... How'd she take it?"

"We both cried. I wasn't going to tell her but she closed her eyes and the next thing I knew she was saying stuff about John. How could she know that? I still shouldn't have told her. I don't know what got into me. This whole thing about your nightmare and a cat burglar has got me spooked. I hardly know what to do. Now Haley comes along and knows what we're thinking."

"Yeah, that's pretty over the edge."

She said, "We're starting to share our dreams; Haley's talking to us in our minds. Who but Mr. Bridger would believe this?"

"Nobody." Kevin shook his head.

"Even though Haley and this dream stuff is helping, I'm almost as scared of it as I am of my step-dad wanting to kill me."

Kevin leaned farther back on the blanket, deep in thought. An unseasonably cool breeze played with Misty's hair and ruffled the loose fabric of her top, making her shiver. A film of moisture formed on her eyes. "What am I going to do?"

A dark shadow flitted across the blanket between them as a large crow swooped through the open space under the spreading branches of the oak and landed on a low limb just five feet past Kevin. The ebony bird gave a loud "Caw." bobbing its head and upper body several times before cawing again. The noise startled Misty.

"That's just Blackie the Crow," Kevin said.

The bird alighted on the ground near their blanket and marched back and forth like a marionette soldier before stopping to "Caw" and bob its head again.

"What does he want—food?" Misty asked.

"Maybe, but he comes and visits me at the homer loft and I never feed him. I guess he just likes company."

Misty's expression showed she wasn't sure what to think about the large black bird. She shifted position so her upper body leaned against Kevin's chest. He automatically wrapped his free arm around her shoulder.

An outraged squirrel descended the trunk of a nearby oak tree. Its head pointed toward the ground as it circled its way down the trunk, chattering noisily as it came. Misty watched the squirrel with less concern than she had for the crow, which flew back to its low branch, intermittently cawing. The squirrel paused three feet from the ground and scolded the crow or the couple. Misty looked like she felt more secure with Kevin's arm around her. When he turned his head and kissed her, she surprised him by returning his kiss with more vigor than he'd anticipated.

Time seemed suspended until their interlude was broken by a high-pitched laugh from the street below the bluff. Haley called up, "I know where you are, and I know what you're doing."

Misty and Kevin separated and laughed despite themselves.

"I'm coming up," warned Haley as she ran around the side of the hill. In no time, she appeared beside them. "I said to go for a walk."

Misty replied, "We did. We walked to here."

"Anybody else hungry?" Haley enquired.

When no response was forthcoming, she tried a different approach. "Kevin, why don't you raid your kitchen and get us some food?"

"Since you're the one who's hungry, why don't you go get it?"

"You know there's way better food in your kitchen than mine. It wouldn't be polite, me rummaging in your pantry."

"That didn't stop you the other day," Kevin pointed out.

To both girls' surprise, he got up and headed down the hill toward his house. Turning after a short distance, he called back, "Anything special?"

"Chips," called Misty.

"Cookies," Haley said.

Misty lay back on the blanket. "He's so sweet."

"Yeah," commented Haley. "Wonder what got into him?"

Kevin smiled to himself. He'd needed a bathroom break for a while and his leg had started to cramp, so a short walk to the house would do him good. He chuckled and made a secret bet they were wondering why he gave in so easily.

"You forgot to draw the blinds." Haley said to Misty.

"Sorry."

Haley seemed excited to broadcast her news, "Misty, you need to go talk with Mr. Bridger tomorrow morning."

Misty sat up, looking horrified. "Haley, what did you do? I told you not to tell anyone about my step-dad, and…"

"You told me not to tell Kevin. I didn't. And Mr. Bridger won't talk to Kevin about it either, unless you tell him its okay."

Misty dropped her head in her hands and sobbed quietly. "What am I going to do?"

In a few moments, she sat back and Haley joined her on the blanket. "I've got to pull myself together," Misty said. "Is my face a mess?"

"Only a little," Haley lifted her soft, cotton top to fix the slight smearing of Misty's mascara. "Kevin's so gone on you he won't notice. You even look good first thing in the morning."

"Oh, Haley, you're sweet, too."

They could hear Kevin's cheerful whistle as he returned up the small hill to join them. In a large, environmentally-friendly cloth shopping bag he'd placed chips, cookies, bananas and oranges.

"Thanks Kevin," said Misty. "See, Haley, he's protecting us from our junk food urges."

Haley peeled a banana and smiled appreciatively as she took her first monstrous bite.

With appetites satisfied, the three friends laid back on their blanket. Haley was first to speak. "Tonight is an important dream night."

"What's so important for tonight?" Misty said.

Haley asked in response, "What do we still need to know?"

"What the guy in black wants, I guess."

"That's right, but for tonight, dreaming will be different. We'll do fun stuff but when we find the ski mask guy, you've got to ask questions. He might not tell you answers, he may show you. Try not to miss anything."

With that, Haley pretended to go to sleep and the other two resumed kissing before all three headed back to Kevin's house.

15: PERCHANCE TO DREAM

The three friends awoke as the sun first penetrated the room. The problem was—it wasn't Kevin's bedroom they'd awakened in. They stirred one after another, lying uneasily on the overstuffed mattress atop the brass bed in Misty's attic, their awareness mounting.

Misty asked, "What's going on?"

"If this is a dream, it's as real as my first." Kevin ran his hand across the big bedspread, feeling the smoothness of the fabric. He reached out and touched Misty's hair, noting its silky fineness, and then Haley's, where her rebellious wavy ringlets smoothed together in her taut ponytail.

"Let's really test this." Misty kissed Kevin.

He said, "It can't be a dream but how'd we get over here?" He felt the pressure ease where Haley reclined and assumed she was getting up to look around. Observing the expression in Misty's eyes, he followed her gaze and his mouth dropped open.

Haley was floating in mid-air about three feet off the bed. There were no visible wires to support her and nothing propped her up. She smiled down at them while rotating in a complete circle, like the hand of a clock fast forwarded from twelve down to six and then continuing back up to twelve again.

She viewed them through her dark, pixie eyes. Revolving again, she paused upside down with her ponytail swinging below her like a pendulum. She finally continued on around to become upright. She'd remained in a calmly seated position through both circular maneuvers. "Are you guys ready to have fun?"

By now, the other two sat straight up, holding hands and looking at Haley with concern. Kevin asked, "How are you doing that?"

"You guys are next."

Glancing about the room, whatever Haley's eyes alighted on began to float in the air, slowly circling the attic chamber.

Misty's voice was tense, "Haley, you're scaring me."

Haley laughed as though she hadn't had so much fun in a long time. Fixing her gaze on Kevin—she focused strongly—and he levitated. First a couple of inches, then a foot, until he finally came to rest about two feet above the bed. Misty had to raise her arm to continue holding his hand.

Perplexed, Kevin looked around and felt beneath him. Nothing there.

"Are you going to join us, Misty?" Haley asked. "Or do you want to let go and watch Kevin float around the room?"

Misty's tone was testier than ever before, "I'm not letting go of Kevin."

"Fine. You can join us. Don't worry; I'm not going to turn you upside down—yet." Haley's eyes focused on Misty, who began slowly rising until she was level with Kevin.

Haley said, "Misty needs some comforting."

Before Misty could protest, Kevin embraced her, saying, "This sure seems real." He thought it couldn't be a dream, but the only other explanation was that Haley had somehow transported them to Misty's house and now defied the laws of gravity.

His blonde girlfriend was calmer since their hug. She'd apparently stopped thinking about being suspended in the air and appeared less bothered by Haley's floating upside down antics, or even the various objects meandering through the air.

Haley said, "Pretend we're at Disneyland on that Mr. Froggy-what's-his-name's ride. You know. I saw it on TV once."

The other two began floating slowly around the perimeter of the bed, maintaining their height in the air, but rising just enough to clear the headboard. They continued to circle, gaining speed, and careening up and down above the brass bedstead. Their movement, though in slow motion, resembled a miniature roller coaster. Misty laughed, leaning into the curves, swaying toward Kevin—even bumping into him. Kevin smiled broadly as they held hands and circled.

"Watch this." Haley halted the other two beside her, above the headboard. Moving away from them, she rapidly circled the room, increasing her speed with each new pass. She wove in-between floating objects, swishing close to her companions. "Are you ready to have fun?"

She apparently took their silence for a "Yes."

"All right." She stopped and hovered, facing them three feet away. Misty's eyes betrayed she was thinking of getting her hands on Haley before things went much farther, but noticed their small mentor was just out of reach.

Haley asked. "Who wants to go first—or both of you together? It's easier, practicing separately."

"Kevin's first," said Misty.

She'd barely finished speaking when he was shifted over beside Haley, and Misty had to let go of his hand. Still, she seemed more secure watching.

"You've had flying dreams, right?" Haley queried Kevin.

"Yes…."

"You know you have to really want to fly for it to happen, correct?"

"I guess…."

She explained, "If a bad guy's after you, your fear can make it hard to fly away…. To start, you're above the bed, so just float down from where you are. Use your imagination. Keep thinking of floating down to the bed. Try different ideas until you find one that works."

Kevin's face twisted in concentration.

"Don't force it…" Haley said, "feel it happening."

Kevin descended a few inches, paused and descended a few more. He repeated until he felt the bedding touch his hips and legs. Smiling, he refocused, returning by stages to his former height.

"You're getting left behind, Misty. Better start practicing." Haley mentally shifted her blonde friend to an open area over the bed. Seeing Kevin's success motivated her to try. Initially, she dropped almost a foot and screamed. She then mastered the slow descent, until she touched the bedcovers. "I did it."

The two neophyte aviators practiced rising and falling above the bed.

Haley said, "Okay, that's good. Deserves a prize, doesn't it? But you each have to go half way. No fair one moving the whole way and the other just sitting."

Kevin moved forward six inches and paused. Misty moved about the same. They continued until they were touching. Soon, they were holding hands and beaming at one another.

"You guys are doing great." Haley said.

In no time, the two mastered solo flight around the room, including the dodging of floating objects. Their maneuvers weren't smooth like Haley's but they demonstrated growing self-assurance.

"You guys rock." Haley announced. "Tag, you're it." She touched Kevin as she zoomed past. "No touchbacks," she jeered.

Misty—seeing that Kevin focused on her—screeched loudly and flew around the bed, keeping it as a barrier between them. Haley opened the attic windows.

Kevin leaned forward and his motion accelerated. Misty screamed as she noticed his increased speed. He unwound from his sitting position; letting his legs stretch out behind, and gained additional speed. He arced farther from the bed, avoiding floating objects even at high speed but with varying degrees of success. Veering to one side, he barely missed a floating candelabra. But collided with a mink stole that draped over his head, temporarily blocking his vision.

Haley smiled as if she had mentally maneuvered the fur into position at the last moment so he couldn't avoid it.

He flung the stole in Misty's direction as he turned and sped toward her. She shrieked in alarm, and glee.

"You guys are getting too noisy in the house," Haley said, "take it outside."

Misty, seeming to know it would be difficult to continue eluding Kevin indoors, soared through one of the open windows, laughing all the way into the darkness beyond. Kevin thought that minutes before it had been daylight, but Misty was obviously too busy evading him to spend much time worrying about the now-vanished daylight hours.

As if shot from a cannon, Kevin zoomed toward the window Misty had just left. Whisking through it, his clothes brushed the sill. In the blackness beyond, he dimly saw Misty flitting above the neighboring house. She was attempting to hide beyond its peaked roof before he spotted her.

With a determined smile, he swooped low into the yard, feeling the wind in his face and a sensation of motion that he sometimes had on amusement rides. Realizing the ground must be near, he swung up and leveled off. The dim light from the courthouse was barely enough to navigate by. Two objects loomed suddenly ahead and Kevin rose in the air, barely missing Cal and Jake as they stood looking up at the enormous house.

Why were they there? He arced past the shade tree and banked around the corner of the smaller house, circling to the far side. Gaining altitude toward the roof, he hoped to surprise Misty. Which he did. She was perched near the peak, and poking her head in the direction she thought he would approach her. Coming from behind, he touched her on the shoulder during his flyby. "You're it."

She screamed, mortified that he'd caught her.

In a continuing burst, he was over the roof, and returning toward Misty's attic.

He wondered where Jake and Cal were as he glanced futilely into the night-shadowed yard on his return trip. Squint as he might, he couldn't spot them.

Hearing Misty in screaming pursuit, he sailed to the right of the dormer, along the inclined roof of her house, aiming for the attic window on the far side. Maybe he could give her the slip. "No touchbacks, remember," he yelled over his shoulder.

A dark shadow appeared before Kevin and he dodged around a figure standing in the valley of the dormer roof. A light flashed from that guy's hand, highlighting the masked burglar at the dormer's peak. Kevin felt chills along his back as he soared higher, over the dark figure, and then dove toward the east-side dormer.

He reached there in a state of turmoil, just in time to see Misty flying straight at him from the interior. He barely eluded her, rising back over the roof in the direction he had just come. She yelled victoriously, confident she would nab him.

From the vantage point of the peak on the main roof, Kevin couldn't locate either of the people he'd seen up there previously. Misty's shouts were nearing, and in desperation he flitted off toward the north dormer. The game was still on, and though he puzzled about what he'd seen earlier, he was too competitive to simply stop and let her win.

Haley seemed to take great delight in observing the other two flying in and out of the attic's three windows. As they coursed through the large room for the umpteenth pass, she stopped them. "Enough! Time to watch the sunrise."

With Haley in the lead, they floated out the west window, hovering in the air past the roof's edge—viewing the sun's first glimmering beyond Mount Hood.

"What direction is that?" Haley asked.

"West," said Kevin with growing concern.

"That's right. Sure is pretty, but what was I thinking? The sun *sets* in the west, doesn't it?"

What had begun as a sunrise transformed into a sunset as the luminous disc sank lower on the horizon. It was a truly beautiful setting sun that bathed Mount Hood in pinks and blues.

"How cool," Misty whispered as she reached for Kevin's hand. The sun disappeared behind distant hills and mountains.

"Come on, guys," Haley rose higher in the air. "There's more to see."

They followed in single-file, crossing high above the street, toward the courthouse roof. Rising over that structure, they saw the sun begin to poke up from due north.

"Hurry," yelled Haley as she flew above an old building. Continuing north over rooftops to Third Street, she dove to almost street level. The other two struggled to keep up.

The threesome serpentined down Third, narrowly missing light posts and a parked vehicle to rise again, crossing toward Second. They rose higher to see the fullness of the sunrise. Then flew faster than ever toward the broad river as the rising sun cast its glow across the mirror-like surface of the broad Columbia.

Waves began to grow from the water. Haley led her companions a merry chase around and between the waves, which stretched ever taller, exhibiting unusually sharp points. Daybreak played its rosy coloration across the water in magnificent hues, flashing up the waves.

Additional setting suns and daylights occurred in rapid succession. Each was unique in color and drama, punctuated by varying cloud formations and mountain backdrops. Some, they experienced in The Dalles, others were viewed from Portland—and one in San Francisco. The three friends were instantly transported to each new locale. Occasional sunups occurred rapidly, others were gradual. Those, along with sunsets, happened from any point on the compass.

Back in The Dalles once again, they navigated downriver and veered south, soon finding themselves floating in the air above a pond near a large building. The current sunrise came from the West, splashing orange light on a massive deck and reflecting off the glass of what looked like a greenhouse attached to the building.

"Where are we?" Misty asked.

"I'm not sure." Kevin's curiosity caused him to flit above the surface of the pond's glowing water toward the building. The others followed.

Rounding the corner of the structure, Kevin saw the familiar rock-work and water feature. "It's the Discovery Center," he declared. "We're back almost to The Dalles."

"What's a Discovery Center?" Misty asked.

"Kind of a museum. We'll take you there some day. It's pretty cool."

At last they were hovering above Misty's house.

"If these were video games," said Haley, "you guys would be at level two or three."

Misty asked, "How many levels are there?"

"Oh, hundreds, probably," replied Haley, "but that doesn't matter. I want us to go up to level five…how's that?"

Kevin said, "Okay by me." He loved video games.

"I guess…." Misty said.

Haley added, "When we get done with that level, we'll come back and see what the ski mask guy's up to. For now, grab my hands. If we get separated, don't panic. Just think about Misty's attic and you'll go there. Then, I'll come back and get you."

16: MISTY'S CHOICE

Haley extended a hand to each of them. "When I hold my arms straight out in front, you do the same. That'll move us forward. If we raise them up, we go up...do you see? All you got to do is follow along. I'll focus on where I want us to go; it's a dream I made a long time ago, which I still use."

Nighttime surrounded them and Haley raised her hands to the front. The other two did likewise, traveling swiftly, in utter blackness. Haley lowered her hands somewhat and they slowed. The darkness became a fuzzy haze. They passed through mists and things began to brighten, then cleared. Haley put her hands straight down and the three descended into the middle of what seemed to be an amusement park—very old and neglected. As they alighted on the ground, some of the rides sprang to life.

Haley cautioned, "Things are not what they seem. If something scares you, don't hit it...don't fight it. Try to find something likable in it."

"I'll try...but please don't leave me alone," Misty begged.

"We'll all stay together. You and Kevin can hold hands. How's that?"

Kevin felt Misty's hand grip his like a vice.

"You're strong." he commented.

Haley asked, "For a girl?"

"For anyone."

They went on some of the rides, including the giant Merry-go-round with large, rotating teacups. They climbed into one cup that twisted around, casting them off-balance—tumbling one against another. Misty squealed and laughed.

On the large Ferris wheel, they paused at the top. Haley had them take turns starting and stopping the giant wheel through mental concentration. Eventually, they went all the way around again until they were back at the apex.

Kevin felt uneasy. The two connecting points for their "car" made the conveyance feel unstable. The slightest movement from a passenger tilted the thing forward or back, as if it would spill them out. From that height, they were above all the rides in the amusement park.

Misty said, "Wow," apparently fascinated by the details of the entrance to the haunted house. There appeared to be statues of ancient warriors, plus a king and queen on their thrones near the entryway. It looked amazingly authentic. "Cool," she said.

"Let's go see," said Haley, but instead of waiting for their ride to end, she lifted the safety bar and leaped out into space. That sudden move caught Misty off-guard. She screamed in Kevin's ear as the large bucket they were in swung crazily to and fro.

Once they'd recovered their equilibrium, Kevin and Misty held hands and rose into the air, following Haley. Theirs was not as dramatic an exit but they were pleased at having flown away from the giant ride.

They pursued Haley, arriving at the mysterious haunted house. Misty looked in wonder at the larger than life statues of the King and Queen. "I wish I were *the Queen.*"

Haley looked at her, then at the monarch's statue, causing it to rise in the air. Haley's renewed concentration caused the ruler to settle slowly back into place on her throne. "Get the idea?"

Misty focused her attention on the Queen, and the statue rose from its seat, floating gingerly into position beside a couple of fierce-looking knights.

Misty rose slowly into the air, turning unsteadily, and settled into position on the throne. The royal seat was an ornate affair. Its thick legs appeared hewed from ancient trees. Large, carved vines wound their way up the throne's legs, around the arms, and twisted across the seat and back of the huge chair. Most of the surface area was covered with gold leaf, having the patina of age.

Intertwined with the vines were two mighty serpents with eyes formed from rubies. Haley looked knowingly at Misty as the older girl scooted her bottom around to get the feel of her coveted seat.

"Aren't you going to be my King?" she asked Kevin.

What was he supposed to say? He did the only thing he could in that circumstance and levitated the king off his throne.

Misty looked downward, noticing the two serpents depicted on her armrests. "I hate snakes," she said bitterly, noting their heads reposed near the ends where her hands should go. In fact, her right-most fingers rested on one. She touched a ruby eye and it glowed. Moving her hand away, she turned her attention to the ornate vines and the many jewels that decorated her lofty perch.

"This is really cool…" she began, but felt something move beneath her forearm. The giant serpents had come to life.

Kevin, seated on the King's throne, looked at Misty without knowing what she was experiencing.

Her voice wouldn't work, and she watched in horror as the serpents wound themselves around her legs, the trunk of her body, and finally her arms. The snakes caressed her skin through the fabric of her clothes. Misty felt violated.

Haley's thought-voice was detectable inside Misty's mind, and Kevin's as well, asking, *'What do they want?'*

In her head, Misty shrieked in terror: *'Get off…. Get off me.'*

Haley's thoughts sounded again, *'I won't let anything bad happen…what do they want?'*

Haley's message apparently soothed Misty, and despite her horror of snakes, her mind began to function. She asked the dreaded reptiles aloud, "What do you want from me?"

There was no reply, but the serpents' coils began to tighten about her body. Kevin psychically felt her heart pounding as if it would burst from her chest.

Haley moved next to the throne and gently stroked one of the scaly coils. "How pretty you are," she whispered to the snake.

The constrictions on that side of Misty's body ceased, freeing her right forearm and hand to move. She followed Haley's example and gently rubbed the other snake's head with her free arm. Its cranium felt unaccountably warm—soft and pliable. She looked into the ruby eyes and saw how lovely they were. "You have beautiful eyes," she said. "What do you want from me?"

There was no answer from the serpent, but both snakes ceased constricting, and the second reptile's head undulated in front of Misty, near that of its twin. It seemed to be jealous of her attention to the other. She used her left hand to touch the second serpent's pate, and it basked in the warmth of her touch.

Both sinewy bodies uncoiled from her and resumed their original positions, intertwined with the vines of the chair. Their heads returned to the armrest positions and Misty's hands followed them, settling on their smooth tops. The ruby orbs were fascinating. They commenced to glow as she focused on them. Their radiance increased, and the rosy light reached in all directions, casting a reddish hue upon Misty and her throne. Kevin watched from the adjacent seat, mesmerized.

Misty saw her immediate world through the suffused ruby glow. Everything appeared soft and warm. She imagined kissing Kevin, and became lost in her caring feelings for him. During her reverie, she felt the serpents move again. Their sinuous bodies caressed her but she was not afraid. She knew they wanted only to experience the wonderful feelings between her and Kevin. Her emotions grew and flowed to the snakes.

Unlike the serpents, she could choose to feel love any time she wished—basking in her warmth and caring for Kevin. Without her help, the reptiles could never experience such emotions. She closed her eyes, becoming lost in her pleasant feelings.

When Misty again opened her eyes, the throne was simply a royal chair, and the carved serpents lay lifeless on its ornate surface. Her hands reached out and tentatively stroked the two inert heads. She floated into the air, returning to the ground beside Haley, and gave her a hug.

"Thanks, Haley. I love you so much. How did you do this? And how'd you know what I needed?"

Haley laughed and hugged Misty in return. "I didn't do this…you did. I only made a place where stuff happens that you want or need."

"This whole carnival," Misty resumed, "the Queen and the throne, the serpents…how did you…?"

"I didn't. Where I brought you, there were just mists and shapes, nothing real. Dim lights hid more than they revealed. Your mind made the rest. This is a place of possibilities. There wasn't a haunted house. No Queen…throne…or snakes…until your mind made them. You and Kevin created the amusement park. The Ferris wheel… merry-go-round… all the rest was both of your doing. The throne and the snakes were strictly of your making. Kevin did none of that."

Misty stammered, "I made the serpents?"

Haley nodded to indicate she had.

"Why would I do that?"

"To learn something about your fears," said Haley. "The things we are afraid of, we bring to us—in our dreams and our lives. It's our fear not what we're scared of that takes control over us."

Misty asked hesitantly, "In our dreams?"

"Yeah, like this one."

"This is a dream?" Misty was mortified, apparently forgetting she and Kevin had bantered the idea about previously. "I created this…?"

She turned toward the statue of the Queen on her throne, but the image was fading—a wayward apparition. The mists returned and with them the fuzziness of objects and the muted lighting.

"A dream…?" Misty's voice trailed off.

Kevin called out to her but the darkness had overcome them all….

17: KEVIN'S TURN

The trio of dreamland adventurers awoke in Kevin's room. According to his alarm clock's luminous dial, it was the middle of the night but they were wide-awake. Misty raised herself on the bed, her body visibly tense from their strange dream experience. Haley lazed about, smiling.

Misty said, "My body feels so heavy now. What happened?"

"We were dreaming," Kevin said as he turned in his sleeping bag on the floor. "Now we're awake."

"Yeah, but we were all dreaming the same thing," Misty said. "Weren't we? Didn't we just come from an old amusement park?"

"Yep," he agreed.

"How can it be?"

Kevin replied, "It's just like when you and I were in the basement, and that ski mask guy came in…."

"No, this was too real. This was super-real." She looked over at Haley smiling at her. "What just happened to us?"

"We were in a dream, and you guys had flying lessons." Haley looked pointedly at Misty. "You gave yourself experience in overcoming fears."

"How come I couldn't tell it was a dream?" Misty wondered.

"Yeah," said Kevin, "it should've been obvious. People don't float in the air and fly around in normal life."

Haley said, "*Most* people don't, but you both came close to realizing it was a dream. You said how real it was. Doesn't that show you knew? If you had fully known, it would have been a lucid dream. Like real life, but you'd of known you were dreaming."

"I love the flying part," Kevin said.

Misty added, "I do too, at least I did once I got over being scared. What made us wake up when we did?"

"You started to realize it was a dream, and that scared you. Your fear woke you up. The 'dream world' and 'awake world' are like different realities. They don't make sense, one to the other. That's way-scary, so we keep them separate, then we don't freak ourselves out. You can learn to combine them, though…. That starts with a lucid dream."

Kevin said, "My nightmare seemed totally real. Nothing was illogical, like a bunch of stuff floating in the air."

"I already told you," offered Haley, "that first one wasn't a regular dream…or nightmare. It was a dream along with another kind of place. That other place is real just like ours."

Misty asked, "What about the snakes? You said I created them."

"It's a place that helps you know stuff you need to see— differently. I didn't make those parts of the dream."

"Why snakes?"

Haley said, "You were afraid of snakes, right?"

"Yeah."

"What did they teach you?"

"I really want love and that's what they desire…except, they can't have it— not the way I can. They want it so badly, they'd do anything, but love doesn't exist for them."

Kevin asked, "So, what did they want?"

"Someone or something to really care for them or about them. I thought they were after me because they wanted to harm or scare me but they wanted to experience what love is like. The more frightened I got, the more agitated they became, and so they tried to force the love out of me, but that only scared me more."

Misty touched Kevin's arm as she said, "Because of Haley, I tried to be more caring and they quit squeezing me. The weirdest thing…I can't say I love snakes, but I don't hate them, even though I've always loathed reptiles."

Haley stated, "Now it's Kevin's turn."

"Yeah," said Misty. "Your turn, Kevin."

He looked reluctant, "What do you mean?"

"We're going back," Haley said, "to see what you will make for us—that we can all try out."

He protested, "It won't work now. I know I'm supposed to be creating something in the dream. I'll be too self-conscious."

"No, your conscious part doesn't have anything to do with it —don't you see?"

It took some persuasion, but Kevin finally decided it was only fair he have a turn.

Misty and Haley lay on Kevin's bed. They held hands as he curled up in his sleeping bag, listening to Haley's ten and one-half-year-old voice direct them on how to proceed.

"Just close your eyes," she said, "and remember that when we first got there it was kind of foggy. Things were fuzzy. Lights dim…. We moved our arms down through the air, into the…."

Kevin noticed the mists, which soon began to clear as before. This time, things had altered. As they settled to the ground, it was apparent they were back at the amusement park, but things had changed. The Ferris wheel was dilapidated. Other rides, including the teacup merry-go-round, were covered with vines. The lighting was more subdued. Kevin's eyes were drawn to a long, low building he hadn't observed on their previous visit.

"Let's see what that is," he said, taking hold of their hands and leading the way.

"We're in a dream, we're in a dream," Misty whispered repeatedly. She noticed Kevin in the lead, and Haley following her.

In a moment, Misty was trailing behind, struggling to keep up. She whispered, "How'd I get back here? I don't remember letting go of Kevin's hand."

They approached a large, log building. The light from multi-paned windows was brighter than others in the park. As Kevin neared, the immense double front doors opened automatically.

The interior resembled the garish opulence of an overly-lit, Las Vegas casino. Two ushers hurried them toward the center of the floor, parting the milling crowd of spectators as they went. A great cheer arose as Kevin and Haley were escorted to the table at the epicenter of the spacious room. TV camera crews were arranged to film the "event." According to a giant banner at the rear of the assemblage, this was the site of the Inter-Galactic Dos Championship.

Kevin and Haley sat opposite one another at the focal-point table. Kevin somehow remembered that Dos was a bit like Uno, a game at which he excelled. As he looked about the room, he saw beings from around the universe. Some were contestants; most were simply observers of the games.

For their playing hands, eight cards were dealt in front of each player. Kevin recognized a well-known game show host but couldn't think of his name. The celebrity emcee came forward through the other nine playing tables surrounding theirs. He wielded a microphone for interviewing the featured contestants.

In his most polished voice, he asked Kevin, "Are you nervous about vying for first place in this fifth-annual, Inter-Galactic Dos Championship?"

Kevin wasn't at all nervous. He was one of the fiercest competitors of games in his small city. It mattered not whether he challenged the toughest levels of a video game, a live opponent at a board or card game or a rival soccer player.

Haley was a strong competitor as well, and unknown to Kevin, far superior to him at video games. The contest progressed rapidly until both players had only three cards left.

The TV crews were placed for the best view of Kevin and Haley's facial expressions and to record their cards as they were played. The cameramen were not allowed, however, to reveal the cards each player still held in their hands.

Kevin had a growing feeling of unease. He knew he could win; he definitely held the winning hand. His dilemma was, he had become aware that if he defeated Haley she would be devastated. In his mind's eye, he watched as the little girl he cared so much about lost her vitality and zest for life. He saw her in the future, not eating and simply wasting away. By the time he had only three cards remaining, he knew playing his winning hand would cause Haley to wither and die.

Kevin had an ideal card and could declare Dos as he played it. He somehow knew that Haley didn't have a hazard card to drop on him. Even if she played, it would be his turn again and he had a "Pass" card to drop on her. He could follow that with his last card of the same suit, to win the game.

Kevin hesitated a long moment. His caring for Haley finally overcame his inner desire to win. It's just a game, he thought to himself.

Instead of playing his good card, he reached down and picked up a card from the draw pile. His new card was a hazard card. He could have dropped it on Haley. Instead, he palmed it with the rest of his hand and drew another card. It was an inoffensive, low numbered card and he played it.

Unknown to the audience or the contestants, a great furor had broken out up in the TV control room. The program producer was Misty, who had realized cheating was occurring at the center table.

"Two earth players," she screamed in outrage. "They have first place sewn-up, and one is cheating—they're probably both cheating."

Although the main TV cameras on the floor were located so they couldn't give away a player's hand, there were two hidden video cameras, with telephoto lenses, placed up high. These recorded the cards each player held as the game was played. The hidden cameras weren't broadcast live, as were the others, but simply videotaped for possible use in recapping the game and to demonstrate key player strategies. There, on the separate monitors for some of the technical crew and the producer to see was Kevin caught in the act of illegally forfeiting his game to his opponent.

"Why? Why? Why?" screamed Misty, the video producer. She grabbed her remote headgear and departed toward the playing floor on the lower level. She called over her shoulder as she exited the control room, "Cue that buffoon of an announcer. I'm coming down. Tell him I'll be replacing him."

When Misty reached ground level, she talked into her headset, "Rewind the part with that guy Kevin's last three cards.

What he held before he made the bogus draws. Be ready to play it on my command."

"Okay, Misty," came the contrite reply. Nobody messed with Misty when she was mad. Not even if she was about to create an international, or rather, an intergalactic incident.

Like a whirlwind, she descended to the central table. "Stop this game." she shouted. The incessant buzzing of the audience turned to immediate silence. Misty grabbed the microphone from the emcee's hand, and waved it in Kevin's face. "Why did you throw this game?" She was livid with indignation.

Kevin looked at her, wondering what this would do to Haley. Why was Misty so mad? He had to say something. "It's just a game."

Misty looked like she couldn't believe what she'd heard. In a strained voice, as though she'd misunderstood, she asked, "What?"

She placed the microphone two inches from his lips.

"It's just a game." He repeated.

Misty screamed, nearly out of control with emotion. "What about right and wrong?"

"Some things are more important than winning." He looked down at the table, then raised his eyes past Misty, to Haley. He focused on her dark pupils and thought for an instant he saw a twinkle there.

"It's my fault," Haley said, "Kevin was protecting me."

In that instant, Misty apparently received a mental image of Kevin's thinking process from earlier in the game. Kevin guessed that she now realized he'd discovered what would happen to Haley if she lost. Perhaps she'd seen the image of Haley wasting away. She nearly dropped her microphone.

"What's right," Kevin said, "or what seems right to others, isn't always what's right. And what's wrong…." His voice trailed off, leaving his sentence for her to complete.

Misty actually did drop the microphone then. Kevin reached up and took hold of her fingers. He also reached across the table toward Haley with his other hand. Haley launched herself along the smooth surface, gripping Kevin's arm.

The bright lights softened. The crowds' mumblings became a gentle lull.

A sensation of moving upward returned and darkness descended....

Moments later, plummeting through the blackness hand-in-hand, the three dropped toward The Dalles. They slowed as they homed-in toward the landmark of the courthouse, with Misty's place nearby. They floated downward at an angle and paused beside one of the dormer windows of the home, gazing through the glass into the lighted interior. The big brass bed was as they had seen it last, blankets still askew, but the electric lantern sat in the center of the floor. As they observed the room, a dark shadow moved and came to life. The man in black paced about in obvious consternation.

"Where is it?" They heard him shout at the walls. He went over and kicked the small floorboard across the room, then stooped and felt inside the dark cavity. "Where?" he moaned in agony.

The black figure raced down the stairs. Doors banged during his frantic descent.

"Come on," Haley urged. She flew right through the closed window without trying to open it, entering the attic. Misty laughed while following suit and Kevin brought up the rear.

They sailed in pursuit down the stairwell, swishing through the air; following the "trail" of noisy clomping along the darkened back stairs to the basement. Inside the rectangular add-on room, they hovered, watching the ski-masked man throwing things around. He searched everywhere.

Misty said, "What are you looking for?"

The man glanced around the room, not seeing the others floating in the air. He returned to his search and said absently, "Where'd he hide the jewels?"

Darkness descended again. The basement of the huge house became dim—remote. The sensation of movement returned.

The three night-flyers raced through timeless space—back to Kevin's bedroom, awakening with a start.

"Whoa," said Kevin, "what a dream."

Misty said, "At first I knew we were dreaming but then I got caught up in it. When we saw the guy in my attic, I realized again it was a dream."

"Me too," said Kevin. "How'd we do that? We started the dream together and we stayed with it the whole time, and sometimes we knew it was a dream."

"What did you learn?" asked Haley.

Misty replied, "We know he wants the jewels. Maybe my step-dad moved them."

"How can we tell which it is?" asked Haley.

Misty said, "We have to look in the floor of the attic."

"What if they're still there, then what?" Kevin asked.

His girlfriend answered, "Give them back to the man with the mask."

"Why?" asked Kevin,

"Because if he gets what he wants, he doesn't have to kill me. What would we do with them, anyway? We can't keep them, can we?"

"No, I guess not."

Haley said, "Way to go, guys." She and Misty were still lying together on Kevin's bed.

He struggled to find a more comfortable position in his sleeping bag. "This is really cool," he said, "but how does it keep Misty's step-dad from finding her? Isn't he going to notice she's gone and start looking? What if he figures out she's here?"

There was a flurry of rapping noises in the wall, followed by an eerie silence.

"Guess he thinks she's still over there…" Haley said matter-of-factly as the stillness resumed.

Kevin whispered, "Thoughts in my head, knocking inside the wall…. What next?"

"My step-dad really thinks I'm still over there?" Misty asked.

"Uh-huh," Haley assured. Her words were punctuated by another bout of rapping sounds.

Just as she was about to fall asleep, Misty whispered, "I'll be glad when this is all over with; I'm getting tired of showering in the locker room at school."

18: RETURN OF THE JEWELS

After school the next day, Kevin and Misty met Haley beneath the giant sycamore tree at the public library. They took their circuitous path to Misty's house, traveling east through the parking lot, then over the fill area: formerly a big chasm. Winding down the hill through the alley beside the old Christian Science Church, they crossed to the back of Misty's house, entering stealthily.

Inside, Haley paused and closed her eyes. "He's not here but he'll be back soon. Hurry."

"What about your step-dad?" Kevin enquired of Misty.

She answered, "I got a message from him at school this morning. The note said he went on a day trip to the coast."

"He's long gone." Haley laughed.

They raced upstairs to the attic without stopping. Kevin wondered if Haley really knew about the step-dad.

"Boy, this is a lot harder than flying," said Misty, a bit out of breath. Kevin went straight for the hiding area, which was still protected by the small board despite what they'd seen in their dream. He retrieved a quarter from his jeans, and pried the wood up with one practiced twist. "Okay, Misty, do your stuff."

Misty looked at Haley, "Your hands are even smaller…you want to try? It was about here." She pointed to a spot on the floor.

Haley was overjoyed. She reached her slender arm into the hole and contacted something solid, which shifted with a scraping sound. She struggled to get her hand around it and then slid the metal box into view.

"All right," whispered Kevin.

Misty said, "It's still here."

She and Haley hoisted the box out, and Misty unfastened the lid, revealing the jewels.

"Whooee." Haley tried unsuccessfully to muffle her excitement at seeing them in real life. Then she turned serious. "He's about to come back—less than a block away. He's putting stuff in a car to leave town. If we're going to do this, it has to be fast."

Kevin replaced the floorboard and Misty carried the jewel box. They raced down the steps—their clomping sounds echoing in the stairwell. In the cellar, the clothes dryer was still going but less than five minutes remained on the dial.

The door to the add-on room was ajar. Kevin pulled it wide open and found that almost everything from their dream visit was gone, except the backpack and a bag sitting in the middle of the room, ready for removal. Misty tipped the backpack down flat and placed the metal box of jewels carefully on top so it wouldn't fall off.

"Let's go," whispered Haley.

"Wait," said Kevin. "He reached into his pocket and retrieved the diamond ring. "We forgot this."

"And this," Misty took the gold chain with its ring and pendant from around her neck. She reopened the box, tossed the last items in and sealed it.

"We're out of here," called Haley, leading the way up the basement stairs. She stopped at the ground floor landing. "Oh-oh," she grabbed Misty's hand and pulled her toward the upstairs. The three got out of sight around the corner just as they heard the back door open. They held their breaths.

At the sound of footsteps tramping into the basement, Kevin felt major relief. In moments, they heard a shout of glee, then some mumbling.

"What if it's a trap?" They heard the loudly voiced question.

Soon, footsteps ascended the basement stairs, pausing at the back door. They overheard the man muttering, "That son of a bitch Shaine better not be setting me up."

After the burglar left, the threesome waited briefly, to be safe, and heard the dryer's buzzer go off.

"He forgot his clothes," Kevin said.

"He's thinking about coming back for them," said Haley. "We better go out the front entrance."

They raced through the main floor and out the front doorway, after which they slowed, presenting themselves publicly as not being in a hurry. They walked a block west, past the large vacant lot, and crossed toward the park on their way to Kevin's. Walking up the narrow, rocky way that turned into a paved cross street, they raced first to Haley's house. Cutting through her yard, they made their way to Kevin's bedroom window. Once inside, they collapsed onto the bed, releasing tension.

"We really did it," sighed Misty.

Kevin agreed and added, "This time it wasn't a dream, right?

The other two laughed at him.

"It's getting hard to tell…"

Meanwhile, the cat burglar was on his way out of town when he decided to stop at a local sandwich shop for a bite to eat. It had been a long day and he'd only consumed a stale donut. He traipsed into the eatery with his backpack slung casually over one shoulder. As he decided what to order, the young woman waiting patiently behind the counter couldn't help but notice the beautiful diamond on his finger.

"What a gorgeous ring. Is it real?"

"Oh, yes." he replied proudly.

"Lou, did ya' ever see a prettier ring'n this?"

Lou approached slowly, not being one to comment on customer's jewelry herself. But, as she beheld the impressive stone, her eyebrow shot up. "Why, no. I can't say I have. Very nice, Mister."

He thanked them and ordered a foot-long sandwich.

"For here, or ta' go?" the girl asked.

"Oh, I might as well eat here, it's awful hot and my air-conditioner isn't working."

Lou found a reason to go to the back and use her cell phone to make an urgent call. That diamond ring looked like part of the jewelry she'd seen in the Chronicle's picture from a recent burglary. Maybe there was a reward? It didn't matter. She hated a thief.

The cat burglar was almost through with his sandwich and considering whether to wrap up the rest and take it with him when two uniformed officers entered the fast food establishment. Before long, they flanked him. "Excuse me, sir, that's a very nice ring. We need to see some personal identification and we'd like to take a look in your backpack if you don't mind."

It turned out the thief didn't mind as much as the policemen might have assumed. No, if Shaine was going to set him up… well, two could play that game. After all, plotting murder was more serious than stealing jewels. With what he'd pieced together about the sailing "accident" on Coeur d'Alene Lake, he figured Shaine would be looking at pretty heavy jail time. Maybe a burglar could turn state's evidence and work out a plea bargain?

Two days later, Misty's stepfather was picked up in Missoula, Montana. He'd attempted going to Wyoming. A paid informant had tipped him to the police investigation started by Mr. Bridger after Haley's visit. Shaine's destination had been a small but remote line shack no longer used by cowboys for tending fence. He had planned to remain hidden there until he could figure out a more comfortable hideout. Hours after his arrest, his fingerprints alerted authorities to outstanding Federal Warrants from two other states.

Under different names, Misty's stepfather was wanted in regard to the deaths of two women, one in Nevada and one in Minnesota. Both had been wealthy and vulnerable. It turned out his real name was Abraham Lincoln Curtin, and he was born in Hinesville, Georgia. His father, a military man, had left his barefoot, fourteen-year-old girlfriend with nothing—but a baby boy.

Misty, being the type of person she was, almost felt sorry for her stepfather when she realized what his early life must have been like. But she couldn't bring herself to forgive him, and she knew she'd never stop hating him for killing her mother. Authorities in Coeur d'Alene assured Misty that Abraham Lincoln Curtin would never again be a threat to her safety. They downplayed the fact that when he was apprehended, he swore he'd kill her.

Mr. Cresswell, from Gridway Investment Company in Coeur d'Alene, called to let Misty know that he'd taken precautions to safeguard her family estate's holdings. He'd also removed her residence in Coeur d'Alene from the real estate market since the pending sale had fallen through. Mr. Cresswell would get her input before making any other major decisions. He encouraged her to return immediately to Coeur d'Alene.

Misty informed him that graduation was in one week and she needed to take care of financial matters in The Dalles as well as Coeur d'Alene. There was, after all, the office supply store that her former guardian had purchased with estate funds, plus the sizeable residence. She had many things to think about and to accomplish in a brief time.

One loomed very high on her list—in fact, right at the top— Kevin. Yet, other things might have to come first.

19: THE TALKS

Kevin discovered a note resting on his bed with Misty's writing on the outside. It was neatly folded and stapled closed—probably so his mother wouldn't read it. He opened it just as Haley burst into his room.

"Hey, Dude." She spoke so loudly someone halfway across the house could have heard.

Distracted by the note he was attempting to read, he absently replied, "Hi."

"What you got? Oh, from Misty…. She's doing some errands and stuff."

Haley's statement confirmed what he'd read in the note. After carefully refolding it, he stashed the paper in his nightstand drawer. Plopping his head back on the pillow, he stared at the ceiling.

He was upset that Haley knew more about what was going on than he did. "I don't think Misty should leave notes in plain sight where my mom can find them."

"Your mom will never find them." Haley replied. She was her usual plucky self, but Kevin was on edge—not ready to deal with her. Still looking at the ceiling, he said, "We've been lucky, but how long can Misty keep sneaking in here, and you spending nights with us, before my mom and dad find out?"

"They never will. I told you before."

Kevin said testily, "Fortune can't keep smiling on us and now that Misty's step-dad has been caught, there is no reason for her sneaking around. I've got to tell mom so Misty can come through the door, and we don't all still need to spend our nights together—right?"

"Do so."

"Why?"

"Because you both have lots to learn. Dreaming is the best way. Besides, they won't catch us."

He rolled partway over, his back to her. "You're overconfident."

"Misty's step-dad never figured things out, and your folks won't either. But that's not important. You're wasting our time." Haley's voice was insistent. "We got to talk."

"About what?"

"Your nightmare—wasn't really a nightmare."

"You've told us, and Mr. Bridger said it was a vivid dream—almost lucid."

"How'd you get all those scratches on your arms?"

Kevin started to look at his now unmarked forearms but felt like somebody had punched him in the solar plexus. He rolled back over, facing her. "What?"

"You heard me. The scratches, how'd you get them?"

"What scratches?"

"Quit playing dumb. I saw them—Misty did too. But you never saw them until she showed you."

Kevin had a bodily reaction so intense he thought he would have to race to the bathroom and retch. "What're you doing to me?"

"Nothing. You're doing it to yourself."

"I can't remember," he lied, trying to block the image from his mind of climbing up through the rosebush.

"Quit struggling. The more you do, the more it's going to hurt."

Kevin panicked. Pulsations ran down his right arm and a stabbing pain surfaced in his wrist. Mental images flooded-in. He and Misty had looked at the scratches on his hands and arms when she held the squab.

Breathing like a panting dog, Kevin struggled but couldn't repel that picture.

"You're going to make yourself sick. What's it mean, the sign in Mr. B's office?"

"What sign?" He held his right wrist with his left hand over his midsection in a vain attempt to relieve gastric distress.

"Believing is Seeing. That sign."

He gasped." What about it?"

"Mr. B says if you don't believe something you don't see it. Like your scratches. They were there all along after your nightmare-thingy." Haley sat down on the bed beside him and placed her small, dark hand over his. Her touch helped in some way.

"You don't have to think on that now," she said. "Ask your questions."

Kevin had no idea what questions she meant.

"The questions about your nightmare. You asked them before. Now I'll answer."

His bad dream played through his mind on fast-forward, slowing at the part where he looked through the diamond-paned window up on the roof of Misty's house, and saw the naked body on the bed. The view seemed to freeze-frame, then zoomed-in on the thin line of dried blood along Misty's neck. He asked, "How come there wasn't more blood?"

"You'd of liked to see lots of blood?" Haley asked.

Kevin shuddered at the mere thought and knew she had the answer. "No. I have to close my eyes in the gory parts of scary movies."

"If there'd been lots of blood, you'd of quit watching your dream, and awakened?"

"Probably."

"Ask another question."

"What happened to the body? Why did it vanish?"

Haley answered. "You gave yourself a message when her body disappeared. She didn't have to die. See? It was both a warning and a hope."

"You're saying that when her body disappeared it showed there could be a different outcome?"

"Yep."

"My nightmare warned me that if we didn't do something she would die, but if we did the right thing, she could live?"

"Sure did."

"Why do you keep telling us it was more than a nightmare?"

"It was way more. In some realities she died. You died in some. She would have died in this one but you helped stop that."

"How'd I know to do that?"

Haley shook her head. "Some stuff we still got to figure out."

He took a breath. "Why were scratches on my arms and the pain in my wrist?"

"Finally." She patted his hands and lay back with her head against the wall.

"Because you were trying to show yourself the nightmare was something more. You wanted to know that you made it. To learn about the alternate universes…and to help me with what I'm doing."

"What about Misty? Shouldn't she be here with us?"

"She isn't ready—yet. You're going to get a bit ahead of her for now. You're the one who made the nightmare, and the one who remembered it."

Haley looked intently into Kevin's eyes. "Nobody is going to catch us all sleeping here…or see Misty sneaking in the window."

Disbelief still filled Kevin's eyes.

"Look in your drawer." She directed.

"Why?"

"Try and find Misty's note."

He reluctantly slid open his nightstand drawer. Finding no note, he searched again and then reached in once more, moving things around. He stared back at Haley.

"Look again."

He turned and saw the note sitting in plain sight in the middle of the open drawer. "How'd you make it disappear?"

"I didn't."

"It wasn't there. I looked everywhere."

She smiled like an older sister showing a younger brother how to work a tricky math problem. "You didn't see it, but it was there. Just like when you look everywhere for one of your socks and your mom comes in and opens your sock drawer—it's sitting right there on top. You looked at it but never saw it. Believing is seeing, and disbelieving…sees nothing. "

He shook his head.

"You saw me in the nightmare when you looked in the window, but you blocked that out too."

Kevin's uneasy feeling returned to the pit of his stomach, like when he'd started to remember the repressed thoughts about rosebush nicks.

She laughed. "Your mom could have looked right at that letter and she'd never see it."

Haley sat up straight, sucking in her breath. A shocked look enveloped her face.

Kevin—whose body had somehow recovered—wanted to sidetrack their conversation. "So, you were spying on me in my nightmare, but what was the deal with Cal and Jake being down in the yard when Misty and I were learning how to fly? And the cat burglar on the roof?"

"You were beginning to fly through your dreams."

"Through them?"

"Yep, just like I told you about when I was a little kid flying through my dreams. Next thing you know, you'll be flying into other people's dreams."

Kevin stared at her but before he could pursue that new idea, he saw a second, troubled look cross her face and asked, "What's wrong?"

"Misty."

He straightened with concern. "What about Misty?"

"Just a minute." Haley leaned back on the bed and closed her eyes. Her features softened and her breathing became slow and regular. "She's at Mr. B's. They're talking about…. She's got decisions to make. You're part of it. She's trying to figure out some stuff…about maybe moving. People are putting pressure on her."

Haley was still for several minutes and it became increasingly difficult for Kevin to remain silent. She finally said, "There's a question she has to ask. She's worried about the answer." Haley's eyes popped open. "There's more, but I can't tell you. That's for

Misty. Some of it, you can maybe.... Oh, just think about your nightmare. You've got to figure it out like it's just a regular dream."

"Interpret my dream like in that book Mr. Bridger loaned me? But not using the Senoi part?"

"Yeah. What's it mean when something's there in a dream and then not there?"

"You mean…like the body disappearing?"

"Uh-huh."

"I don't know; her body totally vanished."

Haley abruptly ran out the door, leaving Kevin with her parting words, "Got to go. See you."

Kevin sat in a daze until Haley returned a few minutes later. "Something else," she said, sounding out of breath.

"What?"

"Remember that time…." she gasped for breath. "With the white pigeons we took to the park?"

Kevin watched in bewilderment as Haley raced out again. She called back, "Or was it white pigeons in the sock drawer…?

"Later, Dude."

20: FLASHBACK TO THE PARK

Minutes after Haley's departure, Kevin watched a scene in which he, Misty and Haley had entered the park. It was as if he viewed a mental video. The park event had occurred after he and Misty got together, but previous to their dream about the cat burglar living in the basement of Misty's house. Kevin now vaguely recalled Haley asking—just before they fell asleep in his room—if they could go to the park on the following day.

In viewing himself and the other two walking toward the park, each carrying a white racing homer, the formerly absent memory sharpened. How could he have forgotten it? Kevin now vividly remembered Haley asking if they could go. He'd tried to be noncommittal, saying *maybe* they could take pigeons to the park. The next morning, Misty sided with Haley, and Kevin agreed.

The threesome made their way toward a hidden spot above the small park near Kevin's home. The reverie became more real as he felt the bird clutched in his hands.... They each carried a white pigeon. Kids in the park took great delight in looking at and petting the birds.

Then, still holding their homers, the threesome clambered carefully up the grassy hillside that had many protrusions of volcanic stone. Few people visited there. Kevin finally found what he sought: the tops of rock formations where ancient Native Americans had laboriously fashioned rounded hollows in which to grind their grain. The hollows now served only as small catch basins for the rains that infrequently visited The Dalles.

The three friends lay on the ground—their heads pointing toward one of the massive hollowed basin stones and their feet positioned outward at right angles to one another. From directly above, they might have resembled three points of a compass.

The laughter of playing children floated from across the park and in the distance there was the faint whine of an emergency vehicle's siren. Wind bandied about through the trees and grass, ruffling Misty's hair. "I just want to lie here forever," she whispered to no one…and to everyone.

At what seemed the appropriate time, Kevin spoke. "Tell us when, Haley."

"Now." she called out and they simultaneously held the white birds up in the air, releasing them. They watched as the three homers rose swiftly above the treetops, gained altitude and circled overhead. The racers enjoyed their exercise as the three friends lay far below, in wonder of the scene revealed above.

Soft blue sky was framed by the greenery of trees and punctuated by the coursing of the white acrobats flying in perfect unison, circling and plunging with abandon. The white avian streaks took turns diving crazily to the treetops and then rising suddenly to regroup.

The enormity of the sky pulled the three friends' minds into its upper limits, making it difficult to shift their attention back to the earth.

Haley finally broke the quiet. "It's strange, you know. People are born into families where they don't belong, and they're stuck like glue. You'd think they'd just look around and find where they fit but it doesn't seem to work that way. Take me. I don't belong.

"Better scratch that part because I'm like—this special case. But you get it, don't you? Anyways, if we three stay friends, it's unlikely we'll last. Even a messed-up family lasts. See what I mean? But you two'll graduate and probably go to college—not here…."

"I see where you're headed," Kevin interrupted. "You're worried we're going to run off to college and ditch you. Misty graduates this year. I graduate next…."

"Oh bummer," said Misty, "I thought you were a senior, too. Now what am I…? Can't you graduate early, maybe in January?"

"I could've gotten through a year early but I figured I'd get a lot of my college credits cheaply through a new program. I'll still be in high school but they'll let me take college courses for free. That'll cut my costs."

"You see what I mean," said Haley, glancing at Misty.

"Yes," Misty agreed. "We're both going to feel like we're losing Kevin."

Haley shouted, "Yes."

"I've been living next to you for two years," Kevin said. "And you've been visiting me through my window for months on end but I never really knew you. I wish you'd told me about the dreaming you've been up to."

"I did. You just didn't listen. I even got you started on making me a Dark-Dream-Girl coloring book."

"I probably still don't know you," Kevin said, seeming not to have heard Haley's comment. "What can we do to fix things? Neither one of us have any brothers or sisters. What if we become brother and sister, even if we don't do it legally? We could tell both our families. What do you think?"

Haley said. "Yes. I hope you don't change your mind."

"I think this is a great idea," Misty added. "Older brother's girlfriends kind of adopt their guy's little sisters. Right, Sis?"

"Uh-huh," Haley agreed.

Misty said, "Then that's what we'll do."

After they'd gotten more used to the idea of their new roles, Haley said, "All right—let's play a game."

"What kind of game?" Misty asked.

"A mind game—what else? Just keep looking at the sky."

Kevin said, "That's easy."

"Pretend you have powers other people don't have," Haley said.

Misty asked, "What kind?"

"Let's say the power to fly, kind of like those white homers up there, or in a flying dream. Not just flapping your arms and barely getting off the ground, but like in the comic books, raising your arms up and flying fast, wherever you want to go. What would you do with your power?"

"Well," said Kevin. "In soccer, I'd use the power to streak across the field to the ball and score a goal before the goalie knew what hit him."

Haley asked, "Misty?"

"I'd have used that power for fun but also to save my Mom. I would have used it to fly away from my step-dad when he was being a, whatever…."

"Okay," Haley continued. "We're pretending you really have the power and you really use it—like Kevin, in soccer. What happens in the real world?"

Kevin said, "I guess they outlaw the ability or somehow keep me from using it in soccer because it's an unfair advantage."

"That's a start. What do you think would really happen?"

Kevin said, "Somebody would want to know how I could do that. They'd probably want to study me."

"How would they find out about you?" asked Haley.

"It would be in all the papers."

"Okay," she clarified, "for real, you'd be famous. People would probably want to turn you into a lab rat. Then they'd want to make a movie about you…or some business would try and figure how to make a fortune off of you. After a year, what would it be like?"

"Yeah Kevin," Misty asked. "What friends would you have? Would you be happy? Who'd be your girlfriend?"

"Hold on," he said. "This is heavy. You're going too fast for me to keep up."

Haley agreed, "That's right. Your life would be moving so fast you couldn't keep up. Now, put yourself back on the soccer field. "Would you use your power?"

"No," Kevin answered quickly, surprising himself.

"See," Haley concluded. "You'd turn out kind of like a superhero, changing clothes in phone booths and leading a double life—even from your girlfriend. Maybe taking a secret flight over the Columbia River at night but not showing off your power."

"That's probably right," agreed Kevin.

Haley turned to Misty. "Hey, Sis, I'm not leaving you out of this. But let's change it. Let's not use the power to fly. Say you have the power to change anything you want. We're going to make you a god. Not the God. Just like...a god for a day."

"Yeah," said Misty, "I can get into this."

"Go ahead; create your change. What'll it be?"

Misty began to think out loud. "Let's see...end death, disease, poverty...injustice?"

Haley suggested, "Why don't you start with one thing?"

"Okay, I'll wave my wand, and puff, there'll be no more bad people."

Haley scooted across the grass near Misty. She laid her head on Misty's shoulder and gazed up at the blue sky. "So you got rid of all the bad people, huh?"

"Yes."

"Now what'll happen?"

"Everything will get better. Everyone will be happier."

"Really?"

Kevin turned onto his side and slid around so he could watch the other two more carefully. He had a feeling—like in his soccer example—this wasn't going to turn out the way Misty thought it would.

"How can we tell you got rid of all the bad people?" Haley asked.

"Because they've disappeared."

"So, what's left?"

Misty replied, "All the good people."

"How do we know?" Haley asked.

"Because they do good deeds. We can tell by their actions."

"Let's see," said Haley. "Don't you figure something is good by comparing it to something else?"

Misty mumbled, "Yeah, I suppose."

"What we got left," Haley clarified, "are good things, maybe some not so good things, but no bad people. What we got left is…. What do you think we got left?"

"A more ideal world?" said Misty.

"What we got is a messed-up world because we threw out free will. To have good, you've got to have evil. When you get rid of one, you take away the other. Remove ugliness and you take out beauty. There'd be pretty people but they'd all have to look exactly the same."

Misty asked, "Why?"

"Any difference will cause a problem, like comparing one kind of beauty to another. Somebody will think one's better. To stop that, everything has to be the same. That's totally boring."

Kevin's head rested on his hand, his smile turned to a look of uncertainty.

"If you make us all rich," Haley said, "or healthy, the world can never change. I used to wonder why Jesus left bad stuff in the world. He cured some people but he left the rest of the world alone. If he could cure some, couldn't he cure everyone? Why didn't he? Because he'd of destroyed the world. This place seems awful sometimes but it's really perfect. Kevin taught me that."

"Me? When?"

Haley sat up. "It's getting late. We better start back."

"This ground *is* kind of hard," Misty said as she stretched.

Kevin stood reluctantly. "Maybe we can talk on the way home?"

"Maybe," Haley agreed but when they descended into the park, some youngsters approached to see if they could pet the pigeons.

"They went home," Kevin informed. "Didn't you see them flying?"

"Nope."

As he led the way out of the park, Kevin's thoughts ran in two directions. He was curious about how he could have told Haley the world is perfect. It didn't seem perfect. His other concern was how the things they'd been talking about might relate to his nightmare and to the danger that Misty—if not all of them—might be in. His mind flitted back to Haley's comment: "Kevin taught me that."

"All right," said Haley. "It happened after I'd just moved next door to you."

Kevin asked, "What happened?"

"What you taught me. The thing I was going to wait until later to tell—but you can't let go of it. When we met, you knew I was hurting inside...about losing my parents. You talked of that one little squab—"

"He told you about a baby pigeon?" Misty asked.

Haley continued as though Misty hadn't spoken. "That was the best little bird Kevin ever saw. He loved it more than any of the others. It grew big and strong— faster and stronger than the rest. It even left the nest early. One day, he saw it sitting on top of the flying pen all alone. He'd forgotten and left the trap door open, never thinking it could fly up there. It'd only been out of the nest a couple of days. Two of the older birds were returning from a training flight and at only four weeks old the youngster flew up to join them. Kevin saw how well it flew and realized it was a future racing champ."

Kevin remembered that fateful day as they neared his house. In fact, they were approaching the very spot where the event had happened.

"Then, life dumped on him. His little bird joined the other two as they made a fast turn. They were all flying through some power lines. That baby had everything going for it except experience. It hit an electric line and fell dead to the earth. Kevin ran over and picked it up."

Misty watched Kevin's face. He was focused on the ground not far from them. Looking up, he saw the power lines overhead.

Haley let the story hang in the air before continuing. "That night as he lay in bed, he couldn't believe God would let that happen. He begged to know why. When he slept, he had a dream in which he again watched the young bird on top of the loft. He saw it flying, only to die once more. But there was an old man standing next to Kevin during his dream. That guy said the greatest gift in the world is free will. But to have that, stuff has to be able to go wrong, as well as right. Nothing can prevent that, or—there's no free will."

"That dream helped Kevin…and me too, but in different ways. I could get in other people's dreams so I went into his and found the wise man. I borrowed him and I still talk to him sometimes. He stayed in your dream too, Kevin. You can go back and see him any time."

Kevin sounded surprised. "I had no idea when I told you about that bird it would help so much."

"That was my greatest gift from dreaming. We can learn stuff we need to know in dreams and that means more to me than controlling them, or making dream video games."

Kevin had the impulse to go over, lift Haley up, and hug her. But he didn't.

She looked into his eyes. "You could do that, pick me up and carry me around—and I'd love it—but Misty's suffering. She needs you to give her a hug."

Misty seemed jolted by some of the things Haley had said, and commented, "I've been worrying about the bad things my step-dad did and the death of my mother. I don't see how having free will can make up for some things people have to go through." She lifted her hand up to stroke Haley's hair and whispered, "How'd you know I needed a hug?"

"Same way I knew Kevin was thinking of coming over and picking me up. He was talking himself out of it, so I let him know I'd like it—for in the future."

Kevin actually hugged them both.

Misty said, "What you said about Christ—that bothers me."

"I know," Haley replied.

Misty continued, "I don't believe the world is perfect. I don't know why Christ didn't make *everything* better, but…. I mean, some things just can't be perfect. Why'd my mother have to die? How come my step-dad's doing all this bad stuff? How's that good?"

"It's not," Haley replied. "I felt the same about my folks. I still feel bad about them."

She paused for some time. "It really hurts."

She sniffled, and then wiped her nose with the back of her hand. Something fierce came into her eyes. "What Kevin told me led to the wise, robed man. And what that guy showed, took me back to what I learned from the beings of light...when I was just little and they taught me about dreaming. It's hard to tell you about it because they didn't use words. Ideas just came into my head—see?"

The others nodded, but they both had uncertain looks on their faces.

"I learned from them in a different way. It was a way of knowing...experiencing something and realizing it was right—until I knew it was real. It's hard to describe. I don't think you're ready, but I'll try because, Misty, you and me suffered the same.

"See, when the world got made, it wasn't finished. If it was finished..." She paused. "Can't think how to say it. We help make the world...to be what it is. If we use our will and get to be what we can..."

The sound of a dog whining down the street attracted Haley's attention. "That's Tiny Terror," she said. "Missing me...." Then she glanced around as though looking for something to help explain what she'd been saying.

She stared down at a rock and Kevin realized how odd the three of them must look—two nearly-adults, listening intently to a ten-year-old girl. He became self-conscious and glanced around to see if anyone was watching.

"It starts in dreaming," Haley said. "We make our dream world. Mostly we don't know that. If we do it knowing we're making it—then we learn how to create what we want in our dreams. If we keep doing that, we can learn how to create stuff in our awake-life. We can only do it if everything isn't already decided on...how it's going to be. We can only become what we want to be if we have free will...and we only have free will if we believe we do...."

The park reverie faded as Kevin heard a noise in his house. He rose partway up on his bed, listening alertly.

21: "TALKS" CONTINUE

Footsteps sounded down the hall, approaching Kevin's room. Misty poked her head in the door. He was relieved to see her, though he'd expected her to be Haley. "Hi."

"We need to talk," she said.

He patted the bed beside him. Misty shook her head no.

"On the hill." She pointed out the window. "Where no one will bother us."

For this second meeting, Misty took Haley's advice. As they made their way outside, she mentally pulled a window blind down as the signal she and Kevin needed their privacy. Kevin, blanket in hand, saw the day was much the same as the previous one, but hopefully, Blackie the Crow and a protesting squirrel would not come to visit.

They spread the blanket carefully on the ground to avoid fallen branches and other pokey things. Misty and Kevin sat facing each other, slouched back, feet touching, supporting themselves with their arms propped out behind. Misty elected, with more determination than before, to go straight for her central issues. "Do you remember when we were talking here before?"

"Yes."

"I tried to tell you about the way things happened between John and me."

"I don't need to hear about that stuff." Kevin tilted farther back. "Now that your step-dad and the masked guy are out of your life we can just forget about the past. Move on with our lives."

Misty looked preoccupied. "I have so many decisions I need

to make. I hardly know what to do, but the thing that means most is you and me getting off to a good start."

"Okay." He believed that whatever it was she needed to talk about couldn't be worse than the 'older guy' thing and having sex with her step-dad. Kevin had gotten through that all right—well, sort of all right.

At the point of telling Kevin "everything," Misty got that sick feeling in the pit of her stomach. There were no little critter interruptions to stop her as there had been before, but something inside caused her to change her mind at the last second. Instead, she decided to discuss her other need with Kevin.

She began, "I know we're kind of young, but I love you and I think you love me...."

She waited but Kevin didn't respond. He thought she was going to continue and he was feeling nervous about the direction their conversation might be taking. He finally said, "uh-huh."

It was hard for Misty to tell if that meant he loved her or he thought they were kind of young, or both.

"I want us to be together," she continued. "There isn't anybody I want to be with but you...."

Again, the silence built between them. Unable to contain her frustrated feelings any longer Misty blurted, "I want us to get married."

Immediately after speaking, she regretted the way it had come out.

Kevin turned his head partway to the side, thinking about what he should say. He didn't want to offend Misty but neither did he want to agree to something he was sure he wasn't ready for. He loved her and felt fortunate she loved him. He wanted them to be together but he also thought he needed to finish high school. Then there was college. He felt overwhelmed—a feeling that translated into tightness across his face—creating a frown instead of a smile.

Misty's fears lay waiting like a crouching cat, ready to pounce. The look on Kevin's face prompted her emotions to launch forth. "Don't you love me?"

He nodded.

"Then why don't you say it?"

Kevin was torn between saying "yes" he loved her and answering her question about why he hadn't already said it. In the past, he'd gotten into these types of "discussions" with his previous girlfriend, Carol. Those had never turned out well. He began to panic and as he did, he couldn't reply to her question.

Misty's anger increased. Her fearful emotions had already been unleashed—particularly her fear that Kevin was going to say no, he didn't want to marry her.

"Why don't you love me?" she yelled at Kevin.

He did love her, so how could he answer her question?

"I thought you loved me, Kevin." Misty stood up, glaring down at him.

He managed to stammer, "I do," but things were terribly out of hand by then. He was still not speaking with conviction. He felt like he was being manipulated into saying he would marry her. He really didn't want to take that big step while he was still in high school.

"You don't want to marry me, do you?"

How much deeper trouble could he get into? He stood up. His anger was rising. Why was she putting him in this position? Why wasn't she giving him time to respond?

"I don't believe this…." Misty started to walk away. Heated tears filled her eyes. She was probably angrier with herself than she was with him, yet her anger focused on Kevin. She was mad because she hadn't taken more time to broach the subject and aghast at the way she'd gone about it.

"We'll talk later," she said in a dismissive tone, heading off the hill toward Haley's house.

"No," said Kevin, feeling hurt to the core by the tone of her voice, and angry at being put into such a difficult position.

"We're done talking." His voice was not raised but a sense of finality was conveyed in his words.

It horrified them both.

All Kevin could do was withdraw. He walked stiffly from the hill toward his home. Afraid he might encounter someone in the house, he climbed through his bedroom window. Flopping onto his un-made bed, he yanked the top cover over his body, curling into a protective ball.

Within minutes, Kevin entered a deep sleep that gave him some relief from the pain that had overwhelmed him.

The solitary blanket remained abandoned on the hill, ruffled by the wind.

Haley obeyed the drawn curtain signal that she and Misty had pre-arranged. Despite her purposely created psychic barrier between herself and the other two, she began to sense that Misty was back at her own house and something was very wrong. Haley speedily made her way toward Misty's.

Reaching the front door of the sizable house, she rang the bell. She tried the doorknob but Misty had taken Kevin's advice and started locking it. After a reasonable wait, Haley sensed Misty was in the attic. On a hunch, she went around to the back of the house and found the rear door unlocked. She climbed the steps to the second floor and opened the door to the attic. She discovered Misty on her brass bed, curled up under the covers. Haley climbed onto the bed, curving her body against Misty's.

"I've lost Kevin…. I've ruined everything. Why didn't I listen? Why did I do it?"

Haley spent that night with Misty, after "calling" and telling her aunt that she would be spending the night with Kevin's mom. Haley's method of contacting Fran was a thought voice resembling that of Mrs. Conners.

The next day, Misty felt a terrible loss. How could she deal with Kevin? In desperation, after several unsuccessful attempts to call him, she went to school and made arrangements to skip the graduation ceremony. She would return to Coeur d'Alene earlier than she had expected. Maybe that would get Kevin's attention?

The situation regarding Misty and her former guardian was known at the school. All due haste was made to help accommodate her wishes to return speedily to her home in Coeur d'Alene. "That poor girl," Mrs. Tedry whispered to herself after Misty left the office.

Misty tried to call and say good-bye to Kevin. She hoped the reality of her leaving would get through to him. His mother said he was sick in bed and couldn't come to the phone but she would give him the message.

Kevin was so physically ill he could barely get out of bed to go to the bathroom. Haley hovered about but he seldom took notice. She was losing her two best friends—her only real friends. She watched in shock as they drifted away from her.

Misty went by Mr. Bridger's office three days before the end of school to thank him and say good-bye. She volunteered nothing more. He asked no questions, although, with Kevin's school absences, he could hazard a pretty good guess. He encouraged Misty to see a counselor when she returned to Idaho. In addition, he asked her, as a favor, to write a small note on a card that he took from his drawer. She gladly agreed to do so. She added a second, folded sheet she'd previously written and gave them both to Mr. Bridger. He sealed the envelope, and she wrote on the outside.

She told him she still had his cell phone number, and she hoped it would be okay for her to keep in touch. He agreed.

On the next to the last day of school, Haley went to see Mr. Bridger. Her visit wasn't a surprise since he'd already spoken to Misty.

"We got to do something, Mr. B, they're both dying while I watch. It's awful…downright pitiful."

"Haley, I'm every bit as worried about you as I am about them."

"All we got to do is fix them and I'll be just fine. Kevin can hardly get out of bed and Misty's already left for Idaho." With her last comment, Haley's eyes teared-up. She tried to hide it from Mr. Bridger, but he simply passed her the box of tissues. Loudly blowing her nose, she looked around for a wastepaper basket, which he held out for her.

"Thanks Mr. B. What're we going to do?"

He picked up his telephone. "Do you know Mrs. Conner's number…?

Haley nodded.

"Actually…." He passed over a small notepad and a pen. "Why don't you write it down for me in case I don't reach her now? I'd look it up but I've already turned off my computer. This'll be faster."

Haley jotted down the information.

"Thanks," Mr. Bridger put the phone to his ear and punched in the numbers.

After a minute of ringing, he said, "Is this Mrs. Conners…? Hello. This is Ed Bridger at the high school. We've spoken in the past, and I'm concerned about Kevin."

From where she was sitting, Haley could hear Mrs. Conners sobbing through the phone. Haley squirmed uncomfortably in her chair.

Mr. Bridger listened attentively to Mrs. Conners' worries about Kevin. "Have you taken him to see the doctor?

"You may want to consider doing that. How long has it been since he's eaten anything?

"I see…. Is he drinking water?

"Well, be sure he has liquids available. Water's best but try anything he'll drink.

"Now, Mrs. Conners—

"Alright…Helen. I want you to make every effort to get Kevin to school tomorrow morning. It's the last day before summer break, you know…. Impress on him how important it is to be here. You might drive him; if you think he's too weak…just get him here however you can.

"If he walks, call and tell me he's left. If you drive him, just come to the counseling center and let me know he's here—after you drop him off.

"If for any reason you can't get him to school, I want you to do two things. First, call and let me know. Then, transport him to the doctor's office. Don't take 'no' for an answer. If he won't come to school tomorrow, get him to the doctor. Okay?

"No matter what happens in the morning, you're going to call and tell me what's going on, right?

"I look forward to hearing from you. Take care, and see if you can get Kevin to watch a funny movie with you tonight—one he really loves.

"I'll talk to you tomorrow, Helen. Good-bye...."

Haley jumped out of her chair and ran over to give Mr. Bridger a hug. He wasn't used to getting hugs in high school but he'd previously served in lower-grade positions long enough to take her hug in stride.

As she headed for the door, Mr. Bridger called out, "I think Kevin's mother is going to need help getting him to school in the morning. Will you assist her?"

"Yep," said Haley, as she rushed toward the doorway. She stopped and turned around. "You hear a lot of crying in this place, don't you, Mr. B."

"Quite a bit."

Haley said, "Changing stuff in my dreams is way easier than changing things in the awake world." Off she ran for Kevin's house.

The small girl was excited because she knew just the movie to put on. Kevin had that little TV with the built-in movie player up on his shelves. He wouldn't even have to get out of bed. He'd be a captive audience.

Kevin's eyes jerked open as he heard the beginning soundtrack for one of the stupidest but also one of the funniest movies of all time. He'd watched it, on average, about six times a year. Usually, it was with a couple of his buddies, and they would stay up late on a weekend night eating pizza or popcorn and watching *the movie*.

Haley climbed beside Kevin on his bed as the opening credits were running. She had a big bowl of popcorn from which he automatically dug out a handful. He ate without thinking about it. She'd placed his favorite soft drink invitingly on his nightstand. Snuggling-up, she wiggled her way in closer. Neither of them said anything but before long, her head rested against his shoulder.

She smiled as she heard his first laugh in days.

22: THE LAST DAY OF SCHOOL

Kevin was better on the morning of the last day of school. He had slept straight through the night and actually felt rested by morning. Watching his favorite comedy the previous evening, he'd laughed loudly while eating the snacks Haley smuggled in. He felt better than he had in days and ate some breakfast. He looked somewhat renewed after shaving.

There was a tapping on his windowpane. Glancing over, he saw Haley's pixie grin shining in at him. Crossing to the window, he pulled it open with effort. "What are you doing out there? Why didn't you come through the house?"

"Come on." yelled Haley. "We don't want to be late for school."

"I'm not late. Come through the house. I don't feel like lifting you up this morning." He wasn't sure he could pull her through the window. She raced away. By the time she got to Kevin's room, he had his backpack on his shoulder.

"Come on," she grabbed his hand, "I'm going most of the way to the high school with you—unless you want your Mom to drive us?"

Kevin gave her a sidelong glance that seemed to say, "What's up with that?"

"Okay," said Haley. Let's go." She grabbed his arm.

Kevin arrived at high school in plenty of time; not knowing his mother had placed a call to the counseling center immediately after his departure. Making his way to his wall locker, he nearly bumped into Mr. Bridger.

"Hi Kevin, it's good to see you. I understand you haven't been feeling too well."

"Been pretty sick…."

"I've got something for you in my office. This being the last day of school, I'd hate to have it get misplaced over summer. Do you have time to come there with me?"

Kevin replied, "I guess so."

The two of them went upstairs to the counseling center and Mr. Bridger began looking through piles of papers on his desk. "I'm really glad to see you up and around again."

Mr. Bridger sat upright. "Now I remember, I put it in the file cabinet for safe keeping." He rolled his office chair over, and taking out a key, retrieved the document he wanted. It was securely sealed in a half-sized manila envelope.

Kevin's name was on the outside and Mr. Bridger handed him the envelope, which Kevin rested on his lap. Misty's handwriting was easily recognizable.

"I hope you'll open and read that, Kevin. I don't know what it says."

Mr. Bridger shifted in his chair, leaning slightly forward. "Something's wrong between you and Misty. I don't want to interfere. If you don't want to talk about it, I'll respect your privacy."

In the pause that followed, Kevin remained silent.

"I won't ask what happened but you're free to tell me anything you wish. I hope you and Misty will learn from your experiences, and that you will both come through this in one piece. As much as I thought you made a nice couple, you're still young. Girls mature more rapidly, so Misty may be ready to settle down with a permanent partner and you might not."

Kevin listened, sitting stiffly. Mr. Bridger continued. "With the loss of both her parents, she likely needs to create a family to regain her sense of security and belonging. You might not have that same need."

Kevin said, "The idea of marriage at my age scares me but the big thing is, when Misty and I got mad, we said things… I'm still upset at her for trying to push me into saying I'd marry her. I felt trapped. I don't know how we can get out of this mess. She's in Idaho but even if she were here, I wouldn't know what to say. I guess she thought if I didn't say I'd marry her, I don't love her."

Mr. Bridger asked, "What kind of relationship do you want to have with Misty?"

"I don't know. I want us to be together but I have to finish high school and there's college to think about. She's already got so much. I'm just starting out...with nothing."

"You want to be with her but you're not sure you're ready for marriage?"

"Yes," Kevin said. There was a measure of relief in hearing his thoughts restated by someone else. "I'm having trouble making up my mind about things. I still don't have any idea where I want to go to college or how much time to take finishing high school. How could we get married and live in two different places?"

"It seems," said Bridger, "like part of the problem is you're trying to solve this without Misty. She's a big piece of the puzzle, don't you think? She may have answers that could help you put other pieces together. The question is, 'Do you both want to continue your relationship?' If so, working out the details must involve Misty."

"I don't know how to talk to her." Kevin rested his head in his hands. "How to start...what to say?" He glanced over at Mr. Bridger. "Last night, I had the strangest dream...

"I was in a play, and I had a prime part. I was supposed to kiss the leading lady. Actually, there were sort of two leading ladies. I was mostly supposed to kiss one.

"I was afraid to do that in front of an audience. When the actresses thought I was going to mess up and not do it—partly because of their doubts—I wasn't able to kiss either of them. I woke up feeling bad."

"Have you thought about what that dream might mean?"

"Not really...never been in a school play—any play for that matter."

"It sounds like you had to commit to a kiss and that was hard for you. Does that sound like it has any relation to waking life?"

"Yes."

"What this makes me think of," Mr. Bridger said, "and I'm not sure why I'm remembering this, but there was a psychologist named George A. Kelly who developed the concept that all people are like scientists. His theory was that we try experiments to make our lives better. He helped people conduct tests and change their lives. At that time, Freud was the king of psychological theory and his followers believed it took a long time for people to make changes.

"Kelly thought people could change more quickly. He helped them describe the type of person they wanted to be and they began playing that role. Sometimes, they changed their first name to go with their new part.

"Dreams are an almost ideal way to rehearse a new way to function. It seems you were doing that in your dream—rehearsing a life role—which is another way to operate in your world. You didn't like the way things were going in the dream, and it seems that's related to your romantic relationships."

Kevin said, "You might be right."

"What do you think you'll notice first," Mr. Bridger asked, "when you see yourself changing in a more positive and assertive way?"

"I'll be able to think of Misty and feel happy instead of cringing like I do now. Yeah, I'll feel happier. I'll wake up in the morning and not be tired."

Mr. Bridger said, "All right, you'll be sleeping better, feeling happier and sometimes you'll enjoy thinking about Misty, is that correct?"

"Yes, my life will be much better…."

The man suggested, "If you have that same dream again, you might take control so it comes out more to your liking."

"I'll try."

"What about your little friend, Haley?" Mr. Bridger asked. "How does she fit into all this?"

"Haley's stood by me through everything. She put on my favorite movie last night. We watched it and ate popcorn." Kevin laughed just thinking about it.

Mr. Bridger commented, "Sounds like there's a ray of hope even in your darkest hour. What will surprise you most when your life turns for the better?"

Kevin placed his elbow on his knee and rested his chin in his hand in marked resemblance to the famous statue of The Thinker. After a time, he said. "I'll read this note from Misty."

"Ah," was all that Mr. Bridger said but his eyes lighted up and he smiled. "When you decide to contact Misty, I know she will appreciate it. I better let you get to class. Here's a pass just in case I've kept you too long."

Kevin stood up to leave and said, "I wouldn't know what to tell her. How to begin…to explain…."

"Some things don't need explanation," Mr. Bridger said. "Contact, in whatever form, that's probably what's important. Good luck and let me know when things are better. I'll be here for a few more days before my trip, and I'll appreciate hearing from you."

"Sure." said Kevin as he left the room.

By the end of school, which only lasted a half-day, Kevin was invited to his friend Jake's to try out a new video game. He phoned his mother to let her know where he'd be. Ordinarily, he didn't bother telling her such things but given his state of the last few days, he didn't want her to worry. She sounded relieved to hear his plan.

Haley also got out of school early. She made a beeline to Kevin's house and was crestfallen to discover he was over at Jake's. She'd been so intent on getting to see him she hadn't mentally checked on his whereabouts. But, like Kevin's mother, she was relieved to see signs of the old Kevin re-emerging. "I'll just go hang out in Kevin's room, Auntie," Haley told Mrs. Conners.

"Okay, Dear…."

Once inside his room, she found herself straightening things up. The two of them had created quite a mess the night before. Popcorn was on the floor and practically everywhere else. Empty soda cans were scattered about and his bed hadn't been made in several days. The more picking-up she did, the more she found things that needed to be straightened or organized.

In the midst of her cleaning frenzy, Haley found one of Kevin's drawing pads had fallen off the end of his desk. It rested in a hidden spot between a file cabinet and the wall. Retrieving it, she wondered what sketches he might have done. She was familiar with his other drawing tablets but this one was new. Flicking open the thick cover revealed the first page. She stared.

Kevin wasn't known for doing people's portraits but there was a good likeness of Misty's face. Haley leafed through the notebook. There were several pages of portraits. Most were good—some better than others—but all were of Misty.

Haley closed the drawing pad and hugged it. She spun around with a little squeal of excitement and carried it with her to sit on Kevin's newly-made bed. She continued hugging it, becoming deeply engrossed in thought.

She, Kevin and Misty had been almost inseparable before Misty's return to Idaho. She looked at the last drawing. He dated all his sketches. He'd drawn it the day before, while Haley was at school and his mother was at work. He'd been sketching Misty from memory, in spare moments. Haley knew Misty could not have seen these and needed to know about them. Closing her eyes and concentrating, she realized no one had seen the drawings except Kevin and her. The pad hadn't accidentally fallen; it had been hidden.

Haley laid it almost reverently on his now-uncluttered desktop. She turned on his computer. He'd been allowing her to do that lately. She connected to the Internet and signed-in to her free e-mail account. She would e-mail Misty about this new revelation.

Haley stopped what she was doing. "I won't just tell her—I'll show her." Haley opened the file cabinet drawer where Kevin kept his digital camera. The more she thought about it, the more she realized how much freedom he'd given to her since they began hanging out with Misty. She found the camera in its small faux-leather case and took it out. Turning the camera on, she found the batteries were good.

She opened the drawing pad, first to one page, then another, and decided on four sketches she thought were the best. She laid the tablet on the floor and focused the camera down until the only thing that showed was the drawing. Squeezing the shutter button, the camera automatically flashed. She checked the result on the small LCD screen. Not bad, she thought.

Haley wished she'd started using Kevin's camera before Misty left, so she had pictures of them both.

Within moments, she'd taken the four photographs she wanted. Only one had to be shot over and it came out much better the second time. Great camera, she thought, makes me look like a real photographer.

Removing the little memory card, she placed it in the slot on Kevin's desktop computer and soon opened the images on the computer screen, pleased with the results. She placed the photos into an e-mail attachment to Misty and sent a second copy to herself, so she'd have the images somewhere Kevin wouldn't find them. She wrote a brief e-mail to Misty, which she read aloud:

> *"Misty,*
> *Kevin Loves You*
> *I Love You- See Attachment*
> *Best Friends Forever*
> *Laugh Out Loud,*
> *Love, Haley"*

After sending her e-mail to Misty, Haley deleted the pictures from Kevin's computer and replaced the memory card in his camera. After deleting those pictures from the camera, she put it back in the drawer. Carefully, she repositioned his drawing tablet in its hiding spot beside the farthest filing cabinet. Looking around, she decided his room was clean enough. Maybe she should go home and straighten up *her* bedroom? No, she thought, I need to spend some time with Tiny Terror; I've been neglecting that little fluff-ball lately....

23: THE AFTERMATH

Kevin and Haley spent quite a bit of time together over the next few weeks. She even got him to take her to the "Nat," short for Natatorium, the local swimming pool. He tinkered around with his motorcycle, replacing the defective muffler so it was street legal again. They rode over to the pool on his "bike," with all their swim gear wedged between their bodies. It was a major sacrifice for Kevin to go to the Natatorium because it was mostly little kids and he felt out of place. But he loved to swim, so he let Haley talk him into going—sometimes.

They occasionally rode his cycle over trails out by Eagles' Caves. Other times, they got lost in the world of video games. The bottom line for Kevin was avoidance. Indecisiveness caused him to miss out on the job he usually had during cherry harvest. In lieu of that, he was filling his time by mowing people's lawns, a surprisingly lucrative endeavor. He managed to keep busy enough so he didn't have to think about the things that still bothered him—like how much he missed....

Kevin finally read Misty's card. It had a powerful effect on him, bringing tears to his eyes. Despite reading her note, he couldn't bring himself to make contact. The reason for his reluctance was unclear and he wouldn't discuss it with Haley even though he'd been tactfully moved in that direction several times. What troubled him was a single word that girls seemed to dote on—commitment. In his mind, that dreaded word translated into marriage, and he wasn't ready.

The sweltering season moved rapidly onward. Procrastination continued to be Kevin's major summertime pursuit. There were a few high points, like water-skiing with some of his friends down by Rowena, in the backwaters of the Columbia River. On one such occasion, he managed to take Haley along. She felt as out of place there, surrounded by juniors and seniors in high school, as he'd felt with her at the swimming pool, with the little kids.

The biggest challenge occurred when Carol showed up and shot mental daggers at Haley whenever Kevin wasn't looking. The other girls that were Kevin's age gave him space, and doted on Haley. In the past, Kevin had been one of the guys they light-heartedly joked with or spontaneously draped themselves on.

Kevin had a recurring experience that unsettled and frightened him. In some ways, it resembled a lucid dream but it occurred when he was wide-awake. It would begin as a daydream. Usually, some remembrance of Misty would sneak into his mind before he could shut it out. It commenced so pleasantly, he would forget to push it away. Whatever the starting memory, and no matter how positive it seemed, it would soon shift. He would see himself lying under the bed in Misty's attic. Registering her presence to the side of the bed, though she was out of his sight.

His eyes focused on the image of her retreating stepfather. He could see the man much clearer than he had seen him in real life, as if through magnified vision. When the man descended the steps, Kevin would focus on the large black mole and the untrimmed hairs on the back of the guy's neck. He would see the pink coloration rising from under the other's shirt collar, as the humiliating sting of Misty's rebuke engulfed her guardian.

Unlike what had actually happened, the man would then stop and turn. Kevin always knew this part was coming, but once begun, he could not switch it off. The step-dad's gaze would sweep under the bed, past the golf bag, locking onto Kevin's eyes. Venomous hatred radiated out, penetrating Kevin's entire being—a look filled with murder, portending the malicious deaths of Kevin and Misty. Kevin could feel the life ebbing out of him.

With great effort, he would jerk away from that image's grip and find himself breathing hard. His body, hot and sweaty, would remind him of the terror he'd felt from the awful fall from the roof in his initial nightmare.

Then he would strain to think of other things, repressing the evil memory and its powerful, negative feelings—until the next time.

Another experience helped to offset the many things Kevin avoided. His dream about being in a play on the high school stage occurred once more. He was again the leading man. Misty was the leading lady and Carol played a strong female supporting role.

When it came time in the production for him to pass by Carol, he knew she didn't believe he'd give her a kiss in public. He surprised her by delivering an excellent kiss. He took her in his arms with conviction, and as she gazed into his eyes, his lips found hers. He kissed her so tenderly, she faltered, nearly unable to continue her role.

Misty, waiting backstage for her entrance, observed Kevin kissing Carol. Instead of being upset, she seemed relieved, hopeful that he'd be able to carry out the dramatic kiss with her in a few moments. He sauntered around the stage with growing confidence. When he and Misty met in the center, their kiss created the grand finale. Kevin's very soul seemed to surge through his lips into her body, throbbing and pulsating with powerful energy.

After the curtain reopened, they ran back on stage to take their bows. Kevin realized he no longer had stage fright in any form. With the final bows executed, the performers went around to meet the audience. His fear of meeting audience members up close had likewise evaporated.

On the following morning, Kevin awoke feeling better. He was on his bed doing another sketch of Misty when he heard a hubbub of voices from somewhere in the house. He guessed his mother had gotten home a bit early and maybe she had some friends with her.

There came a tapping on his bedroom door.

"Kevin," said his mother's soft voice, "you have visitors."

He leaped off his bed, stowing his sketchpad in its hiding spot. He wondered who it was. Not Haley, she would have barged in on him, and besides, she was doing her skateboarding thing. He reached out to turn the knob on his door but it burst open.

"Hey, Kevin, where ya been?" Cal's booming voice bounced off the bedroom walls.

Kevin moved to the side and flopped onto his bed. "Oh, I've been kind of busy. You know…mowing lawns and…"

"Too busy ta see your friends?"

Kevin could hear his mother and a second female voice in the background, through the open door. A peel of laughter from a young woman reminded him suddenly and painfully of Misty, but it wasn't her.

Kevin asked, "What've you been up to, Cal?"

"No you don't, I asked you first and I'm the one visiting you, right? You didn't come to see me. Hardly seen you since the last day of school when we played video games at Jake's, remember?"

A smile played on Kevin's face. He did. When they got together, they acted so stupid. That time, Cal had smuggled some home-fermented grape juice he was trying to turn into wine—except it tasted awful. Kevin and Jake lied, not telling him how bad it tasted.

Cal was pleased with himself for making it, but he didn't want to share more than a little bit with them—which was a good thing. But Cal got mad when the multi-person video game they were playing wasn't turning out the way he thought it should. His friends had to face it, Kevin rocked at video games.

"It's good to see you, Cal." Kevin felt real warmth for his oftentimes uncouth friend.

Cal waltzed over to the desk and straddled the chair, facing Kevin. The chair's back made an armrest he could lean forward against. "Some of us are getting ta-gether to go to the movies tonight…wann'a come?"

Kevin was interested but before he could reply, a movement in the doorway caught his attention.

Long, reddish-blonde hair swung out to one side, shimmering in the light, as Carol turned her head in Kevin's direction. "May I come in?"

Kevin felt like he was lying prone on the floor and someone had jumped on his stomach and chest with both knees, knocking all the wind out of him. He struggled to reply, but words evaded him. He hadn't talked with Carol since he'd connected with Misty. He still felt guilty about the way he'd handled that. She'd been his girlfriend but he hadn't talked with her after he met Misty—he'd simply disappeared.

She said, "I'll take that as a 'Yes.'" And glided into his room. "How have you been?" She moved effortlessly and spoke in a casual manner, as if nothing strange had occurred between them.

Kevin recognized the genuine warmth in her voice and found his words returning—as from a great distance. "I've been holding my own."

"Pity." she said. The look she gave Kevin let him know that she had just made a sexual pun about him. He felt his face warming as Cal guffawed loudly. Carol was, as always, bright and witty.

"Where's your little gremlin?" Carol half-knelt as if she were looking under the desk and then under the bed.

How could Carol go from warm and friendly to...whatever this was...so quickly? He didn't bother to reply, but simply looked at her.

"Sorry," her disarming warmth returned. "May I sit?" She nodded toward the foot of his bed, since Cal occupied the only chair.

"Yeah," Kevin heard himself say. He couldn't very well tell her "No." He changed from his sprawled-out position, covering over half the bed, to sitting at the head.

Carol moved to sit down, passing very near him. He smelled the mixed fragrances of fruit-essence she wore—that she was so fond of. It brought back distinct, highly pleasant memories. Carol settled carefully on the other end of the bed. The glow from the window emphasized the pale, delicate freckling on her face and neck. Kevin had always liked her freckles.

"Oh, say," Cal jumped up, "I forgot, I promised Jake I'd help him get his car started. Just show up at the theater if you wanna join us. Are you gonna come to the movie, Carol?"

"Maybe. We'll see."

Cal left as abruptly as he'd appeared.

Kevin felt uncomfortable being alone in his bedroom with Carol. His mom had always liked her and was unlikely to interrupt them.

Just when he was beginning to think of an excuse why he needed to leave, a strange feeling came over him, one of unaccountable self-assurance.

"You never officially dumped me," Carol said.

Kevin looked her in the eye. "I always liked you way too much to just dump you. I can't explain what happened but someone came along, overwhelming me. It was like…one minute you and I were walking along the beach together and the next moment a big sneaker wave came and pulled me out to sea. You got left standing alone on the shore. I was gone so fast; I couldn't say good-bye."

Carol looked stunned. "I don't know what I expected this to be like or what I thought you'd say, but not this. I get it." she said with resignation. "I don't like it, but I finally understand." She glanced at him. "Thanks for not just sending one of your dudes to dump me."

"It isn't like that." He moved closer, putting his arm around her shoulders. "If I could, I'd split in half and you'd each have part, but I can't. I'm sorry for hurting you. Right now, I'm hurting too, but I can't lie. As much as I care for you, I've been swept away and I don't know what to do.

"The other relationship would have to be totally over before I could think about being with you. That's not fair. If I hadn't cared about you, I would have broken it off the way I should have. I'm sorry. I just couldn't do it. You deserved better."

"That's right." she said. "The thing is…I wanted to hate you, but I couldn't. Hearing what you just said, I know why. I can't hate you because I still love you and I still love you because you've always treated me right—at least, you did till you disappeared with that…Misty."

Kevin put his other arm around Carol and held her tight. The scent she wore seemed to burst forth, enfolding them in its sweet essence and he remembered many wonderful moments they had shared. "I can't blame you if you start hating me," he whispered, "but even when you are at your meanest, I don't think I can hate you." His head turned close to hers as he spoke, adjusting his position so he could again see into her eyes.

After a moment, he kissed her very tenderly on the lips. Not a lingering kiss but what felt right to him. Its softness communicated how much he cared.

"I wish that wave hadn't come along," he said. "My life would be a lot less complicated. But I can't rearrange everything. I can't stop caring about you and I can't change being committed to somebody else."

He hugged Carol again.

"Thanks for the kiss," she whispered. "In your position, I don't know what I'd do but I hope I'd treat you like this. I wish you'd done that before."

"So do I."

She whispered, "I better go, the longer I stay, the harder it'll be for me to leave."

She stood up.

He walked with her to the bedroom door, but she pushed him back so he would let her leave by herself. "I'll see you around...."

She was gone—

24: HALEY TAKES ACTION

"Mr. B," Haley said, "I don't know what to do." She'd been on an errand for Aunt Fran when she encountered Mr. Bridger downtown near the old-fashioned soda fountain. He invited her into the ice-cream shop for a treat so they could talk.

"I'm so glad I ran into you," Haley said, and quickly filled him in about how Kevin had moped around through the summer and hadn't contacted Misty. She talked so fast it made Mr. Bridger appear—and probably feel—slightly dizzy.

"Haley, it's fortunate us meeting like this. I just got back from a trip to Europe, and I've heard no word about what's been happening here."

"It's all I can do, Mr. B, to keep from making them get back together. Sometimes I want to…so bad." Her ponytail had tightened her forehead, so she struggled futilely to produce a wrinkled brow of concern.

She said, "You know I could do it, and they'd never know the difference."

"But you would."

Her eyes lowered. "Yeah, I would…."

"That doesn't mean you're powerless to act."

"How…? What can I do?"

"I won't tell you what to do but you are allowed to intercede with them in the same way anyone else could. Just because you can't use undue psychic influence, doesn't mean you can't persuade them in any of the normal ways."

"Like, how can I inter…whatever?"

"Intercede," he offered. "For instance, you might talk with one or both of them."

"Kevin won't talk to me about Misty. I e-mail her at least once a week. It's tough…not using powers…."

"Of everyone I know, I believe you can sway them if you keep trying."

By the look on her face, Haley had a revelation. She stood up, scraping her chair loudly on the floor. Racing for the doorway, she left Mr. Bridger and their two sundaes sitting nearly untouched on the table.

"Thanks Mr. B," she called back as she hurried out.

He smiled as he took a bite of his ice cream.

He was still savoring its sweetness when his cell phone rang. Swallowing hurriedly, he said "Hello?

"Misty, what a surprise. I was just talking with Haley about… but she's already left. How are you?"

Mr. Bridger's face darkened as he listened to Misty's end of the conversation.

"But he's still in custody?

"Did he threaten to kill anyone besides you?

"The cat burglar, too? Anybody else?

"That must have been traumatic, being terrorized like that.

"No, giving court testimony is never easy, and under those circumstances….

"I haven't seen Kevin. I just got back from a trip. I've been gone a month."

By summer's end, Kevin had turned melancholy—even morose. He'd been in one of his more difficult and testier moods for so long that when Haley went in search of him, she knew even without psychic sleuthing he was hibernating in his bedroom. She didn't need special abilities to figure that out, and simply burst through his bedroom door.

"Kevin," she announced as only she would when he was in one of his moods, "I want you to take me somewhere."

It was obvious from her tone of voice that she had a specific destination in mind.

"Like where?" said Kevin in a tone that meant, "No way."

"Coeur d'Alene."

Surprisingly, he didn't shout, "Forget it," or "Get out." He simply said, "That's pretty far. Why there?"

Both of them knew exactly why she wanted to go there, but since Kevin was going to play dumb, she shouted, "I want to see Misty."

She stood with fierce determination, her eyes unflinching in the presence of his unreadable gaze. Then the tears came. They welled up like miniature pools, clinging at the edges of her eyelids and cascaded down her face. She ignored them and continued staring hard at Kevin, though he tried to look away. He couldn't withstand her deeply pained countenance—yet something in her gaze would not allow him to avert his eyes.

"I love Misty," Haley said softly, "and I miss her and you're going to take me to see her." She knew he would not give in without at least a show of resistance.

"I think," he said, obviously not taking her seriously, "we wouldn't make it on my motorcycle. It's not meant for highways."

Haley replied, "We're going to take your mom's Toyota."

"Won't she have something to say about that?" he asked, knowing his mother's Corolla was brand new and she was very protective of it.

"She already said, 'Yes.'" Haley's voice was strident, playing her first trump card.

Kevin was caught off-guard and said the first thing he thought of, stalling for time. "Where would we stay when we get there and what'll we use for money?"

Haley had been holding her hands rigidly behind her back. She brought them around in front of her and handed Kevin almost one hundred dollars. That was her second trump card. He accepted the money reluctantly, dropping it on his bed. It wasn't a lot of cash for such a trip but it had to be a lot for Haley, he thought. In fact, he doubted most of his same-age friends could come up with that much in as short a time.

An uneasy feeling flashed through Kevin's whole body as Haley continued.

"We're staying with Misty. She says it's okay" Haley played her last trump card. At least, the last one she consciously planned on using. Her tough exterior melted. With tears streaming down both her cheeks, she begged, "Please, please...I miss her so much."

Kevin missed her too, although for many days he hadn't allowed himself to think of Misty. Since reading her note, he'd done his best not to let his mind reenter that painful memory. That was tough to do, because the words on her card were etched deeply in his mind:

Kevin,
I LOVE U —
I'm so Sorry If I Hurt U!
Pretty, Pretty Please. Call me
or write to me.
Love, Misty

Haley's loud sobs jerked him back to the present. "It makes me so mad," she said, "knowing you love her too. But you don't write to her, or anything." She looked him in the eye. "I love you. I never tell you, but I do. This is wrong. We've got to fix it."

She looked away, overcome by embarrassment. She'd actually told Kevin she loved him. She knew he wouldn't say it back, much as she wanted him to.

Unfortunately, Haley's words had the opposite of their intended affect. The feeling engulfing him was anger. Why did females have to be so pushy? Why couldn't they just leave him alone? First it was Misty up on the hill trying to force him to marry her. Now Haley was pressuring him to drive them all the way to Idaho to see Misty. Kevin's buried rage transformed into molten lava, spilling out in scorching words, "Haley, go home! I've had enough of you for today."

Even as he spoke, he couldn't believe what he was doing, especially to Haley. She was the one person who'd stood by him through everything. He knew she was only trying to help him fix things with Misty—knew somewhere inside he desperately wanted such a resolution for his pain.

Haley glared at him as if to say, "How dare you?"

"Leave now," he said in the same clipped tones of his final words to Misty weeks before on the wooded hillside.

Haley stiffened as though he'd slapped her, then settled into a defiant stance.

Kevin grabbed her by the shoulders, spinning her about, and propelled her through the doorway, slamming it behind her. In silence, Kevin felt his hands shaking. What had he done? Yet, another part of him thought she should stay home and never come back.

Awareness seeped through from the other side of the door and he felt the awful impact of his unspoken words on Haley.

The silence deepened, then retreated as soft footsteps moved dejectedly down the hall, pausing at the end. Words echoed through his mind in a final act of defiance, Haley's thought-voice, *'We leave first thing in the morning. So you better be ready.'*

He heard the kitchen door slam as she left the house.

The shaking that had begun in his hands coursed through his entire body. Kevin walked uncertainly around his room. Guilt assaulted him. How could he do this to Haley? What was wrong with him?

Kevin eventually slipped Misty's message out from under his mattress. He opened the envelope facing down so the card could drop out but it snagged. He shook the papers vigorously. The liberated card seesawed through the air, avoiding his hand, and careened to the floor. Meanwhile, a thin piece of neatly-folded paper slid into his open palm. How did that get there? Opening it with curiosity, he read for the first time:

Kevin,

I know how much I must have hurt you. I'm sure there is nothing I can say to totally take away the pain. I always hoped our relationship would be different—better. I love you more than anything but I'll understand if you don't want to talk to me. If you find it in your heart to forgive me for being pushy about something you weren't ready for, I would love for you to call or write to me.

Love Always.
Misty

25: THE ROAD TRIP

Kevin spent a restless night with little sleep. Much of the time he lay on his bed feeling recriminations for what he'd said and done to Haley. The money she'd given him lay scattered on his darkened floor where he'd swatted it off his bed, not wanting to touch it.

Kevin got up extra-early the following morning with a mixture of feelings. He was ashamed of how he'd acted but had no idea how to make it up to Haley. Would she come over prepared for the trip, anyway? Or would he have to go over to her house and beg forgiveness?

He was relieved they might go see Misty, yet jittery, not knowing how he could work out their long-distance relationship.

Haley arrived at pre-dawn, but by the time she entered the Conners' kitchen with her small travel bag and a mid-sized backpack, Kevin already had their lunch in the cooler in the middle of the floor.

"Did you remember your black ski mask, Haley?" He asked when he noticed her backpack—trying to be funny and pretend nothing had happened the night before.

"No," she replied defensively. When she realized he was taking a backpack along as well, she quipped, "But I'm sure you didn't forget yours."

His sly grin caused her a moment of worry.

"You didn't?" She gaped at him.

He laughed. "Got you, Sis." He called her "Sis" as an appeasement and was relieved and pleased she hadn't brought up how mean he'd been to her.

"How long a trip is this—anyway?" She asked him, trying to

steer their conversation onto the journey.

"Mom said it's almost three hundred miles to Spokane when I asked her last night. She thinks it may be another thirty or forty to Coeur d'Alene. It'll take us probably five and a-half or six hours to get to Spokane, depending on how many pit stops we make… maybe another hour to Coeur d'Alene. I haven't been up there since I was a little kid and I don't remember that trip."

Haley had set down her backpack so it leaned against her leg. When she shifted her suitcase, the backpack flopped on the floor. Two small strangely-shaped brown objects slid out of its partially unzipped top onto the rug.

Kevin asked, "What are those, a snack?"

"Naw…they're doggie treats."

"Misty doesn't have a dog." Suspicion tainted his voice. He had a sudden gruesome thought as he watched Haley squish a couple of her stuffed animals back into her pack along with the treats. Maybe she likes to nibble on dog treats? He'd heard old people sometimes ate things like that when they didn't have enough money for food.

"Nope, when we get back I want something to give Tiny Terror and Molly for waiting so long to see us. They're going to miss us awful bad. Let's go," she said. "Because Misty's meeting us in Spokane at noon."

"How do you know that?"

"She called last night and gave me her cell phone number in case we run into any trouble. And…" Haley looked all puffed-up as she reached in the small side pocket of her backpack, "Aunt Fran gave me her mobile phone for our trip. It takes pictures and everything."

"Cool." Kevin was relieved to have a phone along, knowing little about the area where they were going. He remembered Haley sometimes had this one with her after school so she could keep in touch with her aunt. By contrast, his own parents had an aversion to cell phones.

Haley put on her backpack after slipping "her" phone inside the pocket, and grabbed her travel bag with one hand. With her other, she grasped one of the cooler's handles.

Kevin grabbed the other handle and they were trying to get through the kitchen door—with Haley's end of the cooler dragging on the linoleum—when Mrs. Conners appeared. She motioned to a bag of warm English muffins smothered in butter, some cream cheese and bagels, and a bag of grapes on the counter for their take-along breakfast. She suggested, "Go easy, you two. Why not just come back for the cooler? Two trips to the car won't cost you that much time."

They both laughed sheepishly, knowing what a sight they made trying to get through the door the way they were going about it.

In no time, the car was loaded. Kevin got into the driver's seat and his mother came out of the house to give him a quick hug. She slipped him a fifty-dollar bill. Then went around to the other side to hug and kiss Haley, giving her a fifty-dollar bill as well.

Haley was flabbergasted—which didn't happen very often. "Thank you, Auntie," she said, and her eyes teared up as she gave Mrs. Conners another hug. Just at that moment, Haley's Aunt Fran showed up.

Haley said, "You're supposed to be at work."

"They told me I could come in late this morning." She hugged and kissed Haley, and gave her a small roll of twenty-dollar bills. "Share with Kevin."

"I will, thanks." Haley began to tear up again and Kevin thanked his mom for the loan of her car.

They drove east down Sixth Place, turned left at the corner and snaked their way out of town toward the eastbound I-84 freeway onramp.

Before long, they had passed The Dalles Bridge and then The Dalles Dam—with the impounded waters of Lake Celilo behind it. The gorge wind was typically brisk, buffeting the car. A couple of hardy, early-morning windsurfers raced the waves out on the Columbia, just offshore from Celilo Park.

"Those don't look anything like the waves we saw in our dream when we flew across the river," Kevin said. "I think we had it lots easier than those windsurfers do.

"Know what my grandfather said?" Kevin was enthusiastic, wanting to avoid any mention of the previous evening's fiasco. He continued, "Grampa told me that he used to watch the Indians fish at Celilo Falls with their long dip nets when he was a kid. He saw big slices of salmon being smoked by the women over open fires. He told about a little Indian boy who fell in at the upper part of the falls...and a fisherman caught him in his dip net. He pulled the boy out, unhurt."

Haley seemed a little bit interested but said she couldn't imagine the falls when looking out at the flat lake visible from the highway.

He decided it would be pushing things to tell her about his grandfather's stories of seeing Chief Tommy Thompson who was about 100 years old when Kevin's grandfather was a boy. "Are you hungry?" Kevin enquired.

"A little..."

"Why don't we eat a couple of those English muffins before they get any colder?"

She found two of the muffins in the bag, and taking a big bite out of one, she handed it over to him. Then, with a bulging smile, she gave him the uneaten one instead.

After only an hour and a half of driving, Haley was already bored and fidgety. All too soon, they drove out of radio reception into the unpopulated eastern end of the Columbia gorge. She'd played her video game for a while but it just didn't hold her interest. Kevin noticed her mood and guessed she was impatient to see Misty and nothing else held her attention.

Haley started putting CDs into the car's music player one-after-another. Kevin favored blue grass, which was mostly what he'd brought along. Alicia Keys was the only musical performer that he and Haley both liked but he had only one of her albums.

Kevin didn't care too much for any of the music Haley had brought.

"How much longer," she asked, trying not to seem like she was whining since she was the one who'd instigated the whole "road trip" to begin with, and Kevin had reacted so negatively.

"I know," shouted Haley enthusiastically, "let's play twenty-questions." She began immediately, before he could protest, and chose something that was "mineral."

Kevin went along with the game mostly out of guilt but found before too long that he was down by ten questions. Then he asked, "Have we seen it on this trip?"

"Yes," she affirmed and then clarified, "At least, I saw it, but I don't know for sure if you did."

As observant a driver as Kevin believed he was, he decided that if she'd seen it, he had too. After a while, though, he got desperate. He started guessing specific, random things like "the pavement" and "the guardrail," which meant she was stumping him and they both knew it. He was totally blowing it.

"Give up?" she asked excitedly. He had only one question left and he hadn't said anything for five minutes. "I give…what is it?"

"The moon." she hollered with delight.

"Haley, you cheated, it's daytime and there's no moon showing. You said we saw it on this trip."

"Just when we left your house, backing out onto Sixth Place, I looked over and the moon was real light and hard to see, but it was there…at least for a while…before it got brighter out."

He guessed she was right. "Okay, you won that one, my turn." He decided to pick an electron because it could be either a particle or a wave, depending on how the experiment was set up. An electron was so basic, it could be part of almost anything.

He smiled to himself. "I've got it. I think it's a mineral…."

Even as he said that he knew an electron could inhabit any of the three kingdoms—animal, vegetable or mineral. What the heck, he thought to himself, she got me with the moon.

Haley lay back in her seat and closed her eyes. After a minute, she opened them. "Is it really tiny?"

He found himself saying, "Yes."

"Is it smaller than a molecule?"

"Yeah." His mind was racing. What could he change it to that she would never guess?

"Is it smaller than an atom?"

He winced as he said, "Yeah." Then he added, "Want to give up; you're never going to get it."

She closed her eyes again, and after a moment they popped open. "Is it an electron?"

Haley had just guessed what Kevin felt was the most difficult twenty-question target he'd ever picked, and she'd done it in only four guesses. He felt slightly depressed.

She was ecstatic.

"Haley," he accused, "you're cheating. It's not fair for you to read my mind."

She laughed. "Okay, I'll just do regular guessing and you can go first again."

He decided, what the heck, and picked a somewhat rare member of the pigeon and dove family, the diamond dove. He was certain she had never heard of that, and said, "I've got it— an animal."

"Is it this little tiny bird-thingy that has reddish skin around the eyes and little speckle'dees on its wings? ...A dove?"

"Haley, you're cheating again."

She said, straight-faced, "No, I just knew you raise pigeons, and...."

"Okay, what kind of dove?"

"D..dd..ddii...diamond. Is it a diamond dove?" she asked.

He was really mad, and her laughter wasn't helping. "Enough twenty-questions, already," he declared. "You cheated and I'm not playing any more."

"Well," she responded, "I'm just paying you back."

"For what? I'm driving you all the way to Coeur d'Alene for criminey sakes."

"That was for making me cry and beg for you to take me, and you throwing me out of your room. You said you wouldn't kick me out anymore."

He asked, "Truce?"

"Yeah," she agreed. "Let's just listen to music." She put in one of his Gillian Welch albums and promptly fell asleep.

By the time Haley awakened, Kevin had endured one of the loneliest stretches of pavement on the entire continent, all by himself. Well, it felt like he was alone with her asleep. He was glad to finally see Haley awake.

"We're maybe halfway there," he said, "and I'm going to pull over at the next rest stop."

"Good. When we get back in the car," she suggested, "I know another guessing game that you'll like."

"Maybe…" He was dubious.

After they pulled into the rest stop, heat hit them in the face when they left their vehicle.

"I'm glad my mom bought a car with good air-conditioning," he said into the warm wind. The sagebrush bent over in the breeze and several tumbleweeds were snagged on the perimeter's chain link fence. A flock of seagulls flew or walked everywhere they thought there might be a chance for food. When a seagull found a piece of bread, the others all tried mobbing it to steal the morsel away.

Kevin and Haley leaned into the wind as they walked. The closer they got to the restroom, the more they realized how badly they had "to go."

At first, by just walking more briskly they sped up. But then they were both flat-out running for their respective restrooms. Haley shrieked as she ran, whether from frivolity or due to extreme duress, Kevin had no clue. Being older, he tried to look nonchalant about running. He knew, however, there had better be an available urinal or he was in big trouble.

When the Toyota accelerated onto the freeway again, Kevin looked down at the digital thermometer and noted the outside temperature was 88 degrees, although the morning was barely half over.

Haley was excited to get started with their next diversion. "It's a game, but it's not a game," she announced with flair.

Somehow, that statement didn't fill him with confidence. He still felt the sting from their last competition.

"Most questions I ask will be easy and I think you'll know maybe all the answers," she said with eagerness.

"What kind of questions?"

"It's somewhat like Truth or Dare."

"I'm not playing Truth or Dare with you, Haley."

"You can back out any time, or not answer," she began, "the

first question is this. In the amusement park dream you created, what did the game show mean?"

He asked, "What did that show signify or represent?"

"Yeah."

"Let's see…" he talked as he thought, "…well, it was a really big event—bigger than our world. It took in maybe the whole universe."

"Good…what else?"

"You and I were at the table ranked number one. In maybe the entire universe, I guess one of us was going to come in first place and the other would be second out of who knows how many different types of beings."

She prodded, "And…."

"Our relationship was more important than which one of us would actually win." Thinking of that made him feel guilty all over again about the way he'd treated Haley last night.

"Why did Misty stop the game?"

"She felt I violated the rules. She thought I was cheating." Kevin wondered if Haley was about to try and get even again.

"Were you cheating?" Her voice interrupted his thought.

"Technically, yes, but at the level of caring about others—no, I wasn't cheating. I was doing the right thing."

His concentration was interrupted, and then he said, "Here's where we turn off for Irrigon. Mom told me we should get a watermelon at a roadside stand along this stretch of highway, and then keep going to Umatilla. That way we won't mess up on the main freeway and continue in the wrong direction. At Umatilla we'll head north, crossing the bridge over the Columbia River to the Tri-Cities. Now I remember—when we get to the Tri-Cities we're about half of the way."

Haley screwed-up her face, but remained silent. Only half way, she seemed to be thinking—obviously disappointed. Aloud she said, "What are the Tri-Cities?"

"That's three towns close together. Pasco, Kennewick and Richland. They're in Washington."

They stopped and got a watermelon. He put it in the trunk and checked on the three homers he had brought along, giving them some water. They were okay, but he worried about the heat as he put the melon in-between pieces of luggage so it wouldn't roll into his pigeon's transporting box.

Continuing on to Umatilla, they traveled a back road to an RV park and Marina down by the river, and made another restroom stop.

On the way back to their car, Kevin impulsively picked Haley up and threw her over his shoulder like a sack of potatoes. "I think I'll just throw this old bag of laundry into the trunk," he threatened.

"I'm not laundry," she shrieked, trying to hide her delight. "Put me down," she said without conviction. "Put me down."

"Oh wait," said Kevin, stopping suddenly and turning toward the river, "I better throw this sack of dirty clothes into the river and wash it before I put it in the trunk."

She shrieked with glee, obviously knowing he wouldn't do what he'd said, but the thought of it was scary and exciting.

When he turned back toward their car, he tipped Haley gently onto her feet. She gave him a big hug, and kept hold of his hand until they reached the car. She smiled as though she felt like his much cared for—maybe even cherished—little sister.

They crossed the Columbia River on the big interstate bridge into the state of Washington. There was a large truck weighing station on the right as they began to climb the long hill out of the gorge toward the Tri-Cities.

She asked. "Are you ready for the next part?"

"What next part?" He pretended ignorance.

Unperturbed, Haley asked, "Why were there snakes in Misty's dream?"

"Oh, that next part."

"This is so lame, Kevin, you know what I'm talking about."

"Well," he said, "we know she's afraid of snakes."

"Was…. She used to be terrified of them."

"Yeah, I meant she *was* scared of those slimy, underbelly reptiles," he focused his thoughts. "They came to life after she sat on the throne, maybe after she touched them? Misty said they wanted something from her, but I don't remember what."

"How could you forget? They wanted to experience love."

"Oh, yes."

She continued, "Mr. B said snakes are phallic symbols, whatever that means."

Whoa, he thought, there's a lot more in those dreams than I realized.

"Why were you going so slow…getting up onto the king's throne?" Haley asked.

"I'm not ready to get married…the idea scares me. I only went along with the kingship thing because I didn't want to disappoint Misty."

"How did it feel, sitting on the king's throne?"

"Kind of cool. I don't know…important-like, but also scary. A huge responsibility."

"If Misty asks you to sit there again," Haley questioned, "what will you do?"

"I don't want to let her down, but I'm not ready…."

In Kennewick, they stopped to get gasoline and stretch their legs. Just before Kevin turned off the ignition, he noticed the outside temperature was 92 degrees and checked again on his birds in the trunk.

The attendant mentioned the high was supposed to be 106 that day. Kevin wondered about the wisdom of bringing pigeons on their trip. Thank goodness they were accustomed to the warm climate and the car was a reflective color, minimizing the effect of the sun.

26: JOURNEYING

After they filled the car's gas tank in the Tri-Cities, Haley fell asleep again, and continued slumbering all the way to the next rest stop, which seemed like forever to Kevin. He had a long time alone with his thoughts. Many were fearful. What would their meeting with Misty be like? What could he say to her? He felt guilty for his parting remark on the hill by his house.

He wished Haley would wake up and keep him company—divert him. She was a good distraction by inventing games and livening things up. The thought of games reminded him about her questions. He tried not to think about the dream questioning. Why did it make him so nervous to talk about those things?

Here he was with all this time alone with Haley, and she was asleep. Shouldn't they continue the discussion where they'd left off that time in his bedroom? He chuckled and then grimaced as he thought about her reference to his sock drawer. Then the recollection of his rosebush scratches flashed to mind, and his avoidance of that memory. He winced.

At the rest stop, Haley walked zombie-like to the toilets and back, seeming only half awake. In the car, she resumed sleeping.

Traveling the monotonous highway as if he was alone, Kevin's mind replayed the events of his summer. Why had he avoided making decisions? The examples tumbled forth. Not getting his old job in the fruit processing plant. Not reading Misty's letter. Not contacting her. Mostly avoiding his friends.

He began to realize his lawn mowing business had grown to the point where he'd become too busy to think about important things. Avoidance was his way of life, and not just during the summer. Long before then, most of his friends had made definite plans for beyond high school, not counting Cal, of course. Kevin, however, didn't know what college he wanted to attend or what he wanted to study if his choice was finally made. Maybe that part, knowing what he wanted to major in, needed to come first.

A feeling of uneasiness settled over Kevin, becoming so strong he noticed a shiver wiggling its way down the back of his neck. In a flash of insight, he knew what he wanted. It had nothing to do with college. He wished to know all that Haley had mastered. He saw himself diving through his dreams, creating changes with masterful strokes.

Learning from Haley was more important to him than anything else—except for wanting Misty in his life. Aside from those two things, nothing mattered. The feeling of peace that came with his insights was short-lived, however.

A stronger emotion shivered up his neck, prickling the back of his skull as a haunting reverie surfaced. The past summer's threatening glimpses of Misty's stepfather forcefully returned.

Kevin didn't have the presence of mind to oppose the vision that inserted itself until it was too late. The menacing visage destroyed the joy created by Kevin's previous thoughts. He felt powerful fingers strangling his neck, and struggled to shift his mind away to anything else.

Attempting to find solace, Kevin replayed his Alicia Keys album for the third time. He avoided looking in the rearview mirror for fear he'd again see the red finger marks on his neck. The ones formerly left from his haunting vision of Misty's stepfather.

Haley yawned and stretched into wakefulness.

"Hey sleepyhead," he greeted her, attempting to cover up his depressed inner state.

She didn't reply for some moments.

Taking a deep breath, and twisting her neck to one side so she could see him better, she said, "Awake dreaming? It's time for you to remember more stuff."

Even though Kevin had wanted this very thing earlier, he felt apprehensive at her suggestion. His fear from the flashback vision of Misty's step-dad was still strong.

"Like what?" he asked.

Her silence was stifling. Finally, he asked, "Why do I forget things? And why am I so afraid to remember. How come I'm scared when I do remember…and why can't I make important decisions?"

Haley's voice lost some of its sleepy quality. "Some things are hard to believe. They make you doubt what you already know. Nightmares can't leave scratches—but yours did. The stronger your old belief, the harder to get a new one. You have to experience some things more than once to believe them. What ones scare you most?"

Kevin felt relief discussing things that previously disturbed him because they kept the even scarier thoughts away. "When you reminded me I'd seen your reflection in Misty's attic window during my nightmare, that was terrifying. I still don't like to think about it. Why?"

"I was in your dream because I wanted to find someone to do dream-stuff with, and I knew it could be you. I'd already asked your dream self to hang out with me, but your awake self didn't know about that. You and Misty and me had met in our dreams for awhile. If you'd recognized me then, you would have remembered everything when you awakened."

"You said you didn't teach me to do the first 'special' nightmare, right?"

"Nope, I didn't—it surprised me."

He said, "Maybe that's part of what scares me. I thought you should know everything about dreams. If you didn't teach me, how'd I learn?"

She replied, "I don't know—yet."

"See, that worries me."

"Maybe there's stuff," she said, "I'm supposed to learn from you?"

"That's even scarier."

Haley laughed. "No. You don't get it."

"Obviously."

"If one person knows everything, what's the point for the rest of us? We got to all have our specialties. Yours and mine is dreaming. If we want, we can go where nobody ever went before…in our dreams. Next question—"

Kevin was more willing than before, and searched his brain for another query. "What about when I saw Cal and Jake in our other dream?"

"Like I told you…you started to fly through your dreams, from one into the other. You didn't believe you could. If you'd believed, you would have changed stuff. You could have flown into other dreams. Yours, or somebody else's. You could've done different things in them."

"Like?"

"You saw yourself and the burglar on the roof, right?"

"Yes."

"You could've knocked the bad guy off the roof. Or you could have asked him questions. Messed with his mind. Learned things…had fun."

"What kind of fun?"

"Don't know. Flying in his face, or circles around him. He wouldn't know what to do with that. You could have dropped slime on him if you wanted."

"What's the point of that?"

"Learning stuff, and having fun…."

"By doing things in dreams, said Haley…you learn how to do them in real life. If you aren't afraid of him in dreams, you probably won't fear him in real-life. You could help your dream-self in the nightmare to defeat him. See?"

"But what would that do to the dream I was already in?"

"Maybe nothing. You can be in a bunch of dreams at once. We all do that, sometimes, most just don't remember. You can be aware of them all, at the same time, doing different things in each. Even being aware of your body sleeping on the bed while you're in a bunch of dreams—that can happen, too. I told you this before."

"When?" He was genuinely puzzled.

"When we took those three white pigeons to the park."

He shook his head. "I don't know how I forgot about that."

"Too much new stuff—it jarred you—takes time to get used to it. I was trying to teach you guys too much. Wanted you to learn real fast…but had to slow things down. It isn't lost. You'll remember."

"What about the rose trellis?" he asked. "How come in real life it only goes halfway to the roof?"

"You had to have a way up. But it's complicated. Houses in your dreams can represent different levels in life."

"Levels?"

"Yeah. In *your* dreams the main floor means it's your everyday awake life. The second floor is where you think about what life really means, instead of just living it. The attic's where you think of spiritual things."

"How's that relate to the trellis?"

"It was like a ladder, a way to climb up from one level to the next. The basement—that's your subconscious. And the roof's the highest spiritual-link-place in your life."

"Is this just in my dreams, or everyone's?"

"Mostly its in yours and mine, but its somewhat there in everyone else's, too."

"Why was the trellis tall enough to climb up in my dream, but not in real-life?"

"Dreams are where your link is—to the highest levels. Without dreaming, you aren't going to reach where you want to go. The thorns hurt you worst when you got above the first floor, right?"

He nodded.

"I saw that when you climbed up. Your conscious mind was fighting what you could learn in your dreams. When you climbed to the highest point; that's when you got scared. That's what the thorns were all about. The higher you went, the worse they got. Without going to the attic in your dream, you'd of never got there in real life. See?"

Haley became thoughtful. "Was your dream like your life, or was it the reverse? Strange, isn't it, how close they're tied?"

Another question surfaced in Kevin's mind. It seemed unrelated, but he asked anyway. "Why did the washing machine keep running when the power went off—you know, with the burglar in the basement?"

Haley laughed. "Good timing."

"The washing machine had good timing?"

"No, your question. That's good timing. In the awake-world, washing machines don't usually work when the power's off."

"Never."

"Sometimes," Haley disagreed.

Kevin was silent.

"What doesn't make sense in the awake world happens all the time in dreams. If you practice, some can happen in the real world, too."

"A washing machine working when the power is off?"

"Yep."

Kevin yawned, suddenly feeling very sleepy.

"Better watch the road," Haley cautioned, as she turned the air conditioner up a notch, and switched the fan to high. "We better talk about this later, when you're not driving."

27: REUNITED

After awhile, they passed Sprague Lake, and Haley seemed totally refreshed. It was as though the sight of water after the dry, desolate country they'd traversed seemed to revive her.

"How long till we get to Spokane?" she asked excitedly.

"I don't really know, maybe a half-hour, maybe more. Maybe an hour? I just don't know."

"Misty'll know." She reached into the small pocket of her backpack, stowed on the floor by her feet, and pulled out her cell phone. She didn't have to search for the number; she pushed the speed-dial link of the phone's memory. Little beeps issued forth, and Haley hollered at Kevin, "What time is it?"

"It's about eleven o'clock," he reported, after glancing at the dashboard clock.

"Misty." She squealed into the phone. "We're passing Sprague Lake… We don't know how far to Spokane—and what do we do when we get there?"

Her shrill voice filled their car, "Eeeeiiiieei," bouncing around the closed interior. "We can't wait to see you…I luv you, Misty."

Kevin thought how odd it was—feeling the same emotions as Haley—yet not expressing them like she did. Was it, as Misty said, a guy thing?

Haley became unnaturally silent, listening. Then came the "Yeah's" and the "Uh-huhs," followed by, "Wait, wait, wait…."

"When we start coming into Spokane, we go down a long hill….

"Got it. Then what?"

Another pause. "Okay," she said, sounding suddenly adult-like. "We just keep going on this freeway after we get to Spokane, until we come to the Division Street exit.

"Yeah, Kevin'll remember…." Haley looked meaningfully at him. "Division Street exit."

"Then what?" Haley's face contorted with concentration.

"At the stop light, we turn left…go one block and look for Dick's Drive-in on the corner.

"Dick's Drive-in? I've never heard of that. Are you sure?

"Yeah, okay," Haley sounded excited. "Then we'll meet you at the Drive-in, and you'll be in a red Mustang.

"Eeeiiieieieieii." Haley screamed yet again.

"We're in a sort-of silver-colored Corolla."

"I can hardly wait to see you. Oh, oh, oh, Kevin says 'Hi.'

"Love you—Bye." Haley hung up and screamed some more.

"She says she has a surprise for us when we get to that drive-in."

Kevin wondered why she didn't just tune in and see what it was. Maybe Haley still liked surprises—or maybe he would be the only one surprised.

The rest of the trip to Spokane was a blur. Pine and birch trees replaced sagebrush at the freeway edge. Kevin noticed a couple of road signs, but names like Cheney and Medical Lake didn't mean anything to him. He focused more on his surroundings when they started the lengthy decline into Spokane. It was a long hill, but not so lengthy as the upward climb coming out of Umatilla.

Their descent bottomed-out at last. Almost before they knew it, they were at the Division Street exit. Haley screeched, "This is it. We're here—really here…. I'm going to see her….

"When we were at Sprague Lake, Misty told me she was just getting to the other side of Spokane. She must already be here.

"I can't hardly believe it. We're going to see Misty."

After the off-ramp stop, Kevin turned left on Division. Approaching the next intersection, his young copilot and navigator yelled. "It's over there." She pointed with her right arm and waved her left hand in his face. Fortunately, he managed his lane change safely despite her accidental interference. In no time, they entered the parking area of their destination.

Sure enough, there was a shiny red mustang in plain view, with a familiar blond head leaned out the window. Misty waved her arm enthusiastically.

Kevin found a nearby spot to park, amid Haley's continued screaming.

Before he came to a complete stop, she'd unbuckled her seatbelt and started to open her door.

"Watch for cars." His voice was more strident than he intended. He had a sudden fear of Haley leaping out in front of a passing vehicle and getting run over. She turned to him, leaned back across, and gave him a big hug. "I knew you cared… We're here. And Misty's right there." She nearly flew out her door.

Misty hadn't been sitting still, either. She had run halfway to their car by the time Haley got out. The two of them seemed to melt together just a few feet from the Toyota. Kevin clambered out and found he could hardly walk. He was stiff and sore. Some of it was road weariness, but most was built-up tension from the anticipation of seeing Misty. By the time he got to the other two, they were laughing, and teary-eyed.

Misty buried her head in Haley's wavy black hair, which was loose for once—undone after her ponytail poked her while napping in the car.

"Oh, Haley, I missed you so much. I'm so glad you guys could come."

As Kevin got closer, Misty seemed to feel his presence. She looked up. "Kevin."

"Hi, Misty." He felt suddenly awkward. "A long drive," he said. But what he wanted to say, and didn't, was "I missed you so much."

Haley freed herself from Misty, who in turn gave Kevin a hug that said I'm so glad you're here. She held him just long enough.

"Honk, honk." the blaring car horn belonged to the Mustang.

"Oh, I nearly forgot," said Misty. "I want you to meet my friends."

Kevin felt a sudden twisting in the pit of his stomach as Misty led them to the Mustang. In the front passenger seat was a pretty young woman with naturally streaked, summer-blonde hair. In the back seat was a boy about Haley's age. Kevin felt relief.

Misty said, "Kevin, I want you to meet my dearest friend since forever, Candace—and her brother, Brad. He just turned twelve. Candace and Brad, this is Kevin and Haley, my best and only friends from The Dalles. The two people who helped me when my step-dad was planning..."

She apparently thought better about what she was about to say and looked at Kevin, "Of course, Kevin's the guy who...." she might have been thinking swept me off my feet, but she actually said, "I owe so much to...and Haley's like his little sister. So she's my little sis, too. Haley's ten and one-half years old..."

"Ten and three-quarters," corrected Haley.

"Sorry, Sis, this year is just flying by. Make that ten-and-three-quarter-years-old."

While doing introductions, Misty had kept hold of Kevin's arm, pulling it around her waist. She nestled in against his side.

He felt like that was where she belonged.

"I've planned a little surprise for you two," said Misty. "We're going north into Idaho—a place called Silverwood."

Haley interrupted, "Is it like...a place where they have really old trees?"

"No." Misty and Candace both laughed.

"It's a surprise," Misty added, as she looked into the back seat at Brad and held her finger up to her lips. "It's a secret, Brad, can you keep a secret?"

"Yeah," he sounded like anyone should know he was a great keeper of secrets.

Haley's impish grin said she was thinking to herself, no he can't. She seemed to know that Brad had already written her off simply because she was younger, and a girl. It wasn't the first time a boy had underestimated Haley. In fact, that seemed to be more the rule than the exception, with Haley and boys.

"So here's the deal." As she talked, Misty reached out and ran her hand through Haley's loose hair. "Sis, just this once, I want to ride alone with Kevin. Will you ride with Candace and Brad on the way to our surprise?"

Haley hugged Misty. "Sure." Looking into Misty's eyes, she smiled warmly, and attempted a conspiratorial wink.

Kevin noticed, and thought she was going to have to work on the winking thing.

"Okay," Misty began again, "Candace will drive my car and if it's all right with you, Kevin, I'll drive *your* car, because I'm the one who knows where we're going."

Everyone agreed. Candace moved into the driver's seat of the Mustang and Haley—who everyone expected would sit in the Mustang's front passenger seat—invited herself into the back seat with Brad. "Hey…is that a video game you got there?"

As Brad drawled "Yeah," Haley settled her things onto the floor of the car.

"What level you on?" she inquired. Then she added, "Why don't you show me how you're doing?"

Candace, who all kids seemed to love, and had the reputation of being one of the best babysitters around, knew that Brad was in good hands. She apparently recognized a kindred spirit in Haley. Before she started the car, she turned around and made sure both kids had their seat belts on. It was a babysitter's compulsion. She reached back and brushed a stray wave of Haley's loose hair from in front of her eyes. Haley glanced up and smiled. As their eyes met, they became instant friends.

"Thanks, Haley," said Candace. She didn't have to add, for putting up with my sappy brother. Haley already knew. Besides, Haley was going to kick his tail-end all over the back seat when it was her turn to play the video game. She understood that boys respected a tough competitor. She might even teach him a few things that would impress his friends.

By the time they left the fast food place, Haley, Candace and Brad had gotten hamburgers and fries to go. Kevin and Misty opted to snack from the cooler when they got hungry. Their two-car convoy proceeded toward Silverwood.

"I hope this doesn't make you feel like I'm trying to be in control—me doing the driving," Misty began. "If it does, I'd rather you drive."

"No," he said. "I've been driving for hours—I welcome a break."

She reached over and squeezed his hand. "Good. There's so much I want us to talk about," she continued, "I just thought it would be easier if I drove, since I know how to get where we're going."

She automatically chose a back route via Trent Avenue through Rathdrum.

"The thing is…" Misty said. "I don't know where to start. Now that you're really here…and we're actually talking…. I guess I'm doing all the jabbering."

"That's alright, it's nice to hear your voice. Keep it up. I'll cut in if I feel the need."

"You better."

"I will."

"I've thought about so many things since I left The Dalles. Everyone's been so helpful to me, both here and there." Her cell phone rang.

It was Candace. They were going to make a pit stop. It seemed that neither of the kids had gone to the restroom at the drive-in, and now, a few minutes and a large soft drink later, they both had to go.

"We'll follow you, Candace."

They soon located a service station along Trent. While the kids went to the toilet, Misty and Kevin continued to chat.

Sooner than expected, the rest stop was completed and Haley raced toward the Toyota, carrying her burger and fries. Her mouth was full of a large bite.

The car's engine was still running to power the air-conditioner, so Kevin pressed the button and lowered his passenger window. Haley arrived slightly out of breath from trying to run with her mouth full of food.

"Guess what." She didn't have a lot of inhibitions about talking with her mouth full.

Kevin and Misty laughed at her.

"What?" she said with a knowing smile—seeing their reaction to her eating habits. Then she swallowed hard and said, "Brad's only been to level four and I just took him most of the way through level six. He thinks it's okay if I hang out with him now."

Racing away, she called back. "See you at the amusement park."

Misty's mouth opened. "Wait till I get my hands on that little twerp, Brad."

"It's not his fault." Kevin laughed knowingly. "If you'd played twenty-questions with her on the way up here you'd understand."

Soon they were back on the road, wheeling toward their destination.

"Kevin, the place we're going to is fun. Somewhere to talk and enjoy ourselves...just be who we are. It isn't my turf, or yours, and there're no expectations. I think we owe it to ourselves to do something fun. No sneaking around, no worrying like in The Dalles. The only thing I want to happen in these two days is for us to feel reconnected. I don't expect any commitment from you. Not right now—if that's going to get in our way—maybe not ever. Especially today, let's just have fun."

28: AMUSEMENT PARK

Kevin and Misty pulled into the parking area across Highway 95 from Silverwood and got out of the car. Haley ran up to them, "Did you see that big roller coaster? I want to go on it."

Misty said, "Maybe you can go with Kevin, those things scare me."

"Probably..." Kevin tried not to commit himself. If Misty wouldn't go, he wasn't sure he wanted to, either.

Reaching into the driver's side of the car, he pulled the latch to open the trunk, and went around to unload the small pigeon carrier he had brought along.

"We better let these birds head home before it gets any later," he said. "Haley, do you want to let them go?"

Haley got Brad involved and they lifted the lid, allowing three pure white racing homers to rise into the air and circle above the large parking lot. Candace and Brad watched in bewilderment as the birds gained altitude, circling southwesterly.

One of the birds lagged behind after circling in the opposite direction from the other two. It finally reversed course and caught up to the others and the threesome moved farther away, getting smaller until they disappeared out of sight.

The five human adventurers made their way through the tunnel access, passing under the highway and entering the park. Haley excitedly shared her knowledge of racing pigeons with her new friends.

The interior of the theme park was somewhat reminiscent of the Frontier portion of Disneyland, or the ghost town in Knott's Berry Farm. Silverwood had an old-fashioned main street with a railroad depot, and a vintage train powered by an old diesel locomotive.

Haley was ecstatic. Her foreknowledge, based on Brad's view of the theme park, hadn't done justice to the reality of the amusement center. He was somewhat jaded, having been there so many times. Haley couldn't decide where she wanted to go first, but she stayed with Candace and Brad, giving Kevin and Misty some space.

After an hour, the kids were having the time of their lives, but Misty was frustrated. She high-signed Candace to join her in the restroom. Misty had barely gotten through the doorway when she began to vent. "I'm blowing it, Candace. I'm giving him time. But…every minute we're getting more up-tight.

"I'm about to do something really stupid, like throw him in the car and haul him off to a motel…."

Candace's eyebrows arched in dismay. She'd barely survived Misty's "wild" year.

"No, I'm not going to frick-in do that, but I'm getting so freaked-out. I'm losing it."

Haley walked in and stood to one side. Although the other two saw her enter, neither spoke to her, they were so absorbed by Misty's frustrations.

Misty ranted on— "He hasn't even kissed me. Am I a wuss? Is he a wuss? Aw…we're both wusses.

"What am I going to do? I came on too strong before. It was all about me. Now I'm backing off—going slow—but it's still not working. Maybe this whole thing was just a mistake…a big waste of time."

Haley started to cry; covering her face with her arm to hide her tears, she tried to move sideways toward the door, but stumbled.

When Misty saw Haley moving, she looked over and knew immediately how strongly her words had affected her young friend. She ran to Haley and grabbed hold. "No, Haley. I didn't mean it. It's not a waste of time. I'm just so…pissed…excuse my French."

She hugged her young friend, whispering, "I'm sorry, I didn't really mean it."

Candace said, "I'll check on the others," leaving Misty to comfort Haley.

Outside, she found Brad in line for a watery ride. Kevin waited just beyond in the shade, and she joined him.

Brad saw Candace and called over, "Where's Haley?"

"She'll be along; save her a place." She asked Kevin, "How're you doing?"

"Okay. It's a mighty long drive up here."

"Yes it is," she agreed. After another moment, she said, "I don't really know you, but I see how important you are to Misty. She fell apart a couple of years ago and she didn't start getting the pieces back together until she met you.

"I don't know how much Misty means to you, but I know you're everything to her. She won't volunteer this, but I'm telling you—she hasn't gone out with anyone since she got back here. She doesn't even look at other guys. Truth is…you're it…you're the one. I don't know how you feel about Misty…."

Kevin miraculously found his voice. "I love her," he said. "But I don't know what's going on…." He looked off in the distance. "I care so much, but I don't know what she wants—or expects. What if it's more than I can give?" His gaze turned to her.

She smiled, "You're scared."

He was so nervous his left leg shook. Most of his weight was on his right foot.

She continued. "This is about you, Misty, and love. That's all. That's the whole thing. Forget everything else."

She made an on-the-spot decision, and turned toward her brother—still standing in the queue. "Come over here, Brad."

"I'm in line." he shouted.

The baby-sitter's voice bellowed out from Candace. "Not anymore, now come on over here, because we're all going on the roller coaster."

Brad raced to where they were standing. "Really?"

"Yes, wait here while I get the others."

She was back like a whirlwind with Haley and Misty. Haley was so excited she couldn't scream. Misty was reluctant, but Candace insisted, so she agreed to go on the roller-coaster. Candace took Misty's hand and placed it in Kevin's. "You are riding together." Turning to the other two she added, "and you can ride in the same car, or one of you can be with me."

"I'm riding by myself." Brad announced in his most macho, twelve-year-old voice. Haley grabbed Candace's hand.

Misty's worst doubts were confirmed as the ride began. She feared she could not endure the nightmare plunges, but there was no turning back.

Kevin thought she looked like she was already contemplating where to throw-up. By one-quarter of the way through the ride, she clung to him for dear life. He could feel her tension and fear. Reaching out his hand, he touched her encouragingly.

She felt his reassurance and relaxed a little. She sensed something else. Haley said mentally, *'It's just like when you were flying around your brass bed. Feel in control. Reach ahead...meet the corners. Love the plunges. Take charge.'*

Misty remembered their shared dream, and careening around her bed in the attic. She recalled leaning into the turns and enjoying herself. Almost before she knew it, she was having fun. She squeezed Kevin's arm in glee, knowing they were together again—sharing the moment.

As the roller-coaster plunged wildly down through the gift shop, she miraculously reveled in the experience that would otherwise have devastated her.

Back on the ground, they were still getting their land legs. Candace glanced at Kevin and noticed moisture at the corners of his eyes. "Scary ride?"

He wiped at his eyes with his hand. "No, it wasn't the ride." He still had Misty's hand in his. Pulling her around, he gave her the kind of kiss she'd been hoping and praying for since leaving The Dalles weeks before.

As he held her in his arms, he whispered, "I'm sorry. I was scared—and not of the roller-coaster."

They went on the old-time train around the perimeter of the park. Eventually, the rail cars stopped—held up by masked robbers.

"At least they aren't wearing ski masks," Misty said to Kevin under her breath.

Haley was wide-eyed when the robbers entered, but Brad had seen it all before, and became obnoxious toward the desperadoes. "Aw," he said, "you aren't real train robbers."

The fellow with the bandanna pulled up under his eyes called to his confederate, "Want to kidnap a kid this time?"

The other man seriously considered it, and poor Brad gave Candace a worried look, but she maintained a neutral face.

"If we got room on our way back," replied the second bandito, "we'll get him then." They went to the next car.

Brad moved away from Haley, scooting in behind his sister, into her seat. He moved as far from the aisle as possible, taking no chance on becoming a hostage.

When it got hotter, they went on the water ride that doused its riders just enough to cool them off. But the large, circular raft that could hold eight people, dipped unexpectedly, and drenched Misty's back. She shrieked and tried to splash Kevin with some of the water they'd taken in—because he'd laughed at her.

They later attended a magic show featuring a magician and his three beautiful assistants—appearing and disappearing, seemingly out of nowhere.

Throughout the afternoon, Kevin and Misty were inseparable. The ride on the roller-coaster had resolved the initial uneasiness of their reunion. During odd moments, they found themselves reminiscing about experiences in The Dalles...

In late afternoon, they headed their vehicles down highway 95 toward Coeur d'Alene. Haley voluntarily rode with her new friends, allowing Kevin and Misty to continue their private ride in the Toyota. When they were most of the way to Coeur d'Alene, Misty asked Kevin, "Are you worried about tonight?"

"I was, but you've made things so easy today, now I'm not. I look forward to it."

Misty said, "We've done quite a bit of walking this afternoon, but I hope you and Haley are still up to making a two mile hike. It's not a difficult walk and there are beautiful views. I have a special reason for choosing this place for us to visit—and it's right in Coeur d'Alene."

"That sounds fine; we didn't do that much walking at Silverwood, mostly standing in lines. Besides, it was a long trip up here—you know what it's like. A bit more exercise will probably do me good."

"Then it's settled. Haley will be so happy."

"Why?"

"I can't tell. It's another surprise."

29: COEUR D'ALENE NIGHT

After bidding farewell to Candace and Brad, Misty drove her Mustang, followed by the Corolla, to the central city parking area where she and Kevin temporarily left their cars. They were near the Coeur d'Alene Resort, a dominant feature on the lakefront. They walked along the floating boardwalk that formed a perimeter around part of the hotel.

"It's reputed to be the longest floating boardwalk in the world." Misty said.

She and Haley kept surreptitiously watching Kevin, but he didn't notice. The threesome meandered around the walkway, and he was appropriately impressed with its distinctive features.

He stopped and looked about. "You know, I've never been to Coeur d'Alene before…."

"We know," said Haley, barely able to contain a giant chortle welling up inside.

"But this all seems…familiar."

The other two, no longer able to control themselves, burst into laughter.

"What did I say?"

The girls snickered even louder. Misty contained her mirth first. "What do you recognize?"

"This boardwalk, the lake…." His eyes took in more of the panorama. "That hill over there."

The girls guffawed so uproariously they had to cling to one another for support.

He didn't know what to make of their antics. "Come on you two, what's going on?"

That caused them even more raucous laughter.

He sat on a built-in seating area nearby.

The girls at last pulled themselves together and joined him.

"We're sorry," Misty offered. "It's just that...." She began laughing again, but Haley prompted her with a stern look.

Misty said, "It's just...we know something you don't."

"No-duh."

She persisted, "How familiar do these things seem?"

"Really familiar."

Haley asked, "Why?"

"Maybe I saw this in a picture or a movie, or something." He concentrated strongly, but couldn't come up with anything to explain his feeling of familiarity.

"Give up?" asked Haley, as though he were just about to lose at twenty-questions again.

He replied, "Yes, I give up."

Misty declared, pronouncing her words very slowly so he'd hear every word, "You've...been...here...before..."

"When?"

Haley blurted, "It's like this; you weren't awake."

"Aw, come on," he began, but memories surfaced. "No, it can't be."

"Yep," said Haley.

Misty explained, "You were here nearly every night for most of the summer, with the two of us. Your dream-self said your waking-self wasn't ready to remember—until now."

"No way." Even as he said it, he knew they were right. "I was here, wasn't I?" He looked around again, especially at the hill.

"That's Tubbs Hill," Misty said. "I've walked its trail almost every day since I've been back, and then at night—in the dream world—with you and Haley. Those dreamtime walks are what got me through everything. Giving depositions about Shaine, figuring out the estate mess...."

In a short while, the three continued their promenade around the boardwalk, extending their walk partway around the Tubbs Hill trail. Kevin periodically shook his head in disbelief as memories surfaced of local dream experiences. They stopped occasionally at scenic viewpoints.

Kevin and Misty held hands as Haley raced ahead up the trail, begging, "Come on you guys…hurry up." At other times, she clung to Kevin's free arm.

An hour later, Misty escorted Kevin and Haley up the front steps to the ample porch of her Coeur d'Alene home. It was a large and impressive residence, but their dragging feet indicated it had been a long day.

Misty hurriedly opened the front door and led the way in. She couldn't wait to have them feel at home. "We'll take a tour later. There's a bathroom down that hall." She pointed the way. "I know Haley's getting tired. She yawned most of the way over here in the car.

"I was watching in my rearview mirror, Haley."

Misty continued, "I'm so glad to have you both here. But I'm a little nervous now that we're in my house. It holds lots of memories for me—some bad. We'll all sleep in there tonight."

She pointed to the large living room. "That big old couch is a hide-a-bed, but it's comfortable—it'll be like old times, from when we slept in Kevin's room."

Haley raced to the bathroom while Kevin and Misty sat on the sofa. He kissed her before she could start talking again. The more they kissed, the less she needed conversation and the more they hoped Haley would take a long time in the bathroom.

The sound of Haley's footsteps alerted them to her presence, but they couldn't stop kissing.

"Remember, you guys," Haley said, "there's a kid present." She said it in a tone that caused them to break off and laugh with her. Given that opportunity, Haley threw herself in the middle, yawned, and closed her eyes.

"Okay, you two," Misty said. "Get up. Let's pull out this hide-a-bed before we get too tired and end up sleeping in a dog pile."

At the mention of bed, Haley opened her eyes and straightened. They helped pull out the bed and smoothed the blankets. Before the other two could stop her, Haley plunged into the center. "I got dibs on the middle," she called.

Misty locked the front door and turned out most lights. She and Kevin took turns in the bathroom. For reasons she didn't explain, she felt uncomfortable using the second floor restroom. At last, they lay down together for the night.

"Sweet dreams," whispered Haley.

Walking along the Tubbs Hill trail at night isn't recommended practice, but in the case of three dream-travelers, it is acceptable. They meandered down their somnambulistic path until they encountered a wonderful viewpoint overlooking the lake. The site was replete with a plush mini-row of reclining theater seats—an accoutrement worthy of a sumptuous cinemaplex. The three friends smiled to themselves as they sat down in the seats so handily positioned.

They found a large—make that gigantic—bag of popcorn to share. Sodas were nestled in the cup holders of their moveable armrests. For once, Kevin was in the middle.

The sky, which had maintained its helpful, luminous twilight while they got seated, began to darken. Without fanfare, a segment of sky glowed brightly, and a scene materialized in that region, as if it were a giant movie screen.

The three friends knew they were dreaming. Therefore, they didn't have to wonder at the absence of previews to coming attractions. Also—dare they think it—there were no commercials. Not one single sales message prior to watching their movie.

Commercials in the movie theater were one of Kevin's pet peeves. He hated getting bombarded by sales pitches for products when he'd already paid the price of admission. He scrunched down into the comfort of the soft seat, waiting to see what the combined efforts of their dream geniis would conjure up. He thought, based on all the amenities, this was meant to be a really-entertaining experience.

As the "movie" began, the three viewers discovered they were also the cinematic actors. Since they were both the observers and the observed, they felt simultaneous sets of emotions.

In the first feature, the three friends were back in The Dalles. Misty had apparently moved there to be with Kevin and Haley.

They were all three in Misty's large house. The two dogs, Molly and Tiny Terror, lived with them. Kevin had converted the former garage—turned later into a small home—into a superlative, racing homer loft, with large, wire-mesh aviaries. Every night they learned new and wonderful things from their joint dream experiences. Their main task was respect for others and not misusing their burgeoning psychic powers. The movie ended with giant words in the sky.

And They Lived Happily Ever After.

There were lingering effects from the separate sets of emotions that each experienced. The characters on the screen lived platonic lives. The actors seemed perfectly happy with their lots in life. The viewpoints of the observers, in contrast, were colored by dissatisfaction. It was discouraging for them to see the actors behave like insulated brothers and sisters with no outside relationships. In the movie version of their life, Kevin and Misty seldom held hands and never kissed. Romance was nonexistent.

No sooner had the first feature ended, than a second began. All three actors appeared again. This time, Haley became a despot, controlling the other two so their lives adapted to create her favorite outcome. The film was about: Haley, Haley—Haley.

In the third movie, Misty seduced Kevin. The actual seduction took place behind closed doors, and the movie camera panned discreetly away because, after all, it was a "G" rated film. Fiery emotions of love and desire were only hinted at. Haley took a notable backseat in this version, and in the end, only the other two were present. Kevin had become more and more depressed through the course of the film, due to Misty's manipulations, and her incessant nagging. She invariably got what she wanted at the expense of others, particularly Kevin.

The fourth film depicted him as someone who could never make up his mind about anything. He couldn't pick a career path. He couldn't choose a college, and he definitely couldn't commit to a long-term relationship. In the end, Misty moved away in tears.

The next featured Misty, who opened her own boutique in Coeur d'Alene, and soon had a successful string of such outlets.

Her creative talent and business sense served her well. Where guys were concerned, she was a player. Not committing to anyone, she seemed just fine with the singles life style. Kevin and Haley were notably absent in that cinematic presentation.

Another film clip featured Kevin. Wanting to do research in the realm of ESP, he went off to college to become a psychologist and never looked back for Haley or Misty. On the screen, he seemed motivated and happy.

Another film featured only Haley. She achieved unimagined heights in dream experience and understanding. She was able to simultaneously enter multiple alternate realities at will, creating changes in any or all, as easily as she had in her dreams.

There was a pause in the films, and the screen achieved a neutral grayish tone. The three film viewers sat in shocked silence, without physical contact or conversation.

The film viewing began again. Clips were shorter. Some scenes showed one of the three, others showed twosomes in various situations and combinations. Some created positive emotions in all three viewers, but most elicited negative reactions. Interspersed within these were a couple of clips showing all three friends interacting together.

Then came a series of rapid, montaged, sequences. Misty gallivanted around the world visiting famous sights. Kevin was in his own studio surrounded by his great works of art. The three viewers experienced alternating positive and negative reactions, as the final short films played at fast speed.

"Stop." Haley yelled.

The film paused, then faded, leaving a neutral screen.

Haley sobbed. Misty was teary-eyed, and Kevin felt emotionally overloaded.

"I'm not ready for this," Haley said, as she wiped the tears from her eyes.

Misty moved around Kevin and crouched on the other side, sliding her arm around the younger girl. "It's not real; it's just like the movies."

"It's our alternate realities," Haley wailed. "Don't you get it?"

Misty felt less certain about how to console her small friend, but instinctively held the younger girl. Kevin felt drawn to the others, placing his arms around both.

"We need help." Haley cried out. Her voice carried to the lake, and the sky beyond.

The film sequence began again from the beginning, but this time there were three points of view. All three friends were actors in the movie. They were also observers, sitting in the plush seats, witnessing the film. In addition, they floated together in the air, just behind the bench, with their alternate selves seated below.

The three floating selves sensed a fourth presence, and knew instinctively who hovered in the air beside them. His brown, flowing robe and wooden staff were just as Kevin had originally described them to Haley, from Kevin's dream about the young pigeon striking a power line.

"Why are we viewing this?" Haley's question pulsated all through their surroundings.

Warm and caring feelings emanated from the robed figure. He communicated, *'You have attracted these images.'*

'Why?' Misty's question was fright-filled.

The man reached out to her and his "touch" soothed her fear-saturated mind, preparing her for his thought. *'So that you may learn from your mistakes—before you make them.'*

After his thought had time to sink in, he continued. *'Your past fears and unhelpful actions have affected your present choices, which will become your future. You do not create in the past. You do not create in the future. You create in the here and now—only in this present moment. The past can be transformed in the present. The hoped-for future can be assured in the present. Now is your moment of power. All else is illusion.'*

'Misty,' the wise mentor continued. *'Your present moments' creations and thoughts are jumbled because of your past fears. That is why you have so many future possibilities you do not like. Now that you have seen, you may change your present focus. You may select from any alternative you have seen—which you desire—or create anew.'*

Kevin thought, Why am I unsure what to choose? Why don't I make important decisions, and choices?

The other's reply floated on buoyant ethers. *'You have been taught to choose with your conscious mind. For you, that is unwise. Your decisions must come from the heart. That is a problem because you have been trained to rely on logic, not on intuition.'*

Haley was no longer sobbing. "Thank you for coming," her love for their mentor radiated through her words. "Why am I so messed-up?"

The wise one seemed to chuckle. *'Nothing is farther from the truth my precious little one. You are not messed-up. Your emotions are chaotic. That makes you think they are a mess.*

'No other being in this realm touches alternate realities as easily as you. Most people have trouble sorting out their reactions to a single reality. You, however, have touched many at once. It is no wonder you have conflicting emotions. In the midst of these strange and wonderful experiences, you have developed awesome powers that others would give anything to achieve. Wisely, you choose not to display your talents. When you do use them, it is with utmost caution, not out of self-interest.

'Growth is not always easy. Sometimes it is painful. Be encouraged, young friend, the result of traveling your path is worth your effort.'

The movie began again where it had left off, and as the four watched from their suspended positions, the wise man's love and thoughts reached out to them. *'Learn from these possibilities. Do not fear them. Let their wisdom help you choose wisely in your present moment —your point of power....'*

30: THE FINAL DAY

The following morning, Kevin, Misty and Haley didn't talk about their significant nighttime experiences. They knew they might speak of them later, but they weren't ready yet. Misty seemed grateful for the presence of the other two. In the process of being a gracious hostess, she appreciatively touched Kevin or Haley as she passed by them.

Haley moved over to sit beside Kevin at the breakfast table. Misty brought some toast and moved behind them, embracing each before returning to the refrigerator for orange juice.

Haley felt the urgent need to use the restroom and fled in that direction. Shortly thereafter, Kevin reached out for Misty as she passed by, and pulled her onto his lap. She lovingly draped herself on him. Kevin responded, enjoying the touch of her body and her caring feelings for him.

Haley returned and sat in her chair, sipping orange juice. The other two smiled at her. For the first time in their relationship, Haley did not appear jealous of Misty's closeness with Kevin. She didn't display the overwhelming need to wedge.

Misty had another surprise for Kevin. She'd arranged with a diverse group of local friends to have an outing on a Lake Coeur d'Alene tourist boat, the Mish-an-Nock.

With Haley's dreaming help through the summer, Misty had overcome her fear of going out on the lake where her mother had drowned. Before her two friends arrived, she'd taken a maiden voyage on a lake tour boat to be sure she could handle the event she was planning.

Knowing that Kevin and Haley were returning to The Dalles the following day, Misty showed touches of sorrow. She endured the pangs of longing and hurt, knowing they would attack even more when the others left. As emotions rose within, she acknowledged them but chose not to react in old ways. She fought the urge to manipulate Kevin into staying with her in Coeur d'Alene.

Instead, she made herself trust their relationship. She pictured them spending time together in the future, without strings attached. She focused on her love for Kevin and the love she knew he felt for her. Right now, she thought, I appreciate his presence. Right now, I'm happy.

Kevin was surprised and dismayed by the reality of a large boat full of Misty's friends. He didn't know any of them except Candace and her little brother. Feeling intimidated and out of his comfort zone, Kevin wanted to find some lonely spot where he could somewhat conceal himself for the duration of the voyage.

Uncharacteristically, Haley ran off and played with Brad, showing no sign of clinginess to Kevin, who found he missed her hanging on him. Without that, he had to deal with the ugly reality of a boat full of Misty's friends.

The worst feeling came when he realized Misty seemed perfectly content chatting with her old friends—paying no attention to him. He guessed she was tracking him though, because of her concerted efforts not to notice him.

Sensing movement behind him, Kevin turned, encountering Candace's smiling face.

"Are we still feeling a little scared?" she asked with a teasing smile.

"A lot," he corrected, "and intimidated. I feel totally out-of-place."

She slipped her arm comfortingly around his and led the way to the upper deck. Again, Misty seemed not to notice.

"What are you worried about?" Candace asked.

"That no one here will like me and I'll fall flat on my face like some sophomoric imbecile."

She laughed pleasantly and said, "That's pretty harsh."

He enjoyed her laugh. In fact, he liked everything he knew about her.

"Do you like me?" she asked.

Kevin was shocked. Maybe Haley wasn't the only mind reader around.

Candace added, "As a friend, I mean, someone who's really close to Misty."

"Yes," he turned to look her in the eye.

She asked, "You don't feel threatened by me?"

"No."

"Every person here," she said with emphasis, "was handpicked by Misty, just like she picked me to go to Silverwood with you guys. Do you believe me?"

Kevin replied, "Yes. I wouldn't have thought it, but I do believe you."

"The guys on this boat aren't ones she went out with before. Now, let's go meet some of these people." She led the way to the lower deck, with her arm still entwined in his. He felt almost as comfortable with Candace as he did with Misty.

They met Jim Worth and Gayle Mackey, who turned out to be two of Misty's friends from Hayden Lake. Jim was an avid soccer player and Kevin felt instantly at ease talking with him. Gayle was also friendly and welcoming. She invited Kevin to bring Misty and his little "sister," as she referred to Haley, out to Honeysuckle, the public beach on Hayden, so they could all go swimming together. He didn't think he could fit it in. "Probably not this trip," he said, "but I'd really like to do that next time I'm up here."

He felt so accepted by Jim and Gayle that he was reluctant when Candace tugged his arm. "We've got lots more people to meet. Say good-bye."

He grudgingly took his leave.

Within the hour, Kevin successfully met most of Misty's friends on the lake-going vessel. It came as a surprise when he disconcertingly found his arm released by Candace. As he turned, she disappeared. In her place stood Misty, smiling brightly.

"How's it going?" she asked.

He leaned forward and gave her a big hug, whispering in her ear, "You should know, I bet you haven't let me out of your sight for one minute."

"Not a millisecond," she corrected, just before he kissed her.

"I do feel neglected." He acknowledged.

She said in mock outrage, "My friends haven't treated you well?"

"Your *friends* have been great."

"You don't mean," *moi?*

"Yes I do, but I see why you did it and I forgive you. No, I thank you."

She gave him a big hug and returned his kiss. Then she dragged him to the top deck where the wind messed-up their hair, but they could talk more privately.

On his way there, he felt the mental presence of Haley. Until that moment, she'd kept physically and mentally distant. *'Kevin, I hope you want to take some action here. Our futures are partly what you do this moment—we leave tomorrow morning, you know.'*

Misty had selected a semi-remote spot, and everyone on board seemed to be on instant radar alert to avoid her chosen area.

"I really like Candace," Kevin said. "When we arrived in Spokane and you first told me you had a friend waiting in the car, I got nauseous with fear you were going to introduce me to a new boyfriend. When it turned out to be Candace, I was greatly relieved. In that single moment of worry, I knew how much you meant to me."

Misty started to say something, but Kevin placed his finger on her lips. "My confession's not over yet. When I finally read your note…." He became silent, looking off across the lake.

"I read your note and it made me…." He couldn't talk for a moment.

"But, I couldn't contact you. The more time that passed, the less I knew what to do. I don't know how to work out this long-distance thing, how much commitment you want from me, or what I can agree to…but I want something to work for us. I need you in my life."

His gaze returned from the lake's horizon and his eyes bored into hers. "I'm in love with you and I don't know what to do."

She put her arms on his shoulders, continuing to look in his eyes and started to cry. She blinked through her tears to keep looking at him, smiling the entire time.

When her tears let up, she said, "Kevin, a lot of times you don't say much, but when you do…." She paused to take a deep breath and calm herself.

"That was just the right thing to say. I love you so much." She kept smiling through her tears. Kevin kissed her—a slow, lingering kiss. There were hints of passion, but it was primarily saturated with love.

They didn't talk after that. Instead, they sat and held one another. The end to their eventful cruise was a thought from Haley—an intense shout echoing through their minds. *'Yeeeesss. He finally did it.'*

Followed a moment later by a much quieter communication. *'Sorry, I couldn't help it.'*

31: BEATING HALEY'S GAME

In the early evening, the three friends played cards—a game called spoons. The object was to get rid of all one's cards, and quietly grab a spoon. There was one less spoon than there were people. Therefore, the losing player found him or herself spoonless. Problematically, it was more like Kevin playing against Misty, because Haley anticipated when someone was about to go out, invariably grabbing one of the two spoons. No matter how hard the others tried, she always got a spoon.

Misty decided playing cards wasn't working for her, and since it had cooled off outside, she challenged the others to a game of basketball, two-on-one—Kevin being the one. They went out back to the short, paved driveway in front of the garage where a basketball hoop was mounted. He didn't consider himself an exceptional basketball player, but he figured he could hold his own against the two girls.

Not.

Misty had played varsity basketball for three of her four years in high school. She pretty much didn't miss a shot. Haley anticipated Kevin's every move, and ran effective interference against him. In no time, he was down five points, with the score at ten to five.

Then he discovered something significant, at least when it concerned playing games with Haley. He could strongly imagine he would do a certain play when he had the ball. Then, he'd impulsively change his mind at the last second, and do whatever popped into his head. He also imagined a mental fog surrounding him to make it more difficult for Haley to tell what he would do next. Twice in a row, he was able to drive around

Haley, catching her off-guard. He raced straight to the basket for a lay-up. It was a particularly safe shot because Haley accidentally created a blockade that was hard for Misty to get around.

"*Seven* to ten," he said, strongly emphasizing the number seven. "I'm making my comeback." His voice was still echoing off the garage when Haley threw the ball to Misty, who immediately turned and shot from a long ways off, sinking the three-pointer.

"You just stick with those easy lay-ups," she called to him as she and Haley gave each other high-fives. He managed one more lay-in before Haley started anticipating him again, and shutting him down. Misty, meanwhile, made three additional long shots. As quickly as Haley passed her the ball, she would shoot from any distance, and sink it through the hoop.

"Well," said Kevin, "I'd like to say you've got home court advantage, but the truth is, you two are kicking my butt." He wiped the sweat from his forehead. "I concede. You win. I need something cold to drink."

As Kevin and Misty entered the house arm-in-arm, Haley held the door for them. "I didn't know you played basketball," Kevin commented to Misty.

She looked at him and smiled. "That's just *one*, of the *many* things you don't know about me." She gave him a pat on his shoulder and scooted into the house before he could respond.

Kevin and Misty curled up on the couch after cooling off with a glass of chilled orange juice. Haley flopped into an overstuffed chair. She mumbled something about everybody playing a board game, or watching a movie.

"All right you guys," Misty blurted out, "let's play a real game."

Haley asked with enthusiasm, "What sort?"

"A mind game, what else?"

Kevin asked. "How do we start?"

"It's a little like Twenty Questions, and a bit like Truth or Dare. Except, you and I get to ask all the questions, and Haley has to answer truthfully."

"That sounds fair," said Kevin, smiling.

Haley stipulated, "I don't have to answer questions I really don't want to."

"How do we start?" Kevin asked.

Misty said, "You or I think about a power she has that other people don't. Then we ask her questions about it."

Haley was reluctant at first, but soon warmed to the challenge.

"The power I choose first," said Misty, "is your ability to influence others without them realizing you're doing it."

"If Haley could do that, she wouldn't have let me make a fool of myself by throwing a big fit when she tried to get me to come up here. By the way," he turned to Haley, "thanks for doing that...and then forgiving me for how I acted...and for getting us all together again."

"You're welcome," she said, "but how do you know I've forgiven you?"

Her sly smile vanished and she looked thoughtful. "The only way I can show you what Misty asked is to make an example, but that's hard to do without breaking my code."

Misty asked, "Your code?"

"Yeah, it's what I go by so I don't hurt people." Haley leaned back in her overstuffed chair and closed her eyes. Her young face softened in relaxation. In less than a minute, she sat upright and declared, "There's something in your refrigerator's freezer compartment that you and Candace love to eat."

"Yeah," replied Misty. "Some extra-chocolaty, Rocky Road ice cream. We're both chocoholics. How'd you know?"

Haley continued, "Candace is on a date tonight. She's with a tall guy and they're heading to something important."

"Yeah," Misty affirmed. "She's out with Vance, and they're going to a concert in Spokane. Why?"

Kevin interrupted, "Wait a minute. This is impressive...sort of like telepathy, I guess, but it's not what we asked about."

"Give me a second, because we don't have much time," Haley replied. "What're the chances Candace will show up here in the next five minutes?"

"Here?" Misty replied. "No chance—they better be way far out of town or they'll never make it to the concert in time."

Haley was insistent, "So they couldn't come here in the next five minutes for Candace to get a bowl of ice cream—that's what you're saying?"

"Never happen." affirmed Misty.

Reclining in her chair, Haley closed her eyes again. Breathing slow and easily, the peaceful look returned to her face. Kevin became restless, and was about to ask a question when a smile curved the corners of her lips.

"It's going to happen in probably three minutes," Haley said, sitting up, and opening her eyes. "Misty, you'd be doing Candace a great big favor by dishing her a large bowl of that Rocky Road. Just set it on the end-table over there, will you?"

Misty played along without complaint, jumping up to do as Haley had requested. Kevin wondered what was going on. Was Haley already controlling Misty?

She returned with a large, creamy-white bowl filled with dark, chocolaty ice cream. The handle of a spoon stuck out like a small flag on a newly discovered, chocolate-filled planet. She placed it on the end table as Haley suggested. Then she curled up beside Kevin on the couch.

Perhaps two more minutes dragged by. Haley waited calmly. Kevin and Misty became visibly tense, uncertain what would happen.

Haley began to yawn.

Soon, Misty and Kevin yawned as well.

"I don't know why I'm so tired," Haley remarked. Her eyes drooped. Kevin's eyelids also got heavy. Misty's eyes closed. Kevin yawned again and leaned his head back on the couch, shutting his eyes.

The front doorbell rang. Misty jumped slightly and Kevin jerked awake. Before either could rise, Candace burst through the entrance. She raced to the middle of the living room where the three reposed and told them what had happened. "We were on our way to Spokane, but Vance remembered he'd left the tickets for the concert in his other shirt pocket and we had to race back to get them. For some reason, he changed his shirt just before he left the house. He only lives a few blocks from here." Her head nodded in the direction where he lived.

"Anyway, we pulled up in front of Vance's house and he felt in his shirt pocket—and there were the tickets. He'd already checked twice. I'd even poked my hand in there. Go figure.

"We were about to head out when I knew I'd forgotten something over here. Now I don't know what it was. Isn't that funny?" She laughed nervously.

Haley said, pointing to the end-table, "Your ice cream's right there."

"Oh, thanks," Candace shouted, "I've been craving Rocky Road all day. Thanks you guys." She grabbed the bowl and ran out the entranceway without shutting the door, yelling back over her shoulder, "Good-bye everyone, and have a great trip home you two."

Misty laughed uneasily.

Kevin sat up. "What was that…?"

"You got to see mind control," replied Haley. "Any more questions?"

Kevin said, "Tons, but I don't know where to start."

"Me either," added Misty.

He asked, "What did you do?"

"Well," said Haley, "everybody's minds are linked. That's how telepathy works. I just put it out there that I needed volunteers. Candace and Vance showed up. They were already on their way back to find the tickets. I gave them a break. The tickets weren't where he thought. He'd never of found them in time. I just moved the tickets from under a pile of dirty clothes in his room —to his shirt pocket. Then I had him look again. That saved them a lot of time. I figured I'd paid them back for taking the trip to see us, and Candace wanted comfort food. I promised that to her subconscious for coming over here and cooperating.

"I got a parking guy to overlook a parking spot, so there'll still be one when they arrive late. The band was delayed anyway, so the concert won't start on time. They won't miss anything."

Misty said softly, "Haley, when you first told us that dream experts and scientists studied you and they couldn't keep up, well, I'm just starting to see what you meant. What you can do is mind-boggling. Forgive me for not understanding before…and even now. I don't really get it, but I'm trying to."

A small tear formed at the corner of Haley's left eye, but she tilted her head so Misty wouldn't see it. She said in a subdued voice, very different from her usually boisterous tones, "I was so lonely, I put out a call into the thought world—I needed some friends. Then I waited for, like, a whole year. I hoped Kevin might turn out to be one of them, and then you showed up.

"Finally, Kevin's nightmare came along and I knew you were both the ones. Back when a car wreck killed may parents in Portland, and I moved to The Dalles, it was awful. Coming to a new town, a new school, and not knowing any kids here. I was the only…really dark-skinned kid in my class. Couldn't make friends and my teacher said my social skills sucked. Well, those weren't her exact words, but I got the idea…and she was right."

Misty turned and slid her arms under Haley's small body, lifting her out of the chair and carting her to the couch. She sat beside Kevin so they could both hold Haley across their laps.

Haley said, "Kevin was the only person besides my Aunt and Uncle who paid any attention to me. He put up with me and sometimes I felt like he might even like me. Then, you came along.

"When I thought everything was going to work out for us, you two went and broke apart. Kevin looked like he was dying." Haley began to cry softly but she continued, "I was losing the two people I cared most about. I knew I could make you love each other, and me—but I shouldn't. It was hard not to use these powers."

"Oh Haley," Misty said, "When I hear what you've been through, I wish you had used them on us. I don't know how you stopped yourself?"

"Same way you stopped yourself," sniffled Haley.

Misty asked, "What do you mean?"

"You could have snuck into Kevin's room at night on those last days of school before you left The Dalles. You could have changed his mind, stayed in The Dalles and found a way to make him do what you wanted."

"That wouldn't work," Misty replied. "He has to do it out of love, not guilt. Not for sex, or because I tricked him."

"The same thing is true for you guys and me," Haley said. "What I did with Candace and Vance was with their consent— even if it was at a different level—subconscious-like. They kept their free will and I didn't have to break my code.

"You two came to my call for friends. Everything else we have to work out...together. You can't force Kevin and I can't force either of you. It's the same thing."

Misty said, "I understand."

"So do I," said Kevin. "I owe both of you thanks—sticking by me even when I screwed up."

Haley laughed, "Yeah, you do...and don't worry, we'll make you pay." She sniffled, and laughed again.

Misty and Kevin joined in.

When they were calm, Misty asked, "What kind of training program will bring Kevin and me up to speed—in all this mumbo-jumbo stuff you do?"

"It isn't mumbo-jumbo," said Haley. "If we did something like tonight's experiment every evening and we did serious dream training each night... It would take maybe a hundred years... maybe more."

The other two laughed.

"I'm not joking here!"

They watched movies—for real ones—that evening until none of them could keep their eyes open any longer. After they fell asleep, only two slept peacefully through the night....

32: TO DREAM, OR NOT

The following morning, if the three had shared a dream during the night, they seemed not to remember. The only one who admitted recalling a dream was Kevin and he declined to give details—at least for the present.

He used most of his will trying unsuccessfully to suppress memories of his nighttime ordeal—

In his dream, he'd been high up on the flat top of a butte, perhaps two hundred feet in the air. Its sides were very steep and although the top was perfectly flat, it was only a few feet across. It made a nice-sized sleeping area, however. Even in this dream, Kevin slumbered atop the butte, dreaming important dreams. The awareness he gained was inspirational.

Unknown to Kevin, a rock climber laboriously ascended the tabletop mountain. When this peak scaler reached the apex, he was enraged to find Kevin there, and pushed him over the edge. Kevin plummeted down, flailing at the passing bank and inadvertently picking up sticky clay soil as he went. Extremely frightened, he watched the world turn upside down, over-and-over again until he was a round ball of clay with only his head sticking out the side. The descent continued until he inevitably reached the base of the hill.

Instead of smashing him to bits, the butte's curved sides at the bottom made him race through an arc, and roll across the flat ground surrounding the butte. Like a giant bowling ball, he gradually slowed, coming to rest at the upper edge of a steep canyon. Immovable, his head pointed ground-ward at an odd angle. He saw dry grass and weeds in the colorful soil and could tell the steep canyon was just beyond where he'd come to rest.

Some children happened along and playfully began to roll the clay ball back and forth. At first, they didn't notice his head protruding from the round mass. When they finally did, they began pulling on his nose, and yanking his hair. He yelled in pain, seeing little more than the lower halves of their bodies, while they manipulated his clay ball nearer to the canyon edge.

Even though they knew his head was sticking out, and he was more than a ball of clay, they pushed the giant sphere over the rim of the canyon. He didn't protest, but watched apprehensively, wondering what would happen next. Down he dropped for the second time, but this descent was a free-fall. He hit the canyon bottom with great force, bursting the clay apart.

He lay on the ground in a pile of rubble, unable to move, and feeling more helpless and frustrated than ever before. Looking up, he spotted the robed figure from his childhood dream standing nearby.

"You know," the gifted man said, "knowledge, of itself— without action—isn't worth much, even dream knowledge."

Kevin jerked awake, clearly remembering the last words spoken in his dream. In particular, the phrase "knowledge… without action…" reechoed in his thoughts. He shifted restlessly, reaching out for Misty, but didn't find her. His eyes opened to see a dim light coming from the kitchen. Haley snored softly a couple of feet away. He propped himself up with two pillows and heard Misty humming in the kitchen. What a strange dream he'd had.

The subdued but unmistakable sound of the front door opening caught Kevin's attention. He paused, listening for it to close. His mind could focus on nothing else. Where was the sound of the door shutting? Perhaps he only thought he'd heard Misty in the kitchen. She must have stepped onto the front porch for some reason.

He smiled to himself and decided to call out. Opening his mouth to speak, he hesitated, seeing her shadowy movement across the semi-darkened space between the entryway and the kitchen. Except for a slight squeak in the floor, she barely made a sound. As Misty neared the increased illumination by the kitchen door, Kevin froze. It wasn't her.

A bulky shadow more reminiscent of a great ape than a person slowed at the kitchen doorway. Despite its size, it glided silently inside. During the split second that followed, Kevin knew he had seen the familiar form of Shaine, Misty's stepfather.

Sitting there unable to move, Kevin replayed through his mind the spectral shadow. How to make sense of it? Shaine was in police custody, probably on trial somewhere. He should be a thousand miles away.

The dark image flashed through Kevin's mind again, and this time he recognized the telltale glimmer of a thin-bladed knife clutched in the mostly-obscured right hand. He wanted to call a warning to Misty, but his voice wouldn't work. He rolled out of bed, speeding to the kitchen. Peering in, he saw her leaned-over in front of the open refrigerator, still humming.

Just behind—his menacing face brightly illumined in the glow of the open appliance—her former guardian lifted his dagger.

Kevin tried to scream. His heart beat so loudly the others should be able to hear it. His breath—in ragged gasps—allowed him to utter only a hoarse groan. Misty turned her head, not seeing the figure behind her, and squinted toward Kevin. She winked conspiratorially. He could see the carton of rocky road ice cream in her hand.

Her smile disappeared as she perceived the strangled look on his face. She saw his eyes jerking to the figure behind her, and knew she was in danger. Her head craned around, glimpsing her step-dad. The shocked look on her face cut into Kevin as deeply as the sight of the threatening knife.

The carton slipped from her grasp, and she collapsed backward, wilting against the bottom of the refrigerator. Unable to defend herself or flee, she waited like a sacrificial lamb.

The presence behind her slowly rose, savoring his moment of victory, soaking up the terror from her eyes.

Kevin started forward as if in slow-motion. The stepfather glanced, but mentally dismissed the youth, and moved instead relentlessly toward his victim. Her hand protectively gripped her throat just as Kevin finally screeched, "Misty."

All three sensed the inevitable outcome. Her former guardian would prevail—finally killing Misty. Kevin would lose what he held dearest. He futilely tried to increase the length of his steps.

Shaine bent forward, asserting his dominion over Misty as she sat there awaiting her fate. His smile widened in anticipation. Knife poised, he leaned farther down, bringing his face nearer to hers, watching her eyes as he prepared to end her life.

Kevin continued moving futilely on, knowing he could not reach her in time. Feeling the evil force of the man, and hating each second, while knowing he too would succumb to that vile presence.

The glare in the man's eyes foreshadowed the moment of her death. An inner flicker foretold the dagger's plunge. In that instant, Kevin was still too far away, and a scream tore loose from his throat, "Noooooo...."

The full force of the large man's body gathered into the blade, and his knee lowered toward the floor, increasing his leverage. The knife flashed brightly down, but Shaine's lower leg encountered the softening carton of ice cream, which skewed his aim. The knife meant for her heart sliced deep into her shoulder, raking down her arm.

Misty screamed.

Her stepfather seemed pleased by the prolonged ending, taking delight in the blood darkening her nightshirt. Kevin reached for the man to pull him away, but received a backhand and sprawled on the floor. Misty would die despite his efforts, and he would be next.

"Stop." Haley's distinctive voice rang through the kitchen.

Thank God. Kevin thought.

Shaine glanced in the direction the door, flashing a delighted smile before he flung the long-bladed knife at the silhouette of the small girl. It sailed over Kevin, turning end-for-end as it flew through the air, burying its point deeply in the undersized girl's chest.

Kevin could not believe what he witnessed. Haley's shocked look conveyed it was not supposed to end like this. Without a word, she crumpled to the floor, blood covering her chest and flowing onto her midriff. The knowledge that this was her present reality struck harder than the forceful weapon.

Kevin rolled toward Shaine with a vengeance, only to be held at bay by the other's mighty grip, as he viewed the massive fingers of the man's left hand unmercifully squeezing Misty's throat. There was terror in her eyes—and Kevin was forced to watch.

Her step-dad's manner conveyed that there was always plenty of time to dispatch Kevin.

Sounds of a siren became louder but it didn't matter to their tormenter, his resolve deepened as he extracted the last ounce of life from his beautiful victim. Her bloodstained hair contrasted her pale, slackening face. Her head flopped to the side, eyes vacant; a look Kevin had seen once before in his terrible, long-ago nightmare. A harbinger of what he now faced.

A final horrific scream fled Kevin's throat as mighty fingers throttled his neck. His utterance seemed involuntary and as his breath failed, Kevin heard an old woman cackling from the other room, or maybe the front porch, a ghoul's sound....

Darkness—

A final shudder coursed through Kevin and he realized he was finally awake. Wasn't he? Was this what Mr. Bridger called a false wakening? He'd already had one.

Haley's shallow snoring and Misty's rhythmic breathing became more apparent, contrasting with Kevin's frantic inhalations and pounding heart. He fearfully peered around the room. There was no light from the kitchen. He didn't know if the front door was open or shut. Rolling over, he arose partway, sweat-soaked. Neither of the others had yet awakened. Was it not a shared dream?

Hugging his knees to his chest, Kevin reached out to reassure himself of the physical presence of the other two. He hadn't been this scared since the first horrifying nightmare—and seeing Misty dead on the brass bed. What did this mean? It was as real as the first dream.

Was all of Misty's fear about her stepfather justified? Had the man escaped? If not, did this portend that he would? If Misty and Haley had no knowledge of this dream, should he tell them? He curled toward Misty, placing his hand reassuringly on her arm.

Lying in the quiet, he winced at each noise the old house made, praying for dawn's speedy arrival.

33: AND THEY LIVED…

All too soon, it was time for Kevin and Haley to depart. Everything was loaded in the car, and they sat in their respective seats, saying their final good-byes.

Misty leaned against Kevin's car door. There was longing in her eyes, and she blinked back moisture, barely preventing tears. "I don't know when I'll see you again…." Looking across to the passenger seat, she said to Haley, "I'll miss you both…so much. Thanks for coming to visit me. I hoped this good-bye moment would never come." She raised her head and pulled slightly away from the car while still looking into Kevin's eyes. He had started the Toyota, but then turned off the ignition.

He looked away from her, out through the windshield, focusing on the far distance. At last, he said, "Misty, I promised to get my Mom's Toyota back to her by no later than today. With it gone, they only have the pickup, and that makes it tough because Dad works such long hours. The thing is…." his eyes returned to hers, "I can't make myself start the car again…I don't want to leave you."

Misty half-turned her head so he would not see the tear she knew was running down her right cheek.

"It'll be okay," she said with determination. "I can go on, knowing we are still…." She couldn't finish her sentence, so she moved a step away, brushing the tear from her face. "You better go before I start bawling." She rushed back to give him a good-bye kiss, then turned her back and walked slowly toward her house.

The Toyota's engine started, and as Misty made the halfway-point between her departing friends and the house, she turned and waved good-bye.

Haley did not say a word as Kevin drove through Coeur d'Alene and entered the freeway to Spokane. Her silence deepened as they motored beside Post Falls, her face blank, betraying no clue to her thoughts. Kevin left her to her own devices. He had demons of his own to wrestle.

All too soon, the city of Spokane became a distant memory as it blurred in his rearview mirror. They climbed the hill past Fairchild's exit, toward their long journey across desolate lands, returning to The Dalles.

Kevin sat in silence, guessing why Haley was so quiet—but totally centered on his own pain. Separating from Misty and returning to The Dalles were two of the most difficult things he'd ever done.

Mutual silence continued, even as they neared the westbound rest stop near Sprague Lake. Kevin's emotional pain had settled into his midsection in the form of gastric distress. Without mentioning his upset stomach to Haley, Kevin slowed the car and took the wayside exit.

He parked as near the restroom as possible.

"I'll be right back," Kevin said when he was most of the way out of the car. Those were the first words either of them had spoken since leaving Misty.

Walking hunched-over, pain gripping his midsection, Kevin was unsure if he was about to throw up or if he was going to have an attack of diarrhea—or both. Inside the restroom, he found his way to the only empty stall. Even in his uncomfortable state of mind and body, he couldn't help but notice the graffiti revoltingly scraped onto the walls.

He wondered if he should crouch by the toilet in case he threw up.

Misty walked numbly back to her house, up the front steps, entering the door without realizing she'd done so. Pushing it closed out of habit, she neglected to lock the door as she ordinarily would have. Opening the coat closet, she viewed her two suitcases—packed and ready to go—waiting for Kevin to say the words. She dragged forth the larger one, sitting on it, and then she sobbed.

The feeling of absolute aloneness seeped into her being. The contrast between that and how happy she'd felt in the last couple of days with Kevin and Haley visiting made for sharper pain. Closing her eyes, the image of the silver Toyota entered Misty's mind. She watched in memory as it slowed to round the corner onto Sherman Avenue, carrying Kevin and Haley out of sight.

"Why didn't he ask me?" she said through streaming tears, and her mournful wailing commenced.

Kevin slowly awakened. He realized he was on the toilet in the wayside's restroom—still fully clothed. There was no memory of vomiting. His bottom ached from sitting too long on the hard toilet seat. Had he been dreaming? He thought so. There were strange memories, or perhaps just fragments that had replayed in his mind—like a short video clip forming a Mobius loop. His intestinal track felt much better, but he ached with grief at the memory of leaving Misty.

Straightening himself with difficulty, Kevin left the stall and paused to wash his hands. He exited the restroom wondering what had happened to all the people who'd been there when he first entered. The Toyota sat there empty, still parked diagonally from the building.

A flickering fear entered his mind as he neared the car, but then he realized that Haley had probably decided to use the restroom as well. The sun glinting off the Toyota's windshield momentarily blinded him as he moved to the side of the car, opening the driver's door. He sat in the seat, detecting a large lump on the front passenger side. Kevin slipped the ignition key into place and started the engine. He listened absently to the radio while waiting for Haley, and sensed something was wrong.

Glancing at the passenger seat, someone lay curled up, almost like a cat asleep in a chair. That someone was female, and blonde, sleeping heavily. There were tear tracks down her cheeks, but her face looked peaceful, her breathing regular. He knew the sound of those inhalations, knew that glistening blonde head, and the slope of her face—from cheekbone to the gentle curve of her mouth. He knew and loved every facet of the young woman sleeping so impossibly, yet peacefully beside him.

A subconscious prompting caused Kevin to turn and look into the back seat. There was Haley, slumped down, a relaxed look on her face. Her closed eyes opened and stared into his.

'What do you want?' Her thought asked in his mind.

He mentally said, *'What do you mean?'*

'Is this what you want?' her thoughts entered again.

He was about to say something idiotic when Haley added the picture of Misty sitting beside him to the words that were now blazoned in large letters on a banner that floated in the screen of his mind. *Is This What You Want?'*

"Yes," he said aloud, hoping that Misty might awaken.

He turned to look at her but the body shimmered and faded as a mirage might. In a short time, there was no sign of her presence. Angered, he turned back to look at Haley. What game was she playing?

"Is that what you really want?" she repeated.

He yelled at her, "I said, Yes."

She smiled and her lids drooped down, concealing her pupils. Her voice had that familiar ring to it, "Turn around and close your eyes. Get ready to dream."

Kevin did as Haley had bidden and immediately experienced the presence of the mists. Darkness enveloped their car, carrying them mentally to a distant place.

They floated in a gradual descent to the familiar territory of the dreamtime amusement park, but Misty wasn't with them. They landed just in front of the Dos Championship building. The front doors opened and they were escorted inside without the previous fanfare. At the central table sat Misty. She looked angry. Two men told them to sit down, which they did.

"It's about time," Misty stated. "What took so long?"

Kevin was perplexed, but Haley simply shrugged. She said, in what was for her a very diplomatic way, "You know how Kevin is…it takes him a while to catch on to things."

That reply didn't mollify Misty, who peered furiously into his eyes as she asked, "Do you want me in your life, or not?"

"Yes."

"Well…you have a funny way of showing it."

Haley interrupted what was about to become a lecture. "You both need to listen. I have to know…do you want to be my helpers for something really big?"

Misty hesitated, wishing to change the subject back to her own concern, but Kevin said, "Yes," and Misty also agreed.

"You've seen some things," said Haley, "but now it'll get harder to understand—to follow."

"I'm going to help you alter our reality. Are you sure you want Misty with you?" Haley focused on Kevin.

"Yes," he said without hesitation.

"Here we go," Haley warned as the mists swirled about and the darkness descended more quickly than ever before.

All too soon, it was time for Kevin and Haley to depart. Their things were loaded in the car, and they sat in their respective seats, saying their final good-byes.

Misty leaned against Kevin's car door. There was longing in her eyes and she blinked back moisture that gathered to form tears.

"I don't know when I'll see you again…." she began. Looking past Kevin to the passenger seat, she said to Haley, "I'll miss you both…so much. Thanks, you guys…for coming up to visit. I hoped this good-bye moment would never come." She raised her head and pulled slightly away from the car, while still looking into Kevin's eyes.

He hadn't started the Toyota. Looking away from her, out through the windshield, he focused in the far distance. "Misty," he said at last, "the thing is…." his eyes turned back to hers, "it's just that I can't make myself start the car. I don't want to leave you."

The embryo of an idea entered his mind and he said impulsively, "Will you come with us?"

Misty straightened some more, and her arms left the car as she turned, gazing at her house and the Mustang sitting off to the side.

"I know," said Kevin, "I probably don't have the right to ask. It's selfish of me—you've already signed up for college here in Coeur d'Alene. I've got to go back and finish high school, at least until mid-year. But I want us together."

"Yes." Misty half shouted. "Yes, I'll come back to The Dalles with you, at least for a few days—maybe longer."

He could hardly believe it. "Did you say, 'Yes?'"

"I sure did." She leaned down and kissed him on the lips.

Kevin realized Haley was screaming at the top of her lungs, and probably had been from the moment Misty first uttered her agreement.

He opened his car door and got out, wrapping himself around Misty. His whole body shook. "I love you so much. I can't believe this is happening."

She trembled as well.

After a short time, she disentangled from him and took her cell phone out of her pocket. She flipped it open and pressed a memory dial number, placing the phone to her ear. "Candace, guess what. I'm going back to The Dalles with Kevin and Haley.

"He just asked me to. I'm so excited.

"Yes.

"I'm going to get some things and hop in their car. I'll leave my keys on the kitchen table. If you can housesit for me, that'll be wonderful.

"You can? Great.

"If you don't get over here before we leave, I love you and I'll miss you. You're the best friend anyone ever had.

"Yes, that's right...we're leaving in just a couple minutes....

"No, I couldn't tell you before—we just decided; even I didn't know.

"If you miss me too much, you can drive the Mustang down to visit us.

"Yes, but make it quick or we'll be gone.

"Bye."

She turned and ran for her house, yelling—less loudly than Haley—but yelling, nonetheless.

Kevin couldn't believe what was happening. He had two screaming females on his hands. He turned toward the car. "I'm going to help…."

But Haley was already rounding the vehicle on the run. In the next second, the two of them sprinted for Misty's house: Haley, screaming with excitement, and Kevin full of excitement, minus the screaming.

As they ran onto the porch, the front door opened and Misty stood beside two large suitcases, apparently fully packed and ready to go.

Kevin was bewildered. He didn't think it humanly possible for anyone to pack that fast. Misty saw the look on his face and said, "I never really unpacked after I moved back."

That explained it for Kevin, but as he reached down to lift one of the suitcases, Misty gave Haley a conspiratorial wink. Haley laughed, then caught herself, and decided to help her big "sister" carry the second largest suitcase. It probably weighed as much as Haley, but she was an energetic helper.

They were about to load the two cases into the Toyota's ample trunk when a car came barreling around the corner. As it stopped, Candace hopped out of the passenger side. She and Misty hugged and carried-on, while Kevin—with some help from Haley—began loading the two suitcases. Negotiating the second piece of baggage into the trunk beside the empty pigeon box, Kevin mumbled, "What's she got in here, a set of dumbbells?"

In no time, he was once again in the driver's seat with Misty on the passenger side and Haley in the back. Haley was outwardly silent, but at frequencies only a few beings in the collective universes could monitor, she screamed into the vastness of space, *'Kevin, you finally, really, completely did it.'*

Candace gave Misty a good-bye hug through her open window, and Misty passed her the Mustang's key chain. "I forgot to leave it on the table."

"I'll take care of things for you while you're gone," Candace reassured.

Kevin sat behind the steering wheel, still in shock. Thinking to himself about the robed figure from his dream, he said aloud, "Action is good." Then he wondered if he should tell them about his nightmare. Maybe later, he decided. He didn't want to think about that now, or spoil the girl's moods.

Misty waved to the driver of the Honda that had brought Candace as that car motored away. Then she turned to Kevin. "We better get going before half my friends come to say good-bye."

He started the Toyota and Candace came around to his side of the car. Thrusting her head in through the open window, she touched her cheek to his.

Pulling back, she said, "Congratulations, it looks like you're going to get the girl after all. Surprised?"

"Sort of...." He replied.

"I'm not," and she turned, heading toward Misty's house with a joyful, bouncing gait.

Candace stopped at the halfway point and swung around to wave a final good-bye as the Toyota rounded the corner onto Sherman Avenue with a farewell honking of its horn.

The three reunited travelers began their long trip home.

Haley's thought entered the minds of her companions. *This is the beginning of something so cool.... Bigger than you can know....*

Just remember, you agreed to this!

The sky darkened and mists gathered as the silver-gray Toyota and its passengers continued onward...

ABOUT THE AUTHOR

Born and reared in Oregon, EA Bundy grew up in The Dalles, but also lived in Coeur d'Alene and other North Idaho locations. He loves to write and travel and read good books. To learn more about him and see what he's currently up to—or to check out other novels he's written—please visit his website at:

www.eabundyauthor.com